MW01196468

RABBITS IN THE GARDEN

THE GARDENING GUIDEBOOKS TRILOGY
BOOK 1

JESSICA MCHUGH

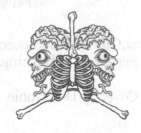

Ghoulish Books
an imprint of Perpetual Motion Machine Publishing
Cibolo, Texas

Rabbits in the Garden
Copyright © 2022 Jessica McHugh

All Rights Reserved

Second edition

ISBN: 978-1-943720-73-6

The story included in this publication is a work of fiction. Names, characters, places and incidents are products of the author's imagination or are used fictitiously. Any resemblance to actual events or locales or persons living or dead is entirely coincidental.

Without limiting the rights under copyright reserved above, no part of this publication may be reproduced, stored in or introduced into a retrieval system, or transmitted, in any form, or by any means (electronic, mechanical, photocopying, recording, or otherwise), without the prior written permission of both the copyright owner and the above publisher of this book.

www.GhoulishBooks.com
www.PerpetualPublishing.com

Cover by Don Noble

ALSO BY JESSICA MCHUGH

The Green Kangaroos
Nightly Owl, Fatal Raven
The Train Derails in Boston
A Complex Accident of Life
Strange Nests

For invisible (not imaginary) friends everywhere.

CHAPTER ONE

NOT MUCH HAD changed since the fire. Long before she set foot inside the hospital, she could smell the patients who hadn't made it out in time. But it wasn't the stench of death that chilled her bones as she approached. It was always a grim place, even to those who hadn't been confined there, and since being gutted by the flames it was grimmer still. But it wasn't the building's cold black shell that made her shiver.

What bristled Avery Norton's skin as she stood outside Taunton State Lunatic Asylum was how stunning its corpse looked in the setting sun.

Pink light poured through gaping holes in the structure, illuminating corridors she'd always found so cramped and suffocating. They were open now, the damage almost playful. It was her first time walking the halls as a free woman, but the asylum wouldn't allow her to feel it. Even in charred death, it ensnared her mind. She assumed it always would.

After six years imprisoned in Taunton, it had become the only place Avery truly felt at home. She knew each tile and brick and barred window, and they knew her just as intimately.

Welcome to Taunton, they whispered. *We knew you'd be back.*

As she ambled across the sun bridge connecting the wings, her mind repaired the peeling paint and walls eaten by fire damage. It swept away leaves and yanked up weeds that had crawled in through the cracks. It filled the silent

1

void with voices and added the echo of frenetic footsteps to Avery's own—which she now realized had changed from the soft patter of muddy shoes to the crisp shuffle of cheap hospital slippers. Her dress had changed too. She'd rarely worn one of the paper-thin gowns after her first few days in Taunton, but the one she wore now told a different story. It stank of cigarettes and isopropyl alcohol as if it was her only piece of clothing since 1953.

But it didn't stop her, didn't even slow her stride as patients and nurses joined her in the hall. Some she recognized, all she pitied, but none paid her any mind, too lost in their own manic business. Except one.

At the end of the cluttered corridor, wearing glee that dripped with insincerity, the woman opened her arms and cooed. *"Sweetheart . . . "*

"Hello, Mother. What lies do you have for me today?"

Faye's smile started small, but when her lips parted, a shrill howl erupted from her throat, and in tandem, the hospital's decaying core. The floor juddered with her widening grin, and as it crumbled away, Avery clung to the wall of the sun bridge.

"You're not real," she growled. "And I'm not afraid of you."

As her expression shrank to a smirk, the hospital gradually ceased its trembling. "We'll see about that." Crossing her arms over her chest, she vanished like a plume of smoke in the breeze.

Like sandcastles devoured by a hungry tide, the past was washed away, leaving Avery alone again in a charred world. Tightening her jaw, she emptied her lungs and locked onto the rigid march she'd made so many times down the hall to the ward where she lost her youth.

Most of the rooms weren't numbered anymore, but Avery knew hers in an instant. It was the only door hanging open, welcoming her with the same threshold creak that greeted her on her first day in the hospital. Smoke damage had blackened most of the interior, but sparse patches of sea green paint remained, rekindling the memory of a thousand hours staring up at turquoise walls.

Her bed was overturned and the mattress baked, and flakes of rust and paint decorated its ebony skin. The bedside table was missing a leg but prevailing over gravity, like it was down on one knee in reverence. The top drawer was open, and the sun flashed against something metallic inside, inviting her closer. A silver mirror with smashed glass granted Avery a broken reflection, her straight hair kinked and lips lopsided. Neither the mirror nor the reflection felt like hers. It wasn't Francine's style, either, though she might've stolen it from another girl at some point. And if she had, it was all that remained of her friend. With that thought, Avery cradled the mirror as if it were precious. She wished it was true, and that retrieving the mirror had been her goal all along. But there was something else she hoped to find, still hidden in the room they'd shared for most of Avery's incarceration.

It was a small thing—hardly even a thing—but like a time capsule, it held steadfast the very moment that ruined her life. She hated it, but she needed it, and like the hospital itself, she figured it was waiting smugly for her return.

Crouched at the third tile from the back wall, Avery blew away the ash and wedged her nail between the linoleum squares, tracing them until she cleared enough grime to free the tile. Inside the putrid pit beneath the floor, her diary sat under a thick layer of dust. It appeared to have been sampled by a rodent or two, but it was otherwise untouched . . . as it had been since her twelfth birthday.

She turned the latch and unbelted the book, but she needed a steadying breath before opening it. Though she'd written in it only once, the sole entry had been poisonous enough to spoil the entire thing. It was a totem for her trauma now, something she could never again touch with love, and something she could never live without.

The diary cracked, almost coughed, and a photograph slipped out from the pages. It landed on her lap, and innocent eyes stared up at her, begging for an explanation she couldn't give. The boy and girl standing hand-in-hand had their whole lives ahead of them. With all the world at their fingertips and the love blossoming between them, how could they expect their futures would be anything but bright? Why would they ever doubt they'd end up together? How could they know then the monsters they'd become?

Now she could see how young they were. Now she could see how stupid.

As Avery ran her fingers over the photograph, she marveled at how much her appearance had changed. Her hair was still cropped at the shoulders, though unevenly, and her bangs were still too long, but the raven color she adored had lost its luster. She remained deceptively thin, her waifish body still trimmed in muscle, but she looked much weaker now. She had sharper ridges and longer shadows, and when emotion overcame her, she trembled like a carousel horse with a few loose bolts, but it would've been foolish to assume she was weak.

She'd always been athletic, and her friendship with Paul Dillon amplified that strength and agility. All those rounds of Tag and Kick the Can made her quick and slender. Hours spent fishing off the Martha's Vineyard Steamship Pier taught her patience and stillness. Scaling abandoned summerhouses in wintertime boosted her confidence and stability. But she knew she wouldn't have been welcome in those games if not for Paul. He was brave enough to be the one who brought the girl and made no apologies to the boys. He endured the mocking and threats from so-called friends because Avery was worth it. And as it turned out, she and Paul were the only relationship to survive the capriciousness of childhood.

All things considered, Paul looked the same: tall and lean with dark brown hair, a beautiful boy even in these terrifying days. His ice blue eyes had a distant, cautionary look, likely the reason for his perpetually guarded air, but they were a warm welcome to Avery. After everything, that boy, that man, that love, still enraptured her with ease.

They first met when Avery was nine. They first played when she was ten. They first kissed when she was twelve. But before Avery reached her thirteenth birthday, it was all over.

It wasn't supposed to happen that way. She should've lived as free as anyone else. She should've been able to trust her heart and mind as she trusted her mother, who claimed to treasure both. She should've played and laughed and cried tears of joy as she and Paul grew together in life and love. But as much as Avery still wished for those things, and as many times as she thought her dreams would finally come true, reality confirmed it time and time again: every hope she had was foolish, every choice she made was cursed.

It was a truth she now accepted, and it didn't sadden her. Believing, even falsely, brought her a modicum of joy, and she refused to deny any moments of joy, however small.

Avery stuck the photo of Paul between the pages of her diary and smiled. That's where she would keep him. Right there. Forever.

She turned to the first page, dated July 2nd, 1953, and as the hastily scrawled words jumped from the page to her lips, her hospital room vibrated with whispers of the past.

"Today, Mom gave me a garden."

CHAPTER TWO

IT WAS THE perfect start to her twelfth birthday. At the Flying Horses carousel, she worked her way up to catching four rings at a time, and though she thought fate might favor her and finally allow her to catch the brass ring, everything from the dispenser was steel, steel, and more steel. When her arm got tired, she turned to Tivoli's penny arcade for a raucous round of pinball, and once all the pinging and jangling got on her nerves, she replenished her energy by picking the flowers that grew along the edge of the Tabernacle. As she was gathering them into a bouquet, she spotted Paul Dillon peeking around one of the pillars.

"Get out here, you chowderhead!"

Paul's jaw dropped as he bounded toward her. "Avery Norton, such language! What would your mother say?"

Burying her face in dandelions, she shrugged coyly. "I'm sure I don't know what you mean."

He chuckled and plucked a flower from her hand. "Stop trying to convince people you're a girl."

"You're right. They suit you much better." She tossed the dandelions at him and dashed away, knowing he'd chase after.

They raced around the Tabernacle until she skidded to a stop, and he slammed into her, knocking them both to the ground in a fit of laughter.

"I did that on purpose," she said, beaming. "I knew you'd never catch me, and I didn't want to make you feel bad."

6

"I'll catch you one of these days, Avery Norton." Helping her up, he said, "Come on, I'll buy you a basket of fried clams."

"I don't know if I have time. I have to meet Natalie at the boat in an hour."

"What kind of Vineyarder are you? We can eat th*ree* baskets in an hour!"

Bellies full and fingers glistening, Avery and Paul waited impatiently as Natalie Norton disembarked the Island Queen. At fourteen, she acted older than her years, which she blamed on an exhausting all-girl environment at Dana Hall, the boarding school she attended in Wellesley. But through her scowl, Avery detected a simmering happiness in her big sister. So, she hugged her. She teased her. She and Paul ran circles around her until she confessed that coming home, even for a weekend, even at the height of tourist season, loosened the noose that was her structured life at school.

Avery, on the other hand, felt her sprightly age in spades. Not even towing her groaning sister from place to place dampened her verve. The salty sweet summer air fueled her as she ran from one side of the town to the other, to the beaches and jetties, to the ponds and parking lots. Natalie's energy was quickly spent, but Paul never once left her side. He bounced from foot to foot and sang songs her mother had forbidden. Avery didn't have radio privileges often, so she relied on Paul to teach her the latest Perry Como and Eddie Fisher so she'd stay in the loop. He'd sing the hits and show off his dance moves and open her mind to a universe of culture she wasn't permitted to know. She even got to watch his family's television set on occasion— without her mother's knowledge, of course. It was an exciting moment, especially when Paul told Avery he had a color set. He bragged about it for weeks on end, so her expectations were sky-high. But when she finally came over, she discovered it was just a black and white set with colored saran wrap stretched over the screen. She didn't rag on him too much, though. It was still new, still a treat, and she was happy to back him up when kids at school asked about his amazing color TV.

In July, the island was teeming with summer blood. Kids ran wild through the streets of Oak Bluffs with their parents trailing lazily behind, more fixated on the architecture than the shiny trays of fudge in the front window of Hillard's. While some Vineyarders rolled their eyes when the ferries pulled in and a slew of eager tourists poured out, Avery couldn't help but latch onto their excitement. Lots of island kids worked non-stop during the summer anyway, and her mother didn't approve of many of the ones who didn't. Each boat brought a heap of potential friends, and because their time on the island was brief, they usually appeared and disappeared before her mother knew they existed.

But she would never hide or deny her friendship with Paul, to her mother or anyone. As he watched the last vestiges of the Holy Ghost Festival draw to a close that evening, Natalie caught Avery staring at him and elbowed her side.

"You like him, don't you?"

Avery's face burned. "I don't know what you're talking about."

"Don't lie. I can tell you like him. Does he like you?"

"Ssh!"

Paul jogged over to retrieve a flower crown that flew off a parade-goer's head. Once he dashed away to return it, she pulled her sister close.

"I think so. The last time we went camping, well, it was weird." She crinkled her nose. "And good."

"Have you kissed?"

She shook her head. "But we've gotten close."

"Close is good. Closer is better," Natalie said with a wink. "Maybe tonight."

As Avery contemplated the possibilities, Paul trotted past and gestured for them to hurry up.

"You should say goodnight to him alone. When we get home, go around to the garden. I'll wait out front."

"Are you sure?"

"If you don't, I will." Natalie chuckled.

When Avery punched her arm, her sister gave her a shove that tripped her up on the path. She skidded and crashed into Paul. She was mortified, but with a snicker that wasn't the least bit derisive, he tilted her back onto her feet, and said, "I knew you were falling for me, Avery Norton."

She swatted his arm playfully as she contemplated the right response, but her mind went blank. She became especially flustered once Natalie began making ridiculous gestures for her to escort Paul behind the house.

"So . . . " He crinkled his nose. "Goodnight, I guess."

She shrugged. "I guess."

"Happy birthday."

Avery wanted the next thing she said to sound elegant. Maybe even sexy; something her mother would think entirely improper. But when she said, "Do you want to go to the garden with me?" it sounded more like her first attempt at a tongue twister.

He didn't laugh at her trip-ups, though. He smiled and took her hand, and all the stars burned brighter as they walked behind the house to the garden.

She intended to bring up their last camping trip casually, then work up to confessing her feelings for him, but she didn't have to. Before she could think of a jumping-off point, Paul Dillon's lips were pressing against hers. His kiss was eager but soft, with just enough pressure to both frighten and draw her in, and the slight wetness that might've disgusted her a year ago made her skin prickle in the most delicious way.

Avery wasn't secure in her knowledge of love and relationships. She had very few memories of her father and mother together, and none extended past the age of five. Whatever love they'd felt for each other before he left made no impact on her either way. But she understood affection and devotion, and she knew what she felt for Paul was real. They didn't need anyone to teach them the how or why. They were already best friends: a love without judgment or pretense. It was beyond reason, yet as natural and beautiful as the bluestars surrounding them in the twilight garden.

Leaning back, he said, "Happy birthday, Avery."

Dazed by the kiss, she purred, "Happy birthday, Paul." She clapped her hand over her face in embarrassment, and he squeezed her tight.

"I just mean I don't think I could've asked for a better birthday present."

"I do have a real present for you," he said. "Can I bring it by tomorrow?"

"I don't know. You know my mom is strange about unplanned visits." Paul pouted, and Avery sighed as she spun out of his arms. "All right, I'm sure it'll be fine."

Natalie peeked around the corner. "Say your goodbyes. Mom's about to flip."

"Goodnight, Paul. Thanks again."

He kissed Avery on the cheek and bounded down the street under ever-brightening stars.

Avery waltzed to her sister and collapsed against her side.

"Good birthday?"

She hummed, cheeks aflame. "I've had worse."

As they approached the front door, Natalie wrapped her arm around her sister and said, "Hold on to that feeling for as long as you can."

CHAPTER THREE

HER MOTHER HADN'T told her when to be home, but Avery knew she was late the moment she entered the house. Decorations sagged, and presents, once precariously stacked, had tumbled off the coffee table. And Faye's "not-so-famous but nothing to be sneezed at" stew, while filling the house with a delicious aroma, was getting cold in one of the three bowls arranged on the kitchen table.

"Avery, sweetie, is that you?"

"And Natalie," Avery replied as she towed her sister into the kitchen.

Faye's face was sunshine when she saw her eldest daughter, but her voice came out deep as midnight. "Yes of course. How was the trip?"

"The same."

"That's lovely, dear."

Faye gestured to the bowl of stew on the table and pulled out the chair. "I'm afraid you've allowed your food to get cold, Natalie, but if there are leftovers after I fill Avery's bowl, you could spoon some more in to heat it up."

"I'll be fine," she said, sliding into the seat.

"If you say so." Faye waved for her youngest daughter to sit. "You look flushed, honey. You didn't run home, did you?"

Natalie stuck her tongue out at Avery, who smacked her sister with a napkin.

"I'm just excited about my birthday. And hungry."

"Ready in a minute," Faye replied in singsong and stirred the pot.

Wherever she was, whoever was speaking, Faye Norton's melodic voice owned the room. Her volume often intimidated those around her, and it shocked folks who heard her voice before getting a glimpse of her. Faye was a thin woman with a delicate frame who looked like a stiff breeze might shatter her before it could knock her over. There were many who believed she couldn't handle the physical demands of maintaining her house and family after her husband left, but then someone would spot her on the roof, cleaning the gutters, ripping off shingles, and all the while singing softly to herself. Despite the demands of caring for two children on her own, she kept her house in order and her demeanor unfrazzled. For practicality, she wore her mahogany hair in a bun that commanded the nape of her neck, and she fully embraced her grayed widow's peak and the silver streaks at her temples, but Faye Norton was hardly the easygoing type. She had high standards and staunch morals, and one sneer from the woman could chill someone to the bone. Then she'd speak, and the melodic timbre of her voice would make them feel warm again, and safe.

She was nothing if not a loving mother, of which she frequently reminded her daughters, and though she could be a tad overbearing, she understood the girls needed their space. So did she, and sometimes went out on weekend nights to play bridge or bingo for that very reason.

Avery once asked Paul's mom if she'd played in Faye's bridge game, and she said she hadn't—didn't know anyone else who had, either. In fact, Faye had never responded to any of Mrs. Dillon's invitations to join *her* game. It didn't make sense to Avery, but it also wasn't any of her business. It didn't matter if Faye wasn't playing bridge; she deserved a break from cooking, gardening, and praying for her daughters' souls as much as anyone.

To call Faye Norton a devout Catholic would've been an understatement. Though she'd toned down talk of the scriptures over the years, she never failed to broadcast that she was in the religious minority of Martha's Vineyard. Except for descendants of Portuguese immigrants from the islands of Azore, most of the island was Protestant, which Faye believed made her faith burn brighter. She seized every opportunity to instill the love of the Virgin Mary and the word of God in her daughters' hearts. But when boredom reared its ugly head, she knew when to put down the Bible and try different, more tangible lessons.

When Avery finished her last bite of stew, Natalie bounced to her side with gifts in her arms.

"Which do you want to open first?"

"I wish there was a way to open them all at once. Boom!" she exclaimed, throwing her hands in the air. "An explosion of paper and presents all over the room!"

"I hope you don't think I'd be the one cleaning up that mess," her mother said from the kitchen. "Besides, it doesn't matter which you open first; they're all going to pale in comparison to *my* gift anyway."

Her head drooping in dejection, Natalie set aside her present. But Avery snatched it up with a cheer and tore away the wrapping paper. Ripping off the lid, she gasped at the plaid pink jumper inside. She held it against her body and swayed from side to side as if dancing with it.

"I love it! It's so pretty. Don't you think it's pretty, Mom?"

Based on Faye's expression of wide-eyed shock and lip-curling disgust, she obviously didn't find it pretty at all. Yanking the dress from Avery, she shoved it at her eldest daughter. "What is this, Natalie? What kind of present is this for your twelve-year-old sister? It doesn't even reach her knees! It looks like something a tart would wear!"

"Mom, it's not that short."

"I don't know what kind of dresses you're wearing off island, but they'd better not be anything like this piece of trash."

"They're not. I didn't think it was trashy, I swear. I didn't know Avery's size, so I guessed."

"Size has nothing to do with it, young lady. I can't believe you spent your money—" Faye's face tightened. "No, you spent *my* money on this. I'd suggest Avery use it as doll's clothes instead, but I'm not keen on her dolls dressing like tarts either." She threw the jumper into the garbage can and exhaled loudly. "Enough of that. Let's move on with the celebration." With a jubilant chirp, she pulled Avery from her seat, covered her eyes, and nudged her to the back door. "Are you ready for the best present of all?"

The lock clicked, and the door opened with a crisp swish. Avery knew she was being ushered outside but she didn't understand why. She didn't see anything special in the backyard when she and Paul were out there. Nothing more special than Paul, anyway.

Pulling her hands from her daughter's eyes, Faye shouted, "Surprise!" and Avery waited.

What was the surprise. There was only the garden. It was a beautiful garden, but it was just a garden. And it was her mother's garden.

"Happy birthday, honey!"

When Avery looked around in confusion, her mother slid in front of her, threw her arms open, and said, "It's yours! I'm giving you the garden!"

"Oh. You are?" She crinkled her nose. "Why?"

"Because it's important for you to learn responsibility. There are other things too, but we can talk about those later."

"What other things?"

Natalie leaned against the door, arms crossed. "Go on, Mom. Tell her."

Faye said her eldest daughter's name like a warning and pointed her back inside. "We'll talk about the garden later, sweetheart. Let's try to enjoy the rest of your birthday."

Avery received lots of presents she preferred over the garden, but with each piece of paper stripped away and every bow untied, her mother hovered ever closer, studying

44

her reactions. She was exhausted by the time she opened her last gift, but her mother insisted she write the first entry in the diary from Grandma Amelia before going to bed. The book open on her lap, she pressed pencil to paper with no idea what to write.

"Why don't you write about your favorite present?" her mother suggested with eyelids fluttering.

Avery nodded but didn't write. The truth was she liked Natalie's gift best, but when rosy eagerness bled over her mother's face, she wrote in clean capital letters:

"Today, Mom gave me a garden."

Faye gasped and kissed the top of Avery's head. "I'm glad you love it so much! And I love you. Goodnight, sweet birthday girl."

She hummed joyfully as she strode out, the stairs creaking under her celebratory dance. Once the house was quiet, Avery closed the diary and gazed out her bedroom window. The moonlit garden looked different now that it was hers. Every growing shadow felt like a threat. Each crunch and flutter filled her with nauseating dread.

Natalie joined her at the window, her hand on her sister's back. "Try not to worry about it."

"How am I supposed to do that? I don't know anything about gardening."

"You don't need to know as much as you think. Gardening isn't the real reason Mom gave it to you."

"What do you mean?"

Natalie swallowed hard. "It's probably nothing. And I don't want to ruin your birthday. We'll talk about it later, okay?" She wrapped her arm around Avery's neck and pulled her from the window. "Has it been a good birthday?"

"It was wonderful. I was hoping Daddy might come, though," she added, red-faced.

"You say that every year. I think it's time to give up on that dream."

"I can't help it. I miss him. Aunt Lily too. They didn't even send cards."

"They're never going to. Look, I have theories on Dad's whereabouts—" When Avery tilted her head, Natalie sucked on her bottom lip. "Forget it. Anyway, after the fight Mom and Aunt Lily had all those years ago, I doubt we'll ever hear from her again. And I don't blame Aunt Lily in the slightest." Flopping onto her sister's bed, Natalie exhaled heavily. "I'm sorry, Avery. I miss you like crazy, and I do love the island, but I don't miss being here."

"Why?" she asked, sitting beside her.

Natalie covered her face with a pillow and groaned. "I hate to say it's because of Mom, but . . . "

Avery pulled the pillow off her sister's face, and Natalie twitched her nose.

" . . . it's because of Mom. You'll understand soon enough."

"At least she doesn't force me to go to church anymore."

"That's because she's giving you sermons right here. She just disguises them better than priests."

"What did Mom and Aunt Lily fight about?"

"I don't know. Sister stuff," Natalie said as she swiped at Avery's hair.

"We never fight about 'sister stuff.'" She batted back, and the girls giggled.

"We probably would if I still lived here. If . . . " Natalie lowered her head. " . . . if Mom hadn't hidden me away like a bad secret."

"Did she ever give *you* the garden?"

"Not the way she did today. She put me in charge, but not for long. I guess I wasn't a very good little gardener." She ran her fingers through her hair and sat up. "She sent me away soon after that, as far as she could."

"Oh Natalie, that's not why I did it." Their mother's voice chimed in the doorway, and both girls yelped. Faye entered the room, pouting, her hands clutched to her chest as if Natalie's words fired an arrow into her heart. "Girls, you know I only want the best for you. Yes, even you,

Natalie. I wanted you to stay, but everyone agreed boarding school would be a more productive place for you."

"Everyone," she scoffed. "Avery, did you have a say in it too?"

"What a horrible thing to say to your sister on her birthday," Faye hissed.

Avery said, "It's fine," but her mother shushed her.

"It's not fine. Natalie should know better. She's smart. That's why Dana Hall is the perfect place for her. She needed to be challenged."

"So I'm *not* smart?" Avery asked, brow furrowed.

"Of course you are. That's why I've entrusted the garden to you. It was important for Natalie, but it will be even more important for you. Within, my love, you have a capacity for faith as I've never seen. And that openness will lead you down all kinds of golden paths. You will learn things you never imagined, things your sister never believed in, when she let the garden go dry."

"It was one time," Natalie said.

"One time too many," she snapped. The cold expression melted fast, though, and she touched both of her daughters' cheeks. "Isn't it nice to be together again?"

She said goodnight and disconnected from Avery, but her hand slid to Natalie's wrist, and she towed her to the door. Head down and voice soft, Natalie wished her sister "Happy birthday," and their mother pulled her out of the room.

CHAPTER FOUR

BACON COAXED AVERY out of sleep. Bounding out of bed at the first delicious whiff, she flew down the stairs to find her mother cooking a breakfast fit for a queen.

"Good morning, Miss Twelve-Year-Old."

Avery gave her mother's waist a tiny squeeze. "Morning. Where's Natalie?"

"I guess she had a change of heart. She caught the first ferry out."

Avery squealed. "What? Why?"

"I don't know, sweetie. I know you were happy to have her back, and I thought she was happy to be back. I'm afraid it might be my fault. I shouldn't have given you the garden in front of her. Maybe she was angry. Maybe she was jealous. I tried to change her mind, but we ended up at the boat anyway. I'm sorry, Avery. I did try."

She exhaled a shuddering breath. "It's okay. I'm just sad is all."

"You have every right to be. We both do. I bought all this food and there's no way we'll be able to eat it all ourselves. Maybe you could call a friend? Stephanie Miller from next door?"

Avery's heart accelerated to a delicious speed. "May I call Paul?"

"Paul? What's wrong with Stephanie?"

"Nothing. I just like Paul more."

Faye stiffened. "You *what*?"

"I like him more."

"I see," she said dryly. "All right then. Call Paul. But we have to talk about your birthday present after breakfast."

"Which present?"

Faye frowned. "The garden, of course."

"I know, Mom." Avery chuckled shakily. "I was just kidding."

Avery skipped to the phone and smacked it off its cradle. She caught it long before it hit the floor, but her mother glared at her anyway. With an apology, she clamped the phone to her ear and asked the operator to connect her with number 1551. A stunning burst of joy surged through her body when Paul answered the phone, and it increased at his ecstatic and grateful acceptance of the Nortons' breakfast invitation.

Avery refused to eat a thing until he arrived. While the food got cold, she stared at the door in anticipation, and Faye stared at her daughter in concern. At the fervent knock, Avery scrambled from the kitchen while her mother hollered after.

"You're a lady, Avery! Please act like one!"

Faye huffed as she caught up with her daughter. She smoothed her dress and fixed her hair, and with a worried pout, stepped aside.

Avery thought she might be wearing history's biggest smile when she opened the door, but Paul's gave it a run for its money. Her stomach fluttered, and his cheeks reddened, and Faye scowled as she gestured for the boy to come inside.

"Good morning, Paul. It's nice to see you today."

"It's nice to see you too, Mrs. Norton. Thank you for inviting me over."

"That was all Avery, dear." As she led him into the kitchen, she peeked over his shoulder. "What's that behind your back?"

"Oh! It's a birthday present." He held out a large box wrapped in newspaper and a pink ribbon. "Sorry I forgot to bring it yesterday."

Paul slipped around Faye and handed Avery the box, which she sat delicately on the kitchen table.

"You two were together yesterday?"

"We ran into each other at the campground." She pulled the ribbon slowly, savoring the silky unfurling, peeled the paper, lifted the lid, and gasped as she beheld Paul's gift.

"I hope you like it.," he said, jittery as she unfolded the dress. "I hope it fits."

Holding up the same pink plaid jumper Natalie had gotten her, Avery giggled in gratitude. She also did her best not to make eye-contact with her mom, who stood with her arms folded and a rigid scowl carved into her face.

"I love it, Paul! Thank you!"

"You don't already have it, do you?"

"Not at all," she said sweetly. "I'll put it on right now."

Faye's brow furrowed. "Avery, do you really think it's appropriate to leave your guest here alone?"

"It'll just take a second," she said and skipped off to change.

When she returned, she twirled the dress dramatically, arms outstretched. Paul clapped in a gleeful rhythm, urging her to spin faster and faster, while Faye's face blanched.

"Avery, sit down," she said, her tone hushed but pointed. "Eat up."

She grudgingly obeyed and sat across from Paul at the kitchen table. After they began eating, Faye resumed tidying the kitchen—one eye always on the children, of course. When she noticed they'd stopped eating and were speaking quietly to each other, she marched over and startled Avery into dropping her fork.

"What have you been up to this summer, Paul?" Faye asked. She lifted her eyebrows at him. "Besides running around the campgrounds with my daughter, of course."

"Working in my dad's garage, mostly. I'm supposed to be visiting my grandparents in Boston soon, but my grampa is sick right now, so we might wait until the fall."

"I'm sorry to hear that," Faye said. "Being around his family might be good for him, though. God willing, he'll pull through on his own, but perhaps seeing his grandson's face would lift his spirits."

"It's my mom's decision. She said he's already on the mend and we can make it a Thanksgiving or Christmas trip. She says summers are important for kids. They give us our greatest memories and always pass too quick."

"I agree," Avery chimed. Her mother's attention shot to her, and she shrank in her chair. "I mean it seems like summer's just starting, and then it's time for school again."

"Sometimes I think the summers are too long," Faye said wearily.

She continued to monitor the children closely, and the moment Paul swallowed his final bite of scrambled eggs, Faye snatched his plate and swept the food from the table.

"Thank you, Mrs. Norton." Paul dabbed his mouth with his napkin and cleared his throat. "So, Avery, do you want to go to the Flying Horses today?"

Avery looked up at her mother in hope, but Faye's expression answered before she could ask. She hung her head and said despondently, "I think I have things to do."

"Speaking of which, we should really get started, honey." Faye loomed over the table, her eyes narrowed at the boy.

"Oh." Paul tried to hide it, but his voice dripped with disappointment as he stood. "Well, it was nice seeing you for even a little while. And breakfast was really good, Mrs. Norton."

Faye gestured to the door. "Have a lovely afternoon, Paul."

Avery ran after as Faye escorted him out, but before they could flash even the hint of farewell, Faye closed the door and flipped the lock. She whined, but it didn't register with her mother. There was no sympathy, not even annoyance—only delight as she clapped her hands and trilled: "To the garden?"

Faye held Avery's hand and led her outside. She guided and spun her, pointing out notable plants and produce as if they'd materialized overnight. It felt odd, but she couldn't deny the beauty of it, and speaking about the garden filled her mother with such vigorous worship, she found herself catching a similar exhilaration.

The eastern bluestars stood tallest, surrounded by a thick crop of yellow daylilies, and bountiful bushes with thorny branches bent by the weight of black raspberries. The bird feeder swayed from side to side as the chickadees hopped around the perches, and sunlight glinted across the tomatoes' dew-kissed skin while blossoms stretched wide to soak up every ray. The flowers looked like a diverse company of dancers too mesmerized by their own beauty to sense the seasonal curtain call, and the vegetables resembled proud soldiers in formation, awaiting a summons to culinary arms. It was a glorious sight, but to Avery, this day in the garden was no more astounding than any other day, and certainly not as magical as her previous evening with Paul.

As mother and daughter sat on the stone bench at the garden's core, Faye breathed in the pleasing aroma and sighed as if life couldn't get any better. But gazing upon Avery, she knew that if the girl was open to her lessons, it could get better still.

"Honey, do you remember the story about Adam and Eve and the Garden of Eden?"

"Yes."

"And how the world got ruined because evil found its way into the Garden?"

"I guess."

"It's not actually true," her mother said. "It's a metaphor, you see. Do you know what a metaphor is?"

Avery scrunched her nose. "Like a symbol?"

"Exactly. The Garden of Eden is a symbol for an ideal world. The serpent that persuaded Adam and Eve to disobey God is the one who poisoned the Garden. There are things that can poison *our* world, too." Faye laid her hands atop her daughter's. "Water, for instance. Good, clean water can give life, it can help the world flourish and its beneficiaries grow. Bad water does the opposite."

"There's bad water?"

"There is indeed. The bad water wilts the garden, makes it pale with disease. Sometimes it will cause the garden to sprout fat weeds that kill the healthy plants. Then the insects come to devour them, and they rot the fruit from the inside out. If even one drop of bad water spills into the soil, the beautiful garden you see before you will lose all its beauty."

"How can I tell if water is good or bad?"

"It's tricky, for certain. Sometimes you can tell right away: the spigot might be rusted, or the water might smell funny. But most of the time, you can't tell by looking. Everything might look clean and pure, and you don't know the water's bad until it starts flowing. Then it's too late. It's much safer to assume all water is bad. The garden—and the world—would rather die of thirst than toxins, and that goes for all of the living things it nourishes: the birds, the bees, the rabbits . . . "

"The rabbits, too?"

"Oh yes, Avery. The rabbits most of all. They eat from this garden as much as we do. And like us, they are very vulnerable to infection, and once that happens, there's not much you can do. It's best to put such damaged creatures out of their misery. That's the ones you see hanging on hooks in butcher shop windows, stripped and skinned, and ignorant to the choices that put them there." When Avery cocked her head in confusion, Faye wrapped her arm around her daughter. "And unfortunately, my darling, bad water isn't limited to this patch of land. There are many veins through which bad water can flow, to all the gardens of the world. You never know exactly where you'll find it, so you must always be on alert and avoid the places it's most likely to run."

"But there isn't any here, is there?"

"Not yet. Not ever, I hope. But that doesn't mean it won't try to get in. It's always trying to get in. You just have to take good care of your garden." She bopped her on the nose, and Avery chuckled.

Maybe it wouldn't be as bad as Natalie said. Just because she never gave the garden much thought before didn't mean she couldn't grow to love tending it. And it made her mother so happy.

She popped up from the bench. "Should I get the watering can?"

"Not yet. Let's sit a while longer." She squeezed her daughter's hand. "There's something I want you to see."

They sat for nearly an hour in silence, all the while Faye's spine remained straight, her gaze attentive and searching. Avery did her best to mimic her, but her eyelids soon drooped. She considered asking her mom if she could go inside—numerous times, in fact—but never mustered the courage.

Faye gasped, and Avery flinched to attentiveness.

"There, honey." She pointed at the cabbage patch. "There, do you see them?"

Avery tiptoed to a patch of rustling cabbage and parted the leaves gingerly. There, below the green canopy, two rabbits stared up at her with large, red eyes. They wiggled their noses, twitched their ears, then resumed their prior activity—which appeared to be some form of rabbit wrestling.

Avery scrunched her face in puzzlement. "It's just rabbits."

"What are they doing? Eating the cabbage?"

"Maybe. There are bite marks, but they aren't eating it right now. They're playing, I guess."

"One on top of the other?"

She leaned in, suspicious. "What are they doing?"

When Avery looked over her shoulder, Faye was standing directly behind her with a paisley gardening bag in hand. Smirking, she withdrew a pair of shears and gave the blades a quick double snip. Before Avery could question it, the shears flew past her face and down into the cabbage patch. Stabbing the top rabbit through the head and the bottom rabbit through the back, Faye gritted her teeth as she lifted the blades. The bottom rabbit slid off, but the top remained skewered, its mouth agape. She twisted them, turning the rabbit's face—frozen in its death rattle—to her horrified daughter.

Avery tried to run, but her mother latched onto her jumper, wadding the pink fabric of Paul's gift in her bloody fist. The rabbit still flopping on the blades, she towed her wailing daughter to the bench.

"Be quiet," Faye hissed, plunking Avery on the seat. Setting the shears aside, she wiped her hands on her apron and sat, arms folded over her chest. "Come now, Avery, you need to calm down. This is just too much."

"Too much?" she stammered through streaming tears. "What did you do? Why did you do that?"

"Because they were trying to poison the garden," Faye replied. "Because they deserved it."

"No, no, it's not fair. It's not right!"

"It *is* right!" Faye crouched in front of her daughter to seize her focus. "What they were doing—it was the bad water infecting them, influencing them. They needed to be put out of their misery. It was the humane thing to do."

Her voice was lovely again, like an angel's song. Angels didn't lie, and if they did, they probably had very good reasons. But it made Avery's head spin and grow heavy, and her sobs changed to intermittent moans and sniffles.

"What were they doing that was so bad?"

"Let me show you." Plucking the skewered rabbit from the ground, she freed it from the shears and flipped it over. "Do you see the mark on its belly?"

Its belly? How could Avery look at its belly when its slack face was staring at her as if begging for another chance to make a different choice.

"Avery, answer me."

"Yes. I see the yellow mark."

"And what about the other rabbit?" she said, pointing to the carcass with her scissors.

Avery squinted through tears. "It's blue."

"Correct. You see, I've marked every rabbit in this garden, always in pairs. When I found two rabbits playing in *that way*, I marked them with the same color: blue and blue together, yellow and yellow, and so on. If we find two with mismatched colors, it means the rabbits are switching partners. They're being brazen, blasphemous. They're being bad, Avery, and we can't have bad rabbits in the garden."

It felt like a pot was boiling over inside her, spilling frothy nausea throughout her body. She was afraid to open her mouth, and the threat of vomiting became more real when she smelled the blood on her jumper. But she swallowed her disgust the way she swallowed the realization that her dad had missed another birthday.

Faye pried the blades out of the second rabbit's back, and Avery's brow furrowed.

"Wait. The colors are on their stomachs," she said. "How did you know these two didn't match?"

Her lips curled slowly, and she sandwiched her daughter's hands between hers. "I've been doing this long enough that I can tell. One day, so will you."

Avery's brain felt like it was filling up with tears. She shook her head and growled between gritted teeth. "No, I can't. I can't kill rabbits."

"No one's asking you to kill anything. I'm asking you to protect the garden from the bad water. If it's clean and pure, this sort of thing won't happen. I set this up to teach you that." Frowning, she wiped away her daughter's tears. "I'm sorry I frightened you, but it's important for you to know what happens when rabbits—and people—are careless with their bodies. Some don't even realize they're poisoning themselves, and that's when good people like us must step in and help them understand the evil they're doing. You are part of a very important process, Avery."

"I don't think I can do it."

"You're already doing it, my love. Open your eyes."

"I'm trying, but . . . why can't you take care of the garden like you've been doing all along?"

"Because you're old enough to do it yourself now. Besides, I have bigger gardens to tend." Faye kissed her daughter's forehead. "You'll do just fine, sweetie. Come on, let's get you cleaned up and throw away that filthy dress."

After a long bath, Avery lay down in her bed to absorb the truths of the day, but she saw the rabbits every time her eyelids drooped. Their red eyes burned, and their jaws slackened as they floated to her, mouths stretching wide enough to swallow her whole. And though she eventually cried herself to sleep that night, it didn't always work. Mismatched rabbits haunted her for weeks, but with each day she tended the garden, the nightmares faded a little more. Every morning, Avery rose with the garden in mind. She enjoyed some aspects of spending her days in the backyard, but she refused to spend one minute enjoying it before she knew the water was clean. She examined the color, the smell, even the feel of it between her fingers. If it was too warm or slightly cloudy, she poured it out and started again. But she did the same thing if she thought it was fine and happened to notice her mom watching her. The weeks passed and the obsession grew, but it was an obsession born of fear instead of desire.

She didn't want any more rabbits to die.

Avery knew it pleased Faye to see her working so hard to keep their little world clean and pure, but she found it difficult to conceal her boredom. She strained her mind and body more than ever before, and for what? Yes, she'd kept the flora and fauna alive, but she felt like she hadn't enjoyed a full day of her own life since her twelfth birthday. She couldn't help mourning all the time the garden had devoured. It was time she could've spent climbing the ornate roofs of Wesleyan Grove or running up and down the streets of Oak Bluffs. It was time she could've spent with Paul.

But she said nothing. She kept her head down and eyes vigilantly searching for any sign of contamination. And for nearly two months, Avery wore fake smiles so her mother could wear real ones.

And she was sick of it.

CHAPTER FIVE

FOR THE FIRST time in weeks, Avery started her day like the garden wanted to sleep in late. While Faye worked in the basement, Avery covertly made her way downtown to fraternize with the summer kids. But it didn't take her long to realize it wasn't summer anymore. The streets weren't empty, but the impending Autumn had stolen the youthful brunt of the crowds. Her mare was one of the few Flying Horses with a rider, so she fought harder than ever for the brass ring. Not that the lack of competition helped.

As she threw her steel rings into the bin and the carousel slowed, a welcome face appeared on the other side of the gate.

"I was wondering if I'd see you before school started," Paul said, meeting her as she dismounted her horse.

"Sorry about that. I've been busy."

"It feels like you're avoiding me. Did I do something wrong?"

"I haven't been avoiding you."

"Avery, I've called your house every day for two months."

"You have?" She stopped so suddenly, she nearly tumbled down the steps outside the Flying Horses. Catching herself, she sat down and stretched out her legs. She hadn't realized until that moment how bruised her knees were from working in the garden every day.

"Your mom didn't tell you I called?"

Avery shook her head. "No, she didn't."

"I knew it." Paul grunted and flopped down beside her. "Why doesn't your mom like me?"

"I don't know, but I get the feeling she doesn't like me much either. I've done nothing but take care of that stupid garden for months, and why? So she doesn't have to? She never even taught me *how* to garden except for the part about the good water and bad water, but I've kept things alive and growing, and none of the mismatched rabbits have been jumping on each other—"

"Avery, what are you talking about?"

"I'm talking about gratitude. She stands in that window for hours with this dumb smile, like she's more pleased with herself than with me. I sacrificed my whole summer for that stupid garden."

Paul's cheeks reddened and he scooted closer to her. "Summer's not over yet."

At that moment, Avery imagined all the things they would do for the rest of the day—fishing, getting ice cream, maybe a long bike ride—but they didn't do any of those things. Instead, they climbed onto the pink cottage known as the Wooden Valentine, empty for the impending off-season, and stretched out to watch the day melt into night.

Avery wasn't sure when her hand found its way into his, but not wanting to jinx it, she stayed quiet. Obviously, Paul didn't have the same self-control. He flipped onto his side to face her and squeezed her hand, eyes brimming with fear.

"Was it the kiss? Is that what made you disappear this summer?" he asked.

"I told you, it wasn't anything you did. It was the garden."

"You never cared about the garden before."

"But my mom gave it to me for my birthday, and she made a really big fuss about keeping the bad water out."

"What bad water?"

She groaned. "I don't know. She keeps getting weirder and weirder. All she does is watch me tend to the garden like it's some kind of show. Then she leaves me alone while she goes off to God knows where. She's going somewhere tonight, too. I'm a little worried about her."

"She's supposed to worry about you, not the other way around."

"I know." She grumbled. "I'm probably just being stupid."

"Hey, don't call my best friend stupid." He poked Avery playfully, and she chuckled. "If you're that worried, we could follow her when she leaves tonight, see where she goes. Then you'll know if there's something to worry about."

"What if we got caught? She would kill me."

"I'll protect you." Paul gallantly threw punches at an invisible foe, and he and Avery sprawled on the roof in a fit of laughter.

When it was quiet again, Avery whispered, "Paul?"

"Yeah?"

"Do you think we'll ever do it again?"

"Do what?"

Hopefully, Avery replied, "Kiss?"

Paul sat up as if spring loaded. Avery sat up slowly, gliding closer as he eagerly scooted forward. The question had been asked, but there was no need for it to be answered in words.

Avery didn't think anything could be more magical than their first kiss, but atop the Wooden Valentine, under a canopy of stars, it seemed they hadn't scraped the surface of magic's potential, or how it could change them. She wanted to shout it from the gingerbread rooftops, but she held it in—and not just because she feared the story would get back to her mom. She didn't want to share it with Natalie either, or even write about it in her diary. It was the kind of moment that couldn't be done justice in the retelling. It belonged to them alone, frozen in time with the power to warm them throughout their lives.

Avery was so caught up in Paul's lips and hands and the way his hair softly brushed against her forehead she didn't notice how late it had gotten. Glancing at his watch, she yelped. "Shoot! I have to get home!"

"Wait, what about the plan for tonight?"

"What plan?"

"To follow your mom."

"I don't think it's a good idea. She might not even go out tonight."

"So I'll wait outside until you find out," he said. "It'll be easy. We'll just hide in the back seat of her car. She still keeps a bunch of quilts back there, doesn't she?"

She nodded. "I used to hide there when it was my dad's car. I'd spring out and scare him. Even though he'd act sore about it, he'd still let me pretend I was driving the car up and down the driveway."

The rare, lovely memory of her father dazed her. She had so few, she wanted to hold onto it. When Paul nudged her, eyebrows raised, she giggled and shrugged coyly.

"I guess it could work."

"Of course it could. It'll be dark. We'll be quiet. And then you'll finally know what she's up to. My money's on a secret boyfriend."

"I don't think that's it."

"A night job, maybe. She's got to get money from somewhere, right? I think that school your sister goes to is pretty expensive."

"I guess I never thought about it."

"That's because you're too busy thinking about me." Paul gave her a playful shove she returned with a chuckle. "Oh! I almost forgot! I have something for you."

"What is it?" she asked, bouncing her knees.

He reached into his pocket and held aloft the prized brass ring from the Flying Horses.

She gasped. "Did you steal that?"

"No, no. I bought it." The ring glowed like the Holy Ghost Festival in the moonlight. Like honor and beauty and faith. "Actually," he said, head bowed, "I got it a while ago, but I guess I was too afraid to give it to you."

"Why?"

"I don't know. You're . . . something else, Avery Norton. You scare me a little."

"I scare you?" She clawed the hair out of her eyes. "Just what every girl wants to hear."

"I wouldn't say it to any other girl. No one scares me as wonderfully as you." Holding it up, he crinkled his nose. "You do want it, right?"

"Of course!" Avery grinned when he hung the oversized ring on her finger, and it swung like a pendulum. "Maybe I should get a chain for it. Until then . . . " She tucked the ring into her dress pocket and kissed him softly on the lips. "Thank you, Paul."

As the pair walked back to Huntington Avenue, Avery didn't let go of the brass ring—or Paul. But she knew Faye would be watching for her, so when her house was in sight, she sped up to distance herself from him. She was just about to cross into her yard when he suddenly grabbed her around the waist, pulled her behind a tree, and kissed her.

When they broke apart, his face burned with joy. "Just in case I don't get to do that later."

Avery beamed as she dashed away, still so focused on Paul that she almost ran into the fence lining her yard. She recovered and burst into the house, but her joy fled when she came face to face with her mother.

Faye tapped her foot angrily, hands on her hips. "Do you know what time it is? Where have you been?"

"Out playing. I lost track of time."

"Playing with whom?"

"Oh . . . just Paul."

Faye inhaled sharply, her body tense. "Avery, this is too much. Did you even water the garden today?"

"I'll do it right now."

"Oh no you won't. Right now, you'll march yourself upstairs and get ready for bed. I don't want you coming out of your room for the rest of the night."

"But Mom—"

"Don't 'but Mom' me. I've been waiting for you long enough, and now I'm late for Bingo. While I'm gone, I don't want you setting even one foot out of your room. Is that clear, young lady?"

"Yes, ma'am." She trudged up to her room and locked the door, then ran on tiptoes to her open window and peered out into the dark.

"Paul?" she called in a whisper. "Paul, are you there?"

He stepped out from behind a tree and waved, his eyes glinting in the moonlight.

"She grounded me."

"Oh." He bopped his head from shoulder to shoulder. "So that means you're already in trouble, and you don't have anything to risk. Don't you think?"

Avery chuckled. "I guess that's true. Okay, I'll be right down."

She climbed out the window, onto the roof, and inched to the beetlebung tree overlapping the side of the house. With a heavy exhalation, she wrapped her arms around the closest branch. The limb bowed slightly under her weight, but she nimbly crept to the trunk and climbed down.

Paul whispered, "Hurry!" and opened the back door of Faye's car.

They scrambled inside and burrowed under the quilts. After a few seconds, they noticed the quilts had a strong sour smell, and they had to position their faces so they could remain covered while breathing fresh air. When they heard Faye's approach, they froze. Paul squeezed his eyes closed, and Avery held her breath.

Faye opened the door, then the car's weight shifted. At that moment, Avery wanted to abandon the mission. She wanted to leap up with frantic apologies and go back to her room where she belonged. But she didn't want Paul to get into trouble too. She made herself as flat as possible in the back seat, breathed rarely and shallowly, and desperately tried not to do something stupid like sneeze. Of course, trying *not* to sneeze made her nose itchier than ever before.

She couldn't tell how long they were on the road, but it was long enough to guess her mother was driving up-island. When the car finally stopped, she and Paul heard music intermingled with joyous screams of laughter. Faye got out of the car, but just as Avery was about to lift her head, the rear driver side door opened. She trembled as she felt her mother grab the blanket covering her lower half. She clenched every muscle in her body and prepared for the explosion. But once Faye ripped away the blanket, the door slammed shut, and Avery sighed in relief.

"Where are we?" Paul whispered.

They gazed out to see a large gray house buzzing with activity. Teenagers stumbled around and through it, drinking and dancing and laughing like hyenas. Paul pointed at a boy and girl who were making out against a tree like the world was about to end. As she chuckled at them, Avery hoped she and Paul didn't look like that when they kissed.

"Where'd your mom go?"

"I don't know," Avery said, looking around. "But she took the other quilt, and this one isn't big enough for both of us."

"Well, we can't stay here. Come on." He and Avery slid out of the car and slipped in and out of the shadows until they reached a small grove of trees. "Now what do we do?"

"Why are you asking me? I was following you!"

"Okay, don't panic. There's got to be something around here we can use to cover ourselves. Look, there's a blanket right over there."

"But there are people on it." She crinkled her nose at the couple rolling around amorously on the checkered throw, confused as to what her mother was doing at such a gathering.

"Hey, is that your mom coming up from the beach?"

Squinting through the dark, Avery and Paul watched Faye struggling with something cumbersome as she trudged up the hill. Dragging the bulging quilt behind her, she panted as she passed the distracted teens on the checkered blanket. Avery and Paul shuffled around the tree to stay out of sight as she passed them too and hauled the sack to the car. Wedging her arm underneath, she hoisted it onto the bumper. She looked like an animal as she lifted it to the lip of the open trunk, her head tilted back and teeth gritted, and her muscles like twisted steel bulging under the gauze sleeves of her tidy black dress. When she rolled it inside, it thumped and rocked the car, and a pale hand flopped out into the moonlight.

Avery gasped, and Paul clamped his hand over her mouth, pulling her behind the tree before Faye turned her head.

"Did you see that?" she whispered against Paul's palm.

"Ssh." He acted calm, but Avery could feel his heart pounding against her back.

The trunk slammed shut. The car door opened and closed.

When Avery and Paul peeked around the tree again, Faye was striding back to the beach with the second quilt. Confusion flopped in Avery's belly like a bluefish, an aggressively fearful thing with razor-sharp teeth that would fight itself to death on a hook rather than be caught. Her fingernails dug into the bark, and her voice trembled.

"What was that, Paul?"

"That was a person, Avery. That was definitely a person."

"But . . . it couldn't be. Why would my mom put a person in her trunk?"

When Faye appeared again, ascending the incline to her car, she was dragging another quilted sack of cargo.

"Correction," he whispered. "Why would she put *two* people in her trunk?"

Faye hoisted the bulky load onto the first, gave the contents a quick shove, and slammed the trunk shut. When the car door opened and closed again, Avery peeked around the tree. As the car rumbled to life, it felt like the fish in her gut snapped the line and swam away. The confusion disappeared into the depths, and all that remained in her was fear.

"Paul . . ." Avery squeaked dryly as her mother turned the car about. "How are we supposed to get home?"

When Faye's headlights flashed over their hiding place, they dropped to a crouch, and as her car vanished down the road, Avery collapsed onto the ground. Hugging her knees to her chest, she wept. It felt like everything inside her was whirling faster and faster, and it wouldn't stop until she spun out, into jagged pieces with no hope of reunion.

Paul rubbed her back. "Don't worry, Avery."

"Don't tell me not to worry," she said. "We just saw my mom put two people in her trunk, and what's worse, we're stranded up-island while I'm supposed to be grounded in my room. There's plenty to worry about."

"It's going to be okay."

"How?" She punched the ground, and Paul recoiled—impressed or afraid, she wasn't sure—but she was glad he was taking her seriously. "I shouldn't have done this. I shouldn't have listened to you." Tears poured down her cheeks as she wailed. "You stupid boy! Why did I listen to you?"

"Because you're my girlfriend, and that's what girlfriends do." He tried to wrap his arm around her, but she smacked him away.

"Of all the times to call me your girlfriend, you pick *now*? Oh my God, Paul, we're going to be in so much trouble."

"Just try to calm down. I can't stand it when you're mad at me."

"I'm not mad. I'm terrified." She whimpered. "What are we going to do?"

"Let's just start walking, and we'll figure everything out when we get home. It shouldn't take too long once someone picks us up."

"*If* someone picks us up."

The snarky response ping-ponged around her brain for the better part of an hour until it became clear no one was coming. She let go of Paul's hand after that, and at nearly two hours of trudging aimlessly, the newly-named girlfriend sat on the side of the road.

"I can't walk anymore. I'm so tired."

Paul sat beside her. "I'm really sorry I got you into this."

He was careful not to crowd her, but once her tears started falling, she scooted close and leaned her head on his shoulder.

"I just need to rest a minute. Then we can keep going."

He hugged her and kissed the top of her head as she nestled into the crook of his arm.

"I'll stay awake," he whispered. "I'll protect you."

Avery was still smiling as she fell asleep.

CHAPTER SIX

BLUE LIGHT SHONE through her eyelids, but it was Paul's frantic elbowing that woke her. Seeing the police officer exit his cruiser, the pair jumped to their feet.

"Are you kids all right?"

"Yes, sir, thank you," Paul said. "We were just resting."

"This isn't exactly a good place to rest. What are you two doing out here?"

"Trying to get home. Our ride sort of . . . left us."

"Sort of left you, huh?"

"Yes, sir. We were trying to walk back to Oak Bluffs, but we had to take a break."

"You're still a two-hour walk away from Oak Bluffs," the officer said. "You'd better let me give you a lift home."

Avery imagined how her mother would react to seeing her brought home in a police car, and her eyes welled. Panic twisted her stomach, and her frenzied heart made her feel faint until she dug her fingernails into her palms.

"That's all right," she said. "We can make it back on our own."

"No, it's not all right, young lady."

The policeman opened the rear door of his cruiser and gestured for Avery and Paul to get inside. With heads drooped, they obeyed and scooted across the backseat.

After an eternity of silence, the officer cleared his throat. "You two were running away, weren't you?"

Avery started to answer, but Paul stopped her. "Yes," he said sadly. "How did you know?"

"It's all too common for young people. But so you know," he said, staring into the rearview mirror, "running away doesn't solve your problems. If anything, it causes more pain. Even though most runaways come home, I've witnessed firsthand the devastation of a parent realizing they might never see their child again; too often, frankly. Especially over the last few years. You might think it's hard living on an island now, but the mainland is no picnic either." He tapped his fingers on the steering wheel. "Listen, I won't tell your parents. I'm sure you gave them enough of a fright. But I don't ever want to see either of you pulling a stunt like this again."

There was a glimmer of hope in the officer's leniency. If Avery's mother had gone to bed immediately after getting home, there was a chance she could sneak back into her room without her mom knowing she'd left.

But when the sign for Huntington Avenue appeared in the dark, Avery's dread was so heavy she didn't know how she'd climb the tree to her window. With her back hunched and eyes to her feet, she sank into the seat until the officer stopped the car. Even after, it took a few seconds for her to budge when he opened the door. She meant every ounce of her thank you when he helped her out of the car, and they started off toward their respective houses. But once the police car disappeared around the bend, Avery and Paul ran back to each other.

"I'm so sorry, Avery. This is all my fault."

They held onto one another in affection, fear, and all the emotions they couldn't quite understand. For reasons neither of them could decipher, there was an urgency in their embrace. They needed to hold on. They just didn't know why yet.

"We're home now. That's all that matters."

"Yes, but . . . " He furrowed his brow. "Your mom."

"She might not even know I'm gone—"

"No, I mean, what we saw . . . "

She stepped back, head bowed. "We don't know what

40

we saw." Something scampered up a tree, and she flinched, moving even farther from Paul. She didn't want to admit it—couldn't out loud—but her jangled nerves didn't have that problem. Deep down, she knew exactly what they'd seen.

"We should go while we still can. I'll talk to you soon?"

He nodded, and she started away. But she stopped short of her driveway and turned back.

"Paul? Am I really your girlfriend?"

With a smile, he said, "Avery, you're my everything," like if she knew anything by that point in her life, it should've been that undisputable fact.

Anyway, she did now. And she didn't feel so heavy anymore.

She climbed the tree and made her way to the awning below her window. Prying it open, she tumbled into the dark and scrambled to bed. As soon as she was under the covers, safe and sound, with no footsteps creaking the hall outside her room, she heaved a well-deserved sigh.

That's when the lights turned on. Avery saw her illuminated ceiling first, then her mother at the light switch.

"I've been waiting," Faye said calmly. "Where have you been?"

There was no point trying to keep her composure. She wept and sniffled and tried to squeak out an explanation, but her words got stuck on the way out, as if blocked by the limp hand that flopped out of her mother's trunk. All she could manage was: "I'm sorry."

"I'm not sure you are," Faye said as she opened Avery's door. "But I assure you, my darling, you will be."

She switched off the light and closed the door with a bang that sent shivers up and down Avery's spine. The girl curled herself into a ball, but no matter how tight she hugged her knees, her body wouldn't stop shaking. Exhausted as she was, she couldn't imagine sleeping. She couldn't stop thinking about what she'd seen. The shape of her mother hauling those bodies. The blue tinge of their moonlit flesh. She felt the same faintness as before, the kind that made her heart race and set her skin ablaze, and she thought she might never sleep again.

The sun burned through Avery's window the next morning with rays that changed every color in her room. As hot as it was, the floor was ice cold and stung her toes so sharply she withdrew her feet and rubbed them warm before trying again.

She didn't bother coordinating her clothes or fixing her hair. She didn't see the point. After the confrontation with her mother, she doubted she'd be leaving the house that day, maybe for the rest of her life. But squeezing the brass ring in her fist, she thought of Paul and didn't feel alone. She needed to keep that sense of support close the next time she faced her mother, so she dropped it in her pocket and released a shuddering breath as she opened her door.

Each step down the stairs creaked louder than usual. The house seemed deathly empty and impossibly ancient, but the instant she passed the living room, she felt the furious electricity radiating off the woman on the sofa. Her head was tilted slightly but dramatically enough to command every facet of the house and its occupants.

"Did you sleep well?" Faye asked softly.

"No." Avery hitched her shoulders to her ears and gulped. "I'm really sorry, Mom. I didn't want to disobey you—"

"Then why did you?"

"I was worried about you."

Faye's eyes fluttered in disbelief. "*You* were worried about *me*? Why on earth?"

"Because of where you go at night. I needed to know."

"You do know. I play Bingo. Sometimes Bridge. Sometimes I go to my quilting circle."

"But you weren't at any of those places."

Her mother shrank somewhat but remained an imposing presence as she tilted her head even more. "This is about that boy of yours, isn't it?"

"What?"

"Paul. This isn't about me at all."

"It doesn't have anything to do with him."

"No? So it wasn't his idea for you to sneak out?"

She swallowed hard. "How do you know that?"

"Because you're my little girl. You wouldn't defy me unless someone forced you."

"He didn't force me."

"No, I'm sure he got you thinking it was your idea. They're all like that." Pinching her chin, she hummed. "And I'm sure he got more than your devotion."

"What?"

Faye's spine seemed to unroll, elongating her neck as she stared down at her daughter.

"Did you let him kiss you?"

Avery's face flushed with heat. That was answer enough.

The moment they met eyes again, Faye slapped her across the face.

"Have I taught you nothing?" she screamed. "Don't you have any self-control? Any self-respect? You're just like your sister. You're a little tramp!"

Clutching her cheek, Avery whined. "It was just a kiss!"

"Well, I hope you enjoyed it because you're never seeing that boy again."

"You can't do that!"

"The heck I can't. I'm your mother."

"You're a murderer!"

Faye spun, her lips trembling in shock. "What did you call me?"

"I followed you to that house. I saw what you put in your trunk."

"I don't know what you're talking about. Obviously, you've had a terrible nightmare. Something that never could've happened. Something you probably shouldn't repeat."

"Only because you don't want to get caught."

43.

A chuckle burst out of Faye as she clapped a hand to her chest. "Caught? I haven't done anything wrong. It's you I'm concerned about."

"I'm fine," Avery muttered quietly, but her brain was near boiling over with anguish, and the hushed words turned to a hiss. "As fine as I can be with a murderer for a mother."

Faye swung at her again and missed. And that time, Avery swung back. She landed a sweaty smack across her mother's cheek, and Faye clutched her face in shock. It quickly shifted to anger, however, and with teeth clenched, she grabbed her daughter's wrist and towed her to the back door.

"Let me go! Where are you taking me?"

"To the garden. You've obviously been contaminated by bad water, and I want to make sure you haven't poisoned anything else."

"I'm not contaminated, Mom!"

"No? Why else would you deliberately try to hurt me like this?" Faye flung open the door and shoved Avery outside. "God in Heaven, what have I done to deserve such wicked girls? Why must I be forced to endure all this filth? Your father with his patients, your sister with her loose morals, and now you with your lies and accusations, and this disgusting tryst with Paul Dillon. You were supposed to be different! What more can I do to keep you clean?"

"I don't understand." Tears filled Avery's eyes. Her mother had always frightened her a bit, but no more than the way she assumed all parents frightened their children. Age, size, and wisdom made adult-sized people seem like a different, more intimidating species. But Avery's fear had evolved overnight; it felt adult-sized now too.

"Stop crying," Faye said.

The command made it worse. Tears spilled down her cheeks, and Faye's face flushed with rising anger. Grabbing her daughter by the shoulders, she spun her around and pointed at the parched earth.

"Tend to the garden. If you can't maintain your purity, you will ensure the cleanliness of every plant, flower, and rabbit." Drawing close to her ear, she added, "Do you understand me now?"

She sniffled. "Yes, but—"

"But what?"

"Nothing."

She released Avery and strode to the door, and with her back to the garden, she added, "I'm very disappointed in you." But Faye was all glare and grimace after the door swished close. She didn't leave the other side for several seconds, staring at the little girl drying her tears.

Even knowing she was being watched, Avery thought about running to Paul's house and begging his mom to take her in. But her resolve shrank with each second Faye stared on, unflinching, unforgiving, and as forlorn as someone watching a performing circus bear that had lost its zeal.

Her mother's disappointment shouldn't wound her so deep, especially after what she'd witnessed with Paul. But for the first time in her life, seeing didn't translate into believing. Faye was frequently overbearing, and she could be cold at times, but Avery couldn't imagine the woman who never failed to provide oyster crackers and ginger ale when she was ill, or who read her Mother Goose stories to lull her back to sleep after a nightmare was the same one who'd given her such sickening dreams the night before.

And maybe she was right. Maybe Avery's relationship with Paul had gotten out of hand. Maybe it was too much too soon. Maybe the bad water *had* gotten into her, and it was doing something to her mind.

As Avery filled up the watering can, her weary eyes rolled across the garden. It was noticeably thirsty, and the leaves wilted, even paled, when she neared with the sloshing can, as if wary of her kindness. As she crossed the garden, the cabbage patch shook wildly and she halted, knees locked. Two rabbits burst out from the plants, and she stumbled off balance as they batted at each other and tumbled across the garden, their blue and orange dots blending as they rolled. They were playing, but it quickly evolved into more.

She gasped and frantically nudged the orange rabbit off the blue with her foot. But they didn't stay apart for long. A second mismatched couple appeared then, followed by a third and a fourth. Before long, the garden was bustling with bad rabbits: red with yellow, pink with blue. A jarring rage built inside Avery, like a knot of nausea and grief unraveling throughout her body until it shook in every atom. Her teeth clenched so tight she thought they might break into jagged shards that would spear her gums. Unable to hold on anymore, she released an animalistic cry, threw the watering can to the ground, and fell to her knees.

As the puddle grew, it soaked Avery's clothes with dark burgundy liquid, and she wheezed in panic. The soil drank up the discolored water just as readily, and though she tried to dig it out of the dirt, she pushed it deeper into the earth, and deeper into her, caking under her nails and dying her hands blood red. And all the while, the dirty rabbits coupled and switched and poisoned the garden.

She swatted them with her hands open at first, but they eventually became fists. Swinging and jabbing, she mercilessly pummeled the bad rabbits. They wriggled and shrieked under her knuckles, but she didn't stop until each and every rabbit was reduced to a furry bag of ruined flesh and bone. She panted at the carnage around her and the rivers of blood dripping down her fists into the sleeves of her dress. It was a hot smell that forced its way into her brain—not blood the way she'd imagined it; more like the smell of days when smashed earthworms littered the rain-soaked paths of the neighborhood—with a hint of rabbit stew. Her head spun and her belly cramped, and try as she might, she couldn't hold her revulsion back. She surrendered to sputtering heaves of sickness that splashed the blood-spattered raspberry patches. As she wiped her mouth, her focus turned fearfully to the window, expecting to see her mother's horrified expression.

It was empty. A small mercy.

But Avery had to hide what she'd done. She held her breath as she collected the corpses, her mind rattling off justifications her heart combated. The rabbits were poisoned. They were doomed whether she killed them or not, right?

Except, it was her fault they'd been poisoned. She'd brought in the bad water. She'd doomed them to death before her fists ever fell.

She gathered the bodies in her arms and started toward the cellar, but the matted fur tickled her nose. A sneeze blasted one of the rabbits out of her arms, and it hit the stone walkway with a wet smack. She crouched to pick it up but was only able to grasp it between two fingers. It swung like a fleshy anchor as she hurried to the cellar door and hooked her foot under one of the handles. It swung open and bounced on the concrete with a clang that shook her bones—and the rabbit out of her grip. She kicked the bunny down into the dark, and its body rolled with soft thumps and clicks against the stone steps. At the bottom, the rabbit lay twisted, staring up at her with bulging eyes speckled with broken blood vessels and a grisly grin. She squeezed the bodies tighter, the dried tufts of bloody fur poking and tickling her arms as she retrieved the rabbit and began the search for a place to hide the evidence of her crime.

She hadn't opened the cellar storage closet in years, probably because it held all the things her father left behind. Neither Faye nor her daughters were eager to delve into the memory of his sudden abandonment. She turned the lock with her knuckle and yanked the stubborn door open. Illuminating the closet revealed pillars of boxes marked with her father's name, almost confrontationally. But she didn't engage, too distracted by the musty, sour smell that thickened as she wove between the towering dregs of her father's life.

Her arms ached from the dead weight, and the cellar dust irritated her eyes. They teared when she squeezed them shut, and the tears ran harder when she stubbed her toe on a bump in the floor. The corpses flew out of her arms as she stumbled and skidded across the concrete. Aching, shaking, her head buzzing, she scraped herself off the floor and wept at the sight of so many dead creatures scattered around her father's things. But as she collected them again, she realized the bump that tripped her was a latch . . . belonging to a small wooden door in the floor. The latch squeaked as she flipped it open, but not as much as she would've thought. It couldn't have been used often, though, because the sour smell intensified like a punch to the face when she pulled up the door. Her body spasmed with revulsion, and despite her best efforts to hold on, her weary arms released the rabbits into the darkness below.

Thoughts clashed and converged, and she couldn't decide what to do. Her mother would return to the window eventually. When she discovered her daughter missing, she'd search the house for her, and it was only a matter of time before she searched the basement.

At least she was getting used to the smell.

On her belly, her head hanging over the edge, she heaved a shuddering breath that became a yelp when her weight shifted and something fell clanging into the abyss. Cold panic juddered her insides as she dipped her hand into her pocket.

Empty.

She peered into the void, trembling at the thought of venturing into the dark to retrieve the brass ring. But the notion of losing Paul's gift forever frightened her more. On the edge, the reinvigorated stench making her gag, she forced himself to reach for the cold iron ladder that would take her down into the fetid dark.

Rung by rung, she descended, breathing through her mouth, but the increasingly putrid odor found its way inside, anyway. She was swallowing back bile when her feet found floor, and she fell to all fours to gather her bearings. But nausea stayed close, like the squishy, matted bodies of the murdered rabbits. Backpedaling in revulsion, she smacked against something damp and cold that swung after impact. Moving around the space, she discovered more clammy objects hanging around her. She hit several before feeling something metallic attached to a string and shrieked in joy at finding the pull string for the lightbulb. She tugged it with a triumphant grin, but the light blasted it away.

Avery shrank to the floor with a choked scream. Spinning and swinging, casting ghastly shadows over the girl and her dead rabbits, a half dozen naked humans hung from the ceiling, their slumped bodies skewered by large black hooks. The corpses swayed, smacking against each other, smacking against her. Everywhere she looked, sheared bone peeked between soggy chunks of flesh, tufts of thin hair fluttered across dry scalps, and gaping mouths hung stretched in fright. Avery's senses waged war on her mind so intensely she found she couldn't process it all. Her legs buckled and she flattened herself on the floor, but even with her cheek against the cold concrete, the people, the rabbits, the blood that pumped behind her eyes like bad water—it swirled around and within her. Her breath thinned, her body tingled with sickness, and she felt herself slipping away.

Then, comfort glinted at her from beneath a bunny's wet belly. She reached out, her fingers quaking as they dove under the knotted fur and closed on the brass ring.

CHAPTER SEVEN

PAIN WHIP-CRACKED HER skull when she woke. Light stabbed her pupils as she struggled to focus and piece together what had happened.

"Avery?"

She lifted her head to a policeman crouching beside her. For a few seconds, she thought she might still be asleep—until she saw the other officers gathered around the small room.

And that's all she saw. Not the ghastly bodies, not the hooks. There *were* no hooks.

The blast of a flashbulb captured her attention, and she saw a barrage of people snapping photographs of something in the corner.

"Avery, do you know where you are?" the policeman asked.

She looked down at her feet, where one of the dead rabbits lay twisted, and she burst into tears.

"I killed them," she mewled. She lifted her hands to wipe face, but seeing the dried blood on her palms made her wail louder.

The officer quieted her down, but the sound of screaming continued from the crowd of police in the opposite corner. There, Faye Norton sobbed and pounded her chest as she panted in mounting grief.

"Avery, can you tell me what happened?" the officer asked. He touched her arm, and she flinched.

She felt displaced from the world she knew, and though her gaze found her mother's through the madness, she didn't recognize what shone out.

"Avery?"

The girl's focus shifted back to the officer, and her throat tightened around the words attempting to rise. "I . . . I didn't . . . "

Her mother's head cocked suddenly as if already refuting the answer.

"I didn't mean to do it," she continued.

"Do what, Avery?"

"They were being bad. I was trying to save them."

"Who was being bad?"

"The rabbits." She sniffled. "I didn't want to hurt them, I promise. I was trying to stop them from being bad."

The policeman glanced at the pile of bludgeoned rabbits and patted Avery's shoulder. "It's all right. I believe you. But what about the people? Why did you kill the people?"

The crowd of photographer's parted, and she at last saw the dead bodies piled sloppily in the corner of the cramped space. It felt like someone squeezed the last centimeter of her windpipe shut. She coughed and gasped, and the words she eventually sputtered up came out as strained and staccato chirps.

"No! No, I didn't kill any people!"

"But you did kill rabbits?"

"Yes, but it was an accident. I didn't have anything to do with those people. They were already here when I came down. But they were hanging."

"I'm sorry," another officer said, "did you say hanging?"

Faye whimpered into a handkerchief, and a policeman draped a blanket over her shoulders.

"Yes. Dead and hanging, from giant hooks. I didn't even know they were down here or . . . " She looked around the tiny room and crinkled her forehead. ". . . what she did with them."

"She?"

Avery locked eyes with her mom, and as Faye lifted her

waxy gray face from the kerchief, the officers looked in her direction. "Yes. If you want to know what happened to those people, you should ask my mother. I saw her put two dead bodies in her trunk last night."

Faye wailed into the handkerchief, shaking her head and speeding through a Hail Mary with her hands clasped at her heart. "Oh Avery, not again."

The officer beckoned to Faye. "Mrs. Norton, could you join us, please?"

"Yes, of course. I just feel so weak. Would you help me?" She held out her arm, and four officers hurried to her rescue. They escorted her like helping an old lady cross the street, but within a few feet of her daughter, she pulled free and crumpled against Avery with a bone-crushing embrace.

She sobbed. "Oh honey, I'm so sorry. I wanted so badly to protect you. I wanted you to be healthy. My good little girl, my sweet little lamb."

Avery burst out of her embrace and crawled to the officer, howling. "Keep her away from me! She's a murderer!"

Faye gasped, clutching her neck as if the accusation was a piece of metal stuck in her throat. "Mother of God, no, no. My poor girl. It really is happening again." She reached out to an officer. "I can't take this. The smell." She fanned her face, and her voice cracked. "I have to get out of here."

"Take them upstairs, will you, Franco?"

The man helped Faye stand, then guided her up the ladder, but he let Avery stand on her own while the police looked on in derision. The climb out of the crypt wasn't as long as she remembered, and the pillars of her dad's things in the storage closet weren't nearly as tall. And yet, she'd never felt smaller.

A man with a wide-brimmed hat and a stark white mustache greeted Avery and Faye and introduced himself as Police Chief Blake. He sat them across from each other at the kitchen table, but Faye closed the distance between them with a glare, unwaveringly fixed on her daughter.

Avery's head pounded and her vision blurred for a moment. She squeezed her eyes shut, and Faye sighed.

"It's happening right now, isn't it, sweetheart?" she said, her voice dripping with false concern. "It's all right. Just let us know so we can prepare ourselves. I'm certain someone here has handcuffs."

Chief Blake rapped his knuckles on the table. "I don't know what's going on here, but I'm going to need an explanation right now, because in over thirty years with the Oak Bluffs Police Department, I haven't seen anything close to that mess you've got down there."

"Of course," Faye said. "I'm more than willing to help you in any way I can. I've been silent about this for far too long."

"About what exactly?"

She deflated. "It's my fault. It must be my fault. I'm her mother. I wanted to protect her. I thought maybe if I could help her stop, she'd never have to know what she'd done."

"Which is?"

Her fingers traced the wood grain of the tabletop as she spoke, her focus downcast as if seeing her story as clearly as the future in a crystal ball. "It started when she was four. I'd come into her room and find her dolls torn apart or gruesome drawings she'd done. It happened so rarely I didn't give it much thought. But then . . . " She swallowed dryly. " . . . there were animals. A stray cat, a few birds. Rabbits, of course. She killed them all."

"What?" Avery howled. "I've never done anything like that!"

"Except for today, correct?" Chief Blake sat beside her and folded his hands on the table. "You told the officer down there you killed those rabbits to keep them safe."

"I—yes, I did, but it was the first time. And it was an accident. I've never done anything like that before."

"Yes, you have," Faye said. "I'm sorry I didn't tell you.

You never remembered doing it, even seconds later, but I thought one day it would stick, and . . . I'm just so sorry for all of it."

"This is crazy! She's lying, Chief Blake!"

"Mrs. Norton, why didn't you tell anyone? This isn't nicking candy when the clerk's back is turned. This is murder."

"I didn't murder anyone!" Avery roared, and Faye's fingers flew to her temples.

She rubbed them furiously as she wept through her words. "I know, I know. Trying to ignore what she was, lying about her blackouts—I never thought it would get so bad. I didn't know what she was capable of until—" She buried her face in her hands. "Oh God, it's just too much." Lifting her head with a huff, she forcefully wiped away her tears. "But I knew, even back then, I think. Even though I hid it, so many times."

Avery chin trembled. "Mom, why are you doing this?"

"I've been asking you the same thing for years, my love. And I'm sorry, but I can't keep it a secret anymore. I can't— I—" She breathed heavily, her chest jumping under curled fingers. "Chief Blake, there must be something we can do. Avery's not an evil child. She just has these . . . spells. Hallucinations, blackouts, whatever they are—she's sick. But I believe she can get better."

The policeman hummed as he nodded. "A mother's love."

"No," Avery whimpered as she reached across the table. "You can't believe her. You can't." She grabbed the police chief's hand and stared at him, eyes brimming. "Please. I've never hurt anyone. Before today, I never hurt any*thing*. She did this to me. She set me up."

He cocked his head and pulled his hand free. "Why would your own mother do something like that?"

"I don't know," she said, voice wavering as she flicked her focus to Faye. "Why are you doing this to me? What did I do to deserve this?"

Faye's face was harder and colder than ever before when she said, "How familiar this all seems." But her expression softened quickly, and she leaned over to cradle her daughter's cheek. "I tried so hard to help you, sweetheart. I tried to guide you down the path of righteousness, but you've strayed too far this time. I never wanted this to happen, not to you, but I can't protect you anymore. You've made it perfectly clear you don't want my help anyway."

"I've heard enough." Chief Blake stood and beckoned two officers to the kitchen table. "Mrs. Norton, these men will take you to the station for further questioning."

"Of course. Anything I can do to help. And Avery's going to cooperate too, aren't you, dear? I know it's hard to remember everything, but you're going answer everything the police ask to the best of your ability, won't you?"

Faye lay her hand atop her daughter's like such things could still comfort her, but the moment their skin touched, Avery's body shrank into itself. Sickness and rage swelled up in her like a blooming matchstick.

"Don't make this harder than it already is, sweetie. Be a good girl."

The rage simmering in Avery's gut reached a sudden boil. She lunged at her mother with a scream, swiping at her face and drawing blood as she pushed her hard against the counter. Faye crumpled to the floor as the police yanked the girl away and closed handcuffs on her wrists. It was like snuffing a candle flame—and all of Avery's energy with it. Drenched in cold sweat, she wilted, but the policemen wouldn't allow her to fall. While others fanned Faye and dabbed her cuts, they spun Avery toward the hall, pushed her past clusters of scowling officers, and shoved her out the front door.

Whispering neighbors crowded both sides of Huntington Avenue. And why shouldn't they? Things like this didn't happen on Martha's Vineyard. They were supposed to be invincible to the problems of the mainland, protected by the island . . . and all its good water.

"Don't worry, honey!" her mother shouted from the hall. "Everything will be right as rain soon. I'll see you at the station."

"She's not going to the station," Chief Blake said as he escorted Faye outside.

Avery struggled against her restraints to swivel around. "Wait, where am I going?" she asked, mouth dry.

"Considering the nature of these crimes, we feel it best we take you somewhere with people who are equipped to help you."

Every muscle tensed, and she repeated the question. "Where?"

"It's a facility off-island, in Taunton. They'll look after you while all this gets sorted."

Avery's stomach dropped. "Taunton *Asylum*? The crazy people place?"

"It's a hospital."

"But I'm not sick. And I'm not crazy." She jerked her head tearfully. "She did this, not me. Please don't send me away."

Her pleas were ignored, if not treated with disdain by the officers pushing her back toward the cruiser.

The onlookers weren't much different, their eyes blending into one intrusive, accusatory glare as the men marched the girl away from her home. Except, of course, for Paul Dillon.

He screamed Avery's name as he forced his way to the front of the crowd. He was only a few feet away, so close she could've swerved and grazed his outstretched hand, but the officers steered her away from him. He followed her closely, though, every step a battle to reach her.

"Avery, what's going on?"

"They think I'm a killer, Paul! But I didn't do anything! You know I didn't do anything!"

"Of course you didn't. Let her go!" he screamed. "You have to let her go!"

"I told them what we saw, but no one believes me. They think I'm crazy. They're taking me to Taunton Asylum."

"Don't worry, Avery, I'll get you out of this. I'll tell them—"

"No, don't! Don't you dare. I can't bear the thought of her hurting you too."

Paul dodged the officer controlling the crowd long enough to slip his arms around Avery's neck, but police promptly tugged him away and held him at arm's length.

She'd never felt so small, or so ancient when she sobbed, "Don't forget me, Paul."

"Don't talk like that," he said as the officer pushed Avery into the car. "I'm going to get you out. I'm going to save you. I love you, Avery Norton!"

That, also, sounded small and ancient behind the glass of a police car.

Paul's voice echoed inside her once the car door slammed shut. Everything else was hollow and shrill and as cold as the window separating her from everything she loved. With panicked breath flowering and withering on the glass, she stared out at her best friend and truest love. She noted every molecule of his beauty, memorizing it as best she could before her mother, ragged in her mask of grief, stood between them.

Drawing her face nearer to the glass, Faye sneered, and for that moment appeared as slickly coiffed as usual: hair knotted, lip tight, and voice torturously musical as she said, "I told you you'd be sorry."

When she pressed her hand to the window, Avery's chin trembled in devastation. Cupped in her palm, scraping the glass, was the brass ring Paul had given her daughter, shining nearly as bright as Faye's grin.

Avery deliberately turned her focus to Paul, beautiful even in his sorrow, and clung to him for as long as she could. But as the police car sped away and turned the corner out of her neighborhood, she dropped her gaze to her dirty shoes and wondered if she'd ever see anything beautiful again.

CHAPTER EIGHT

"ABOUT TEN MINUTES left." Turning onto Tremont Street, the policeman glanced at her in the rearview mirror.

She didn't respond; couldn't. The words "ten minutes" stampeded through her mind too loudly to find any others. Ten minutes until Avery was at Taunton Asylum. Ten minutes until she was just another one of its crazies and her life was never the same. As the clock counted down, she replayed everything she'd heard about the place in Bristol County, Massachusetts. Or "Curse County," as some kids called it. Even on the island, the kids knew of Taunton. They said you could see true insanity in the eyes of people who'd lived there, even for a short time. Avery wondered how long it would be before she got that look. Maybe just ten minutes.

When the hospital appeared, Avery's body quaked. Even under a clear blue sky, bordered by a lush lawn, Taunton had a forebodingly harsh appearance, every arch imposing, every corner a warning. Though, she supposed they could've dressed the buildings in velvety flowers and happy little bluebirds and she would've reacted the same. The one-hundred-and-twenty-year-old asylum looked every year of its age, maybe even older, and lost any charm distance had granted when the car pulled into the drive. Broken brick and peeling paint greeted Avery with corroded apathy, but its most unappealing attributes didn't compare to the wild eyes glaring at the approaching car from barred windows.

As the policeman helped the prisoner out of the car, a cluster of nurses emerged as if called to it by destiny. They wore their friendliest faces, which looked less genuine the closer they came, especially with hands half-hidden in their pockets, wrapped around the syringes peeking out of the cloth. Avery didn't understand why they'd need them. She was up to date on her vaccines; the remnant scar from her smallpox shot was a constant reminder.

A nurse with a sharp nose and a gravelly voice extended her hand. "Good morning, Miss Norton."

"Morning," she whispered.

"I understand you're going to be staying with us for a while."

"Until this gets sorted out, Chief Blake said. A few days maybe."

The woman nodded, and when she shot a look of pinched amusement at her colleagues, they nodded too. "Indeed. These things do take time, though. I'll help you get settled, just in case."

"In case of what?"

"Thank you, ladies. That will be all." She waved to the staff, who disappeared inside while the officer handed her a piece of paper. They both signed, and after a brief documentation exchange, it was settled. Avery belonged to Taunton and the nurse with the pointy face.

Clapping her hands, she grinned. "Let's get down to it, shall we? As Head Nurse of the juvenile ward, I'm proud to welcome you to Taunton Hospital. You may call me Nurse Day, Nurse Meredith, or Meredith. Whichever you prefer."

"Okay," she muttered, eyes to the ground.

"There's no need to be frightened, dear. Taunton is the safest place you could possibly be. We're here to help you."

As Meredith spoke, Avery's gaze climbed from the muddy base of the building to the tarnished cupola at its peak, then down to the tidy nurse with her clean white uniform, angular face accentuated by blush and cropped brown bangs. She gave Avery no reason to fear her, but considering where the woman wanted to take her, she also had no reason to trust Nurse Day either.

She confirmed the fear when Avery hesitated. Grabbing her hand, she tugged her toward the building and said, "Like it or not, you have nowhere else to go."

Her heart ached, because Nurse Day was right and she knew it. As Avery deflated, the nurse lifted her chin and towed her new patient into the hospital's bustling administration area. She quickly ushered her through the hectic space, however. "You won't be spending any time here. The other wards, either. Juveniles are heavily restricted. No children with adults, no boys with girls. Although," she said, wagging a finger, "there are some exceptions where safety is concerned."

As she pulled Avery down twisting corridors, scores of judgmental eyes from staff and patients alike burned the child to the core. They shamed and pitied her, and though their stares filled her with fear, it was nothing compared to the terror that whipcracked her insides when a shrill scream exploded from somewhere below. It vibrated the floor, even shook the pale green walls. Then again, everything was shaking to Avery, like her panic had leaked from her body and infected each plank of wood in the asylum. She thought her contagious terror might've created the scream too, but it came again like a barrage of tiny fists under each footfall.

There were other voices too—anger and pain and joy resounding in facets she'd never heard on the island—but the moment Nurse Day opened the doors to the juvenile ward, the din dropped to a hush, albeit one as cacophonous as a stormy sea.

"Don't be afraid," Meredith assured her again. "You're safe now. You're home."

Her body tensed. "For now."

"Yes, of course." The nurse nudged her over the threshold into the ward, and before she knew it, they were walking in stride down a cream-colored corridor. "The girls here range from ages seven to seventeen. And they're all here for different reasons. Some don't like to share those reasons. Some are all too keen to share them. You might bond with some of them instantly, some may take time, and some you might never bond with at all."

"Is anyone here like me?"

Nurse Day batted her eyelashes. "A murderer?"

Avery clenched her jaw as hot tears swamped her eyes. "Is anyone here innocent? Waiting for a trial?"

She didn't speak, but her amused expression was answer enough. It was, in all technical senses, a frown, but there was warmth in it that made Avery confident about her choice not to trust Nurse Day. As they entered the juvenile ward, she introduced the staff as if pointing out inconsequential cracks in the ceiling.

"This is Nurse Moore, Nurse Mathis, and that's Nurse Radcliffe in the Nurses' station. Lavatories are to the left, and the common room is straight ahead. You're restricted to daytime hours only for the common room, but that might change pending your first evaluation with Dr. Aslinn." Passing the patients gathered in the common room reminded Avery of sweltering days on the island— days so hot you couldn't do anything but sprawl out, sweat, and complain. Some of the girls looked at her in intrigue, but most glanced with deep disinterest, which suited her just fine. She wasn't going to be there long enough to get to know them, or allow them to know her.

She was in denial, she knew, even then.

As Meredith introduced the nurses they passed, it felt like Avery was living the same moment over and over. They all looked and sounded so similar, neat and fresh like they'd gone through the wash and press with their uniforms. Most had soft, sweet faces with fatigue encircling their eyes, and though many of the nurses looked like their hair hadn't seen a comb in days, the most unruly coifs had been fastidiously stuffed under a cap, giving them the illusion of tidiness. None appeared inherently evil, but that didn't mean they were kind.

And yet, that was exactly how Nurse Day looked when she gestured at a door marked with a plump number eight. "You'll be staying in this room," she said, smiling warmly. She reached for the door gracefully, as if poised to twist a ripe apple off a branch, but it flew open before she could turn the knob, and a tall girl with sleek blonde hair tumbled out. "Rachel, what on earth is going on?"

"Ask Flint," the girl said with a huff. "She started it. She always starts it."

She ducked her head into room eight. "Well, Francine? What happened? Why did you push Rachel out of the room?"

Avery peered inside at a wiry teenager with strawberry blonde hair and skin that would've been stark white if not for an abundance of freckles. Calm, she sat on the bed, legs crossed and arms folded as she pouted her bottom lip.

"Not *the* room," she corrected wispily. "*My* room."

"It's not your room, Francine. Nothing here is yours."

Avery's gut clenched as the nurse scolded the freckled girl, who bowed her head in shame.

"But we've been over this many times, haven't we, Francine?"

"More times than necessary," she grumbled.

"You make it necessary. Why did you push Rachel out of the room?"

The girl tightened her mouth and looked to the ceiling.

"Rachel?"

"I found—" When Francine shot her an icy look, Rachel muttered, "Nothing. I don't know. It was my fault."

"Don't avoid the issue, Rachel. What did you find?"

Wringing her hands, she whispered, "Matches."

Without blinking an eye, Nurse Day shouted, "Sandra! Matches!" Moments later, Nurse Radcliffe ran over, readying a syringe.

"She's lying!" Francine screamed. "I don't have anything!"

But neither nurse was convinced. Radcliffe grabbed her arm as Francine wailed.

"Sandra, stop! I'm not fighting you!"

"Where are they?" she demanded.

After a defiant grimace, Francine ripped the book of matches out of her pocket and threw them on the bed.

"Take it. There's only one. It's not a big deal." She tried to pull free, but the nurse didn't relent. She swung the whining redhead to the door and steered her out.

Meredith scrunched her nose at Avery. "I'll be right back," she said and marched down the hall after her screeching patient.

When their frustrated stomps had been reduced to soft patters, Rachel hummed at Avery, an eyebrow raised. "So, what are you in for?"

"Me?"

"You see anyone else?"

Avery's shoulders hunched. "I'm in for a lie."

"Oh, you're a compulsive liar?"

"No."

With an annoyed groan, Rachel removed a pack of cigarettes from her pocket and pinched one between her teeth. "So . . . yes?"

"I'm not a compulsive liar. I'm here for something I didn't do."

She scoffed. "Right."

"It's true."

Rolling her eyes, she strolled out of room eight and shouted at the lounge. "Does anyone have a match? Flint nicked my last one."

Teetering between the corridor and the room that didn't belong to her, Avery avoided making eye contact with the girls strolling the ward. But acting aloof gave her no power. If anything, guarding herself made her feel weaker. She stood hunched, her focus downcast, when Nurse Meredith returned and ushered her back into the room.

"I'm sorry about that." She gestured at a bare mattress and a pile of pilled sheets atop a thin cushion that barely qualified as a pillow. "We've provided you with these linens, and it will be your responsibility to take care of them." She slung a ratty towel on a dresser knob, and its bleach-spotted folds created a grotesque face in the faded terrycloth. "I'm sure you were accustomed to such chores in your last home."

"It's my *only* home."

Nurse Meredith sniffed, and her lips shriveled to a red bow of a smile. "There are also plenty of clothes in the drawers."

"What about *my* clothes?"

"They'll be shipped in time, I'm sure. What's most important now, Avery, is that you allow us to help you get well. And the best way to kickstart this whole process is for you to blend into the community."

"I'd probably feel more comfortable doing that if I had my clothes, my books, my pictures, from the real world."

Bending at the waist, her face a jagged shelf of rosy rock, the nurse said, "This world is very real, my dear. If I must live in that truth, so must you."

Avery's throat tightened. "But I don't belong here."

"I think you'll find that response will become tiresome before long. For everyone, and especially for you. It's also the worst kind of attitude for recovery." Meredith looked to the wall clock and her spine snapped straight. "You've had a long day. We'll start fresh in the morning."

Until that second, it hadn't occurred to Avery that she wouldn't sleep in her bed that night—or any night after, perhaps—and she was farther from home than she'd ever been, alone, in strange new clothes, and with no clue to when she'd ever see the island again.

"But . . . " Her chin trembled as she whispered, "What am I supposed to do?"

"I'm sure Francine wouldn't mind if you borrowed one of her books. She won't be back for a few hours anyway."

"Why? What did she do?"

"She knows the penalties for breaking the rules. And there are few rules more important than keeping matches away from arsonists." When Avery blinked in confusion, Meredith continued. "An arsonist is someone with an overwhelming compulsion to set fires."

Avery gasped. "And you put me in the same room as her?"

"Snap judgments won't get you far here. Besides," she said, "Francine probably won't be happy when she learns what *you've* done."

"I haven't done anything!"

"The books are over there," Meredith continued, undeterred. "There's a good variety, but I always recommend the Bible. It can be a great comfort in times like these."

Though the nurse didn't close the door when she exited, a door closed nonetheless, and it shook every bone in Avery's body. She stared at "Holy Bible" stamped in gold along the spine of the leatherbound volume on the shelf, but her head ached and tears welled as if Nurse Day had smacked her with it. Collapsing onto the bed, she buried her face in the pillow and prayed for the longest nightmare of her life to end.

Somewhere between grief and exhaustion, she vanished into sleep. A loud click eventually woke her, her eyes burning and pillow damp as she lifted her head. She didn't know how much time had passed, but the room was pitch dark for a moment before the hallway light spilled in through the opening door, and a burly male orderly carried a young girl into the room. Gently, he deposited Avery's roommate onto the empty mattress and backed out, gaze sweeping the beds. When he caught Avery's wide, watering eyes, he offered a small, apologetic blink and shut the door.

Avery turned her focus to the girl the nurses called Francine and the patients called Flint. Moonlight shone through the barred window and striped her with shadows.

With her mouth hanging open and arms limply outstretched, she looked dead, and Avery was glad for the slight rise and fall of her belly. For a moment, she looked like the people in her mother's cellar, bloodless and rotting inside.

But maybe Avery was the one rotting, and maybe it was spreading. Because every time her eyelids fell, she saw the garden and felt its hunger.

The deeper she sank into sleep, the brighter the image became, and less terrifying. Twisted stems righted themselves, and petals opened with beams of colorful light. There were no rabbits to reprimand, no plants to water. No one was scrutinizing her every move. She stood with arms open to embrace the supple felicity of the garden, but she hadn't seen its true grandeur yet. That lay just beyond the border, where sunlight glinted on his skin like he was doused in diamond dust. Paul Dillon, striding toward her in refined confidence, was more beautiful than any flower in the garden.

He caressed Avery's cheek. "There's no flower more beautiful than you," he said, and she giggled.

"I'm not a flower."

"No?" Paul crinkled his nose and pointed at Avery's feet.

Looking down, she shrieked at the knotty roots bursting out the tops of her feet and coiling around her legs. There was no pain as the garden burrowed in and out of her and the wet soil swallowed her body, save when it wrenched her out of Paul's embrace. He screamed with the same helpless devastation as the moment the police tore them apart. She cried and wriggled and reached for him, but the garden's appetite was too strong. It devoured her without effort, and her best friend's tortured expression stayed with her until a voice ghosted through her groggy brain the next morning.

"Who's Paul?"

Avery flipped over with a groan and blinked at Francine perched on the edge of the bed, furiously twisting a blanket's tassels between her fingers.

She yawned. "What?"

"You said the name Paul. Who's Paul?"

"Oh. He's my friend."

"Your *boy*friend?"

"He *was*. Probably not anymore."

"Did he break up with you?"

Avery huffed as she sat up. "He can't very well be my boyfriend if I'm stuck in here, can he?"

"Why not? Sheila's got seven different boyfriends on the outside who come to visit. One time two of them missed each other by five minutes. It was pretty funny."

Avery's face cracked in amusement. "Your name's Francine, right?"

"Only the nurses call me that. Everyone else calls me 'Flint,'" she said, bouncing off her bed. "And you must be Avery Norton, the girl behind the Martha's Vineyard Massacre."

Avery couldn't catch a breath. It was like she was back in the garden of her nightmares with the roots filling her insides so entirely, the air had nowhere to flow.

"How do you know about that?" she said, her hand pressed to her racing heart.

"It's all over the news. The papers, too. You didn't think killing seventeen people would slip between the cracks, did you?"

"No, I didn't . . . I mean, I didn't kill anyone."

Flint pursed her lips. "Oh, that's right. Someone mentioned you have blackouts."

"No, I *found* the bodies, and *then* I blacked out . . . at least, I think so." Growling in frustration, she threw aside her covers and jumped out of bed. "It doesn't matter. You won't believe me anyway, just like everyone else."

"You're probably right. It wouldn't make a difference if I believe you or you believe me." Grabbing a towel off the back of the door, she said, "Just don't kill me, okay?"

With a wink, she opened the door, and Avery muttered, "Don't burn me up, okay?"

"You got it, Lizzie!" Flint disappeared around the corner before Avery could ask what she meant, but another girl heard Flint's remark and chuckled as she strolled past.

"What's so funny?" Avery asked.

The girl stopped with a snort. "You've never heard of Lizzie Borden? The girl who chopped up her parents?"

"Oh. Yeah, I guess I have, but what—"

The girl popped her hip. "She was in Taunton for a while, too. One of the biggest big-shit killers the ward ever had . . . until you." With her face screwed up to one side, she said, "You're our new Lizzie."

Avery groaned. "Great. Everyone's calling me the same name as a girl who killed her parents?"

"Well, you *did* kill your father, right? I just saw it on the news."

"What?!"

Avery rushed to the common room where several girls resembled smoky blankets draped over the furniture. Huddled in front of them, she watched in increasing horror as the stone-faced reporter disclosed the newest facts about the aptly-named "Martha's Vineyard Massacre."

" . . . her own father, thought to have abandoned the family eight years ago, which makes Dr. Jason Norton the oldest of the bodies discovered in the Oak Bluffs home."

"Daddy?" Avery's head spun, and she had to focus on a cigarette burn in the carpet until she stopped spinning.

"The police have yet to release the names of the remaining sixteen victims, and no official charges have been brought against the accused as of yet, but we've received confirmation that Avery Norton is indeed confined to Taunton State Hospital."

The girls hooted and clapped at the mention of Taunton and cheered for Avery when her picture appeared on the screen.

A plump girl with a crooked mouth stood and said, "Lookie at this, ladies. We've got a star in our midst."

Flint scratched her scalp, causing her hair to puff up in

back as she strode into the room. "Leave her alone, Pam. She just found out her dad's dead."

"Doubtful, since she's the one that offed him."

"It's her first week."

"But not her first rough-and-tumble, from the looks of it. She shouldn't have any problem defending herself." She cracked her knuckles, and Avery recoiled.

"I don't even know you."

"Oh, you will, Lizzie."

"It's Avery."

"*Lizzie*," she sang, a sneer crinkling her face.

Fury scalded Avery from the pit of her belly to the roof of her mouth, inch by inch clawing closer to her brain. Her hands tightened to fists, and her face got so hot she thought it must've been beet red. Pam's resonating singsong constricted the area behind her eyes, making her feel like she was being pinched and pushed from within. And then, like a rubber band snapping, she released.

A tornado of rage and sorrow, faith and shame, she felt each one like hunger pangs as she throttled Pam's cheek and shoulder and anything else she happened to hit before the nurses pulled her away. The next thing she felt was pain in her neck, starting cold but quickly flowering into a hot, itchy mass she couldn't scratch. Her fingers were too heavy, too numb, and as blistering fluid surged throughout her body, dizziness followed. The faces around her spun, and their voices swamped her thoughts. They became everything then, all her love and fear streaming through her at once and the familiar sensation of anger washing over her like unmaking waves.

Then there was darkness.

Then there was comfort.

Then there was Paul.

CHAPTER NINE

PAIN ROUSED AVERY from unconsciousness and threw her into a fit of involuntary shivers. Her mind screamed at her to get up, get out, get away, but the cold was all around her. Helpless and restrained, Avery thrashed madly in the freezing bath, kicking at the chunks of ice on the surface. She thought she was tugging at the straps on her wrists, but she couldn't feel them, or anything anymore, except the emptiness of her lungs. She couldn't catch a breath, and the harder she tried, the more it felt like her lungs were full of stalactites piercing the delicate tissue. Her screams were thin and ragged, but she cried until her throat burned and her head pounded, and she could no longer hold it up. It smacked on the back of the tub, and colorful explosions filled her brain as she floated on the cusp of unconsciousness, somewhere between hypothermia and her new torturous version of life.

She was unsure how long she lay in the freezing water before the nurses appeared beside her, gently calling her name.

She tried to say, "Help me," but her lips wouldn't move, and her voice sputtered out like the engine of a rusted out junker trying to turn over. But a different overturning should've worried Avery more. That of the basins held by the nurses surrounding the tub. Her vision was blurred and her thoughts sluggish, but it wasn't hard to figure out what was happening.

An avalanche of ice tumbled into the water, and she

screeched, kicking the ice at the nurses, but they weren't fazed, and left the patient once their basins were empty.

Avery didn't think she could be colder, but the fresh ice started the agony anew. Her chin trembled so violently she thought her teeth might shatter, or her skull might split and crumble to useless chunks. Alone again, broken, her body dim and flickering as the lights, she found herself in an icy wasteland with mountainous drifts of snow. Beneath the wind, she heard her own screams and the walls of ice screaming back, but she couldn't feel her voice inside her body. Her skin, muscles, blood, and future were utterly frozen. She wasn't even shivering anymore. She stopped fighting and accepted the end was near.

When feeling returned, she figured she had to be in Heaven, enfolded in an embrace of perfect love. Except, Heaven shouldn't have barred windows. They sailed past her as a large man in scrubs carried her through the hall.

She shivered. Her head pounded. Of course, Heaven wouldn't want her.

It was Patrick, the same orderly who'd deposited Flint back to their room. Avery expected he was taking her back there too, so panic set in when she didn't recognize the corridor. She whined and wiggled in his arms, but he held her tight.

"Calm down, girl. No one's going to hurt you."

He sounded sincere, but she didn't believe him for a second. The staff and Avery clearly had different ideas about what it meant to hurt someone.

In a room the color of a ripe apricot, a plump woman filing her nails dropped her emery board and snapped to attention.

"Patient 8-1-5," the orderly said, and the secretary checked her clipboard. Popping out of her seat, she scuttled to a gray door so narrow the large orderly would've had to walk through sideways even if he weren't carrying a patient.

The apricot unripened in Dr. Aslinn's office. It was

paler, more comforting, but Aslinn himself made Avery shrink against the orderly when the doctor rose from his chair.

He dwarfed his chestnut desk, and when he gestured to the large white sofa, his hand appeared bigger than Avery's head. She clung to Patrick as he set her down on the couch, her stare a pleading scream, but he avoided her watery stare, his focus firmly fixed on the exit. The moment his arms disconnected from the patient, he was gone, not a word of remorse uttered. She wasn't sure why it felt like a betrayal until she pulled the blanket tighter and realized someone had dressed her in unfamiliar clothes. Had Patrick done that? Or the nurses who'd buried her in ice? Neither seemed a reasonable or forgivable answer.

As the doctor approached, she retreated into the deepest corner of the couch, her chin trembling.

"Avery Norton. So nice to finally meet you," he said softly, his catcher's mitt of a hand extended. "I usually like to speak to new patients by their second day, if not the first, but something prevented that, didn't it? A lot of things. But rest assured, I've had plenty of discussions *about* you since your arrival, so I'm well versed in your case." Dr. Aslinn's subtle European accent landed roughly on certain words, making him sound sinister, but the natural musicality in his speech and gestures made her feel ashamed of her fear.

"You look dazed, my child. Do you know where you are?"

Her voice cracked as she said, "Yes, I'm in Hell."

Dr. Aslinn chuckled. "So you haven't lost your sense of humor. That's good."

"I wasn't joking."

His mouth tightened and he stiffly reclaimed his place behind the desk. The bulbous yellow light hung too low above him, casting a heavy shadow over his brow when he sat.

"I see. Well, I suppose we should get to know each other. I'm Dr. Aslinn, Chief Therapist for the juvenile ward here at Taunton Hospital. I've been working in this field for over twenty years and written several books specializing in—"

"I don't care," Avery said flatly.

"No? Usually, people your age care quite a lot about being treated by someone they don't know or trust. I'm just trying to set your mind at ease."

Stressing each word, she repeated, "I don't care."

He tilted his head. "Why are you so angry, Avery?"

"If people accused you of crimes you didn't commit, wouldn't you be angry? If you were taken away from your home and friends and locked up in a dungeon for crazy people, wouldn't you be angry?"

"Actually, I think I'd be relieved for the holiday," he said, leaning back in his chair. "You could think of it like that, you know. Some time away to think, to rest."

"Being tied up and left alone in freezing cold water for God knows how long isn't my idea of resting."

"Have it your way. Let's talk about something else." Dr. Aslinn straightened his spine and folded his hands on the desk. "Why do you think so many people believe you committed these crimes?"

"Because my mother set me up. I saw her put two dead people in her trunk, so she told everyone I killed them, and that she was covering for me."

Dr. Aslinn opened a manila folder and sifted through a pile of papers. Drumming a pencil on a page, he hummed. "Can you explain why your fingerprints were on so many of the bodies?"

"The light was out in the cellar. They were hanging on hooks, and I couldn't see them. I was pushing them away to look for the light. I didn't know what they were."

He shook his head sadly. "Avery, there were no hooks."

She sniffled. "I know what I saw."

He pegged his pencil eraser to another part of the paper. "Tell me about the rabbits."

"It was an accident. I didn't mean to hurt them."

"So you admit to killing them."

"Yes. But it wasn't on purpose—I mean, it *was*, but I didn't *want* to do it."

Dr. Aslinn leaned back in his chair. "So you feel like killing them was out of your control."

Avery pouted. "I guess. But I never would've done it if my mom hadn't told me to."

"Why would your mother tell you to kill rabbits?"

"I guess she didn't put it exactly like that. But she did kill two rabbits in front of me."

He checked his notes. "When she was teaching you about taking care of the garden?"

"Yes."

"What other pests did she instruct you to keep out of the garden?"

"It wasn't like that. They weren't being pests. They were—" Her face flushed, and it grew hotter the longer she felt the doctor staring at her. "They had the bad water in them, and it made them do bad things."

The doctor tilted onto his elbows, his forehead creased with contemplation. "What kinds of bad things?"

"Playing with one rabbit, then playing with another. Switching. Being dirty. Being bad."

"I see. So you killed the rabbits because they were having sex with each other."

She shrugged. "I . . . guess?"

"Just like those teenagers. And your father."

"No!"

"Your mother told the police you were the one who discovered your father's infidelity. That you caught him with another woman."

"What?!" Avery hugged her body and shook her head. "No, that can't be true. I don't know anything about that. She's trying to make me sound crazy, but I'm not. I didn't even know my father was dead until—" Her voice caught in her throat. "I thought he left us."

"No one is saying you're crazy, Avery. You're just a very

confused girl, and you need help from people who understand you. People like me." The doctor tented his hands in a sort of professional prayer. "But I can't help you if you won't let me. That's why I've decided to call in your mother. I think speaking with her face-to-face will be beneficial for you both."

Speaking into his intercom, he said, "Please send in Mrs. Norton."

Avery's body juddered with revulsion. "No. I don't want to see her."

She'd barely finished the sentence when the door flew open, and Faye Norton entered on a gust of air that chilled Avery all over again.

Rising from his desk, the doctor shook her hand. "Good morning, Mrs. Norton. Thank you so much for coming."

"It's actually 'Hayworth' now. I'm going back to my maiden name in the hopes of distancing myself from this awful business."

"This is all because of you," Avery hissed, and when Faye wilted to the couch, she scooted as far away from her as possible, her body rigid as her mother's hand fell gently upon her leg.

"I know you're angry with me. I'm angry with me too. I should've done something about your problems before they got this bad."

"You're the one with the problems," Avery spat. "What are you even doing here? Why aren't you in jail right now?"

Faye threw a sad puppy dog gaze at Dr. Aslinn. "Maybe this wasn't a good idea."

"We just need to open the lines of communication," he said. "Ms. Hayworth, how do you feel knowing your daughter thinks you committed these crimes?"

Faye stared at her hands. "Horrible. It breaks my heart, frankly, but better me than her. I tried to convince the police it was me, that I killed all those people, but . . . " She lifted her head, her cheeks marked with fresh tears. "I wish

I could carry this burden for her. I wish I could be the mother she needs."

"I don't need anything from you. Especially not your pity. And I won't be the only one carrying this burden. I might get most of the blame, but you're still going to jail for your part in it."

"You're right, I will. And I'm happy to. I deserve it for the horror I allowed you to inflict on those innocent people." She crossed herself and folded her hands in her lap as she looked to Dr. Aslinn. "Of course, I only knew about the earliest victims, so my lawyers are optimistic about a shortened sentence. I'm not being held accountable for everyone she killed."

Avery jumped to her feet. "You're a lying bitch!"

"Avery!" Faye clutched her chest and apologized to the doctor. "I understand you're upset, but please don't speak to me like that. I came here because I thought it would help. And I brought some of your things: toys, clothes, your diary. And I can bring more." Moving closer, she grasped Avery's hand. "Do and say whatever you want to me; I will keep visiting for as long as it takes you to get well."

Avery pulled free and held the blankets so tight her fingers went numb.

"I'm not going to yell at you," she said rigidly. "And I'm not going to fight you. I know how they punish you for fighting here."

"What do you mean?"

"Avery had an altercation with another girl the other day," Dr. Aslinn said.

Faye popped up on the couch. "Oh my goodness! She didn't hurt her, did she? Oh dear, that poor girl."

"She's all right. Bumps and bruises, nothing serious."

"Thank God for that." Faye crossed herself again, and Avery groaned.

"So you've seen this behavior before," he said, head tilted.

She nodded like agreeing with him exhausted her.

"Yes. When Avery was five, she was playing with a girl in the backyard, a tourist's child she met in town. I was in the kitchen making lunch when I heard a scream. I ran outside and Avery was standing over her with my gardening shears, both of them covered in blood. She'd slashed the girl across the leg and was planning to cut off one of her toes when I found them."

Avery threw herself against the doctor's desk, knocking a jar of pencils to the floor. "That's a lie! This is all a lie!"

Faye dropped to her knees to collect the pencils, her head shaking. "No control," she muttered as she set them on his desk. "I'm so sorry, Dr. Aslinn."

"It's fine. Please, take a seat, both of you."

Faye quickly reclaimed a spot on the couch and sat perfectly straight while Avery grudgingly slumped into a chair.

"She's lying, Dr. Aslinn."

"I told the police the same story I'm telling you, Doctor. Not a detail has changed. My memory's as steadfast as my faith." Turning to Avery, she said, "How's yours, sweetheart?"

Avery shook her head at Dr. Aslinn pleadingly. "I killed rabbits, that's it. And I only did it because she told me if they got bad water inside them, they'd have to be put out of their misery, for their own good."

"Honey, you really need to stop spinning that yarn. It makes you sound a little, well, I'm sure you hear this sort of thing all the time, Doctor. She said the same thing after she—after she—" Faye pressed her fist to her lips to contain a sudden swell of emotion, but as Avery suspected it would, it exploded out of her like a busting water pipe, and she wailed. "After she killed her father!"

Her stomach turned. It couldn't be true. She couldn't have hurt her dad. She loved him. She hardly knew him, but she loved him. It terrified her to think she was wrong.

"That's not true! I didn't even know he was dead!"

Dr. Aslinn gestured to Faye. "Can you speak to that, Ms.

Hayworth? Did you tell your daughter her father left Martha's Vineyard when you knew he was actually deceased?"

"I told *everyone* that. To protect her. What else could I do? She's my daughter."

"He was your husband."

She sucked on her bottom lip and nodded. "And I'll pay for what I've done. I knew it was wrong to hide her crimes. I thought I could love her into being healthy, but I guess my love just wasn't enough." Offering Avery a half-smile, she said, "I did try. And for all my love, I've had such ghastly nightmares, long before the arrest. When I was awake, too. I kept thinking she'd come after me next, or after her sister. That's why I sent dear Natalie away. To keep her safe."

"This is complete bullshit!" Avery shouted, and Faye covered her ears.

"This is too much. I can't bear the kind of person you're becoming."

"What are you going to do, Mom? Ground me?"

Dr. Aslinn poked the folder with his pencil. "This party up-island—"

Faye dropped her hands and sniffed. "I told the police I have no idea what that's about. I can't confirm if she went or not—"

"Oh, she did," he replied, looking up from his papers.

Avery's head lifted too, and Faye inhaled deeply.

"Really?"

"A Chilmark police officer has gone on record as having picked Avery up on the State Road the night of the murders, allegedly coming from that party."

Avery buried her face in her hands, and Faye scoffed.

Then, in a voice as smooth as browned butter, she said, "Was a boy named Paul Dillon with her?"

Dr. Aslinn's brow furrowed. "I'm not at liberty to speak about any other potential suspects in this case, nor is it relevant. I'm here to help Avery get well. Both of you, if possible."

"Maybe you could introduce me to some of the girls," Faye said, and Avery flinched. "If that's all right with you, Dr. Aslinn."

Avery opened her mouth to protest, but nothing came out. Faye and the doctor had managed to turn every defense into a condemnation, and she didn't have the energy to hear one more person disparaging her truth. Closing the arguments behind her teeth made her feel woozier, though, and her body grew heavy in the chair. Rolling the back of her throbbing skull on the headrest, she heard her voice clashing with her mother's as if she hadn't held her tongue. The confusion sent electric shivers down her spine, and she clenched every muscle in her body. When her curled in her shoes, she realized they were filled with pebbles and dirt. Garden dirt. She could smell it, wet and wormy, with notes of rusty spigot. Squeezing the earth between her toes, she sat up perfectly straight, praying they couldn't detect the rancid odor. Her skin flushed, and sweat formed on her upper lip as her mother and the doctor discussed a future tour of the ward. Their joyful voices echoed and expanded, making it feel like the room was strangling her.

Clapping her hands over her ears, she screamed. "Stop! I don't want to give her a *tour*! I don't want anything to do with her! She's a *murderer*!"

The room was silent but for Avery's breathing, and when she reclined on the sofa again, her mother gawked at her, hands folded and eyebrows raised.

"I thought you said you wouldn't yell."

"I lied," she said. "Just like you."

"There's no need to get so upset," Dr. Aslinn said. "Everyone understands that you need time to assimilate and get comfortable, and we'll give you that. Once you're feeling more grounded, we'll revisit the idea. I think your mother showed tremendous courage coming here, and you've shown a great deal as well, Avery. There's a long road ahead of us, but we've taken some bold steps today, and I'm proud of you both."

While Faye Norton lifted her chin in delight, Avery's head sagged lower.

"Now," the doctor continued, "I'm willing to ignore the incident with Pam and lift your common room restrictions, if you promise to behave from now on."

"That sounds reasonable," Faye said.

She clenched her jaw. "Fine."

"That's my girl," her mother chirped. "I suppose I should be off then, but I'll be back soon if that's all right."

"Of course it is," Dr. Aslinn said, beaming. "I must say it's refreshing to see a parent so devoted to their child's recovery. I'm sad to say the parental visits around here are few and far between."

"Oh dear, what a shame."

"I want Natalie to visit," Avery said firmly. "I want to see Natalie."

Dr. Aslinn checked his notes. "Natalie is your sister, yes? Of course she's welcome to visit."

A gloom fell over Faye, and she shook her head. "I'm afraid my other daughter has no interest in visiting. Apparently, one of the boys they found in the house was a friend of hers. An old boyfriend, actually." She patted Avery's hand reassuringly. "She'll get over it, honey, but right now, Natalie doesn't want to see you."

Avery's gut tightened, and nausea swelled through her. It couldn't be true. When the world was against her, she thought of Natalie as someone who'd always be on her side. She couldn't possibly believe her sister was a murderer; it had to be another of Faye's lies.

But maybe not. Natalie didn't know what Avery and Paul had seen up-island. She hadn't even told her about the rabbits, or their mother's strange gardening lessons. If it was true, if Natalie could believe her little sister was a killer, maybe what Faye said about blackouts weren't lies at all. Maybe Natalie had seen them too. As much as it bewildered her, she had to consider that side of it. If she'd blacked out and done some unspeakable thing, her mind might have substituted the memory of murder with something nicer, something mundane, giving her everything she needed to blame someone else.

No. Avery knew herself. She knew her heart and her soul. She couldn't have done anything so horrible. Teeth clenched and face trembling from the pressure, she wanted so badly to scream and cry and punch holes in the pale green walls, but she refused to give her mother the satisfaction of knowing she'd won.

Dr. Aslinn stood beside her and patted her shoulder. "I'm sorry, Avery. There's always a chance she'll come around once you're well."

"Just like those few and far between parents?" she replied, her words bitter on her tongue.

He flared his nostrils and extended his hand to Faye. "Thank you for coming, Mrs. Norton—pardon me—Ms. Hayworth. I think Avery could do with some rest."

"Of course." She shook his hand and turned back to her daughter. "Goodbye, sweetheart. I'll see you soon."

The news about Natalie devastated her so entirely, Avery almost didn't want her mother to go. She'd fixed so many boo-boos and chased away all manner of monsters when Avery was little, that as much as she hated her, she longed for her love.

It was a fleeting feeling, though, gone by the time Faye kissed her forehead. As her mother leaned over, her necklace slipped out of her blouse, and a brass ring swung in Avery's face. She gasped, and Faye tucked it away, but she also cradled it, twirled it, and treasured its slick warmth as it disappeared under her shirt: an extra twist of the knife before she abandoned her daughter in the lunatic asylum.

While Avery sat stunned, Dr. Aslinn shook Faye's hand, thanked her for coming in, and escorted her out. When she was gone, he extended his hand to Avery's, but she wasn't sure what to do with it. She sure as hell didn't want to touch it. Eventually, he retracted the gesture and returned to his desk. "It was nice meeting you," he said. "I'll see you again very soon."

She couldn't respond. She was too angry, too sick, and when Nurse Meredith arrived, her stomach churned harder, like a sour sea trying to empty itself. The woman and her cohorts had tortured Avery for God knows how long, and she was supposed to act like nothing happened?

"Some of your things have arrived," the nurse said as she escorted her back to the ward.

"I know."

"Excellent. Your first group therapy session is in a few hours, so I hope you're feeling a little more at ease now."

Avery groaned. "Do I have to?"

"As long as you're not catatonic, yes." She said it jokingly, but Avery detected a solemnity in the answer, like it had been a viable excuse more than once.

She went to her room to lie down, partly hoping for catatonia to follow, but the shock that awaited her guaranteed any kind of sleep was off the table. The boy sitting on Avery's bed in a tailored hospital gown and a blue bonnet waved at her, and she yelped as she dashed for the door. Jumping in front, Flint crossed her arms over her chest.

"Calm down, Lizzie."

She shook the girl away and barked, "Don't call me that."

"Sorry. *Avery*. Don't flip out, okay?"

"There's a boy on my bed," Avery whispered.

Flint chuckled. "In a way, yes." Dragging her to the willowy boy with raven hair, she said, "Avery, this is Frankie. Frankie, Avery."

"Nice to meet you," he said. Frankie's voice was so wispy and gentle, the force of his handshake surprised her.

Avery shot Flint a curious look. "Is this your boyfriend?"

Frankie and Flint erupted into howling laughter, and the boy fanned the tears from his eyes.

"Frankie's a patient like us," Flint said, giggling. "Well, not *exactly* like us . . . "

"I thought girls and boys were supposed to stay separated."

"I was on the boys' side for a few months, but they moved me over here last year because my presence made the other boys . . . a little testy." With a hum, he added, "Prudes."

Avery smirked, but it didn't last long under the weight of the last few hours. Natalie didn't want to see her. Her mother was walking free, and she was wearing—no, *flaunting*—the brass ring Paul had given her. Chin quivering, Avery fought to hold back tears.

"Are you okay?" Flint asked.

She swallowed her grief as she looked at the boy in the bonnet, the girl with the twitchy fingers, the random patient who stripped down to her socks and danced past the room singing, "Polly Wolly Doodle," and all the other girls with one loose screw too many for the outside world. She felt so normal compared to them—yet, allegedly, she was the most disturbed girl in the bunch. Who was she to judge anyone there?

Flint sang a few bars of "Frankie and Johnny" as she and the boy danced around the room. She spun him into Avery's arms, and he held onto her shoulder as he dipped himself. He elegantly extended his arm as he tilted back his head, and Avery giggled.

"No," she said. "I'm not okay. But I hope I can be."

RABBITS IN THE GARDEN

CHAPTER TEN

"**F**INISH THE FUCKING story, Brianne."

The young girl bounced on the sofa. "Right. Like I was saying, it was the worst day ever—horrible, ghastly, the worst word you can think of to describe the worst day ever. I mean, oh my God, I couldn't believe so many things could go wrong in one day. So, I get up, go downstairs, and—hey look, that bird is back." Brianne flew to the window, leaving Sheila to groan in frustration.

Pam strolled over, her eye on Brianne's spot on the couch. When she started to slip into the space, Brianne whipped around and said, "Don't. Tyler's sitting there."

"Well, tell him to move. I want to sit down."

"Just sit down," Sheila said.

Pam flopped onto the sofa, and Brianne's eyes peeled in horror. Dashing over, she wrenched the girl from the spot and scooped up her invisible companion.

"I can't believe you would do that! Can't you hear he's in pain?"

She glanced from side to side. "Uh . . . no . . . "

"Look, you broke one of his whiskers. I should report you to the ASPCA."

Avery sat back and watched the events unfold. After more than a month in Taunton, she'd become accustomed to most of the patients, but they hadn't stopped amusing her. Brianne was one of her favorites. She was crazy, no doubt, but it was an endearing sort of crazy. She never said an unkind word to anyone, even when they accidentally sat on her invisible—*not imaginary*—companion, Tyler. While

Brianne was only a year younger than Avery, she was far more immature. She was almost never out of her braids and pink nightgown, and in those rare times she changed clothes, she replaced them with ragcurls and pink jumpers.

Avery also enjoyed being around Sheila, mostly because her mother would've disapproved of her friendship with "that kind of girl." Though she had no one to impress, Sheila never neglected to doll herself up: makeup on, hair done, ensemble carefully and proudly coordinated. But Avery suspected that beneath Sheila's brazen confidence, the girl was insecure and lonely, which was why her door was always open, literally and figuratively.

"Marlon Brando could walk in here at any moment," she said frequently. "And which one of us do you think he'd go for? You look like you're ready to go to sleep, but I'm ready for a night on the town."

She was never able to give a reasonable explanation for why Marlon Brando was looking for a date in a madhouse, but she did explain her other common phrase, "Boys want BJs, not PJs" to Avery—who, once filled in, bubbled with intrigue, and begged to know more.

Avery and Pam made up after their spat and acted friendly to one another, but they were not friends. Pam still called Avery "Lizzie" behind her back, and Avery knew it. But as long as she didn't have to hear it, she didn't mind. Not enough to risk another punishment, anyway. There was also the matter of Pam's past. Boorish as she was, she was also one of the most mysterious girls. Except for the staff, no one knew what brought Pam to Taunton when she was ten years old. As a resident of the asylum for over seven years, she'd been committed longer than anyone in the juvenile ward and often acted high and mighty about it. But whenever patients discussed the reasons for their incarceration, Pam clammed up and shut down.

Violet was much the same when it came to her past. Her present, too. She never talked to anyone, and she rarely moved from her chair in front of the lounge window. After so many years of choosing the same seat, the nurses painted the chair purple, forever differentiating the girl from the rest of the population.

"She used to talk," Flint told Avery. "When I first got here, she talked and moved around more, but now . . . nothing."

"What's wrong with her?"

"All I know is she's an orphan. Someone left her on the hospital doorstep when she was three."

Avery frequently caught herself staring at Violet. The girl was several years younger, but her hunched back and dull gray eyes made her look like a little old lady. She sat like a lump of skeletal clay in her purple chair, exhausted by too many ages of the world to bear any sight but the view out the common room window. She was a typical fixture in that area, but every few months, she'd be absent for days at a time. Avery assumed she spent those days in bed or staring out the window of her own room, but when she investigated during one of the absences, she found Violet's room empty.

Taunton was a puzzle with oddly-shaped pieces Avery had to force into fitting. None locked tight, and there were slivers of space into which no piece seemed to fit. Slivers like Violet. And the horrible, blood-curdling screams that blasted from the bowels of the hospital. By the time Avery's first month turned into two, and two into four, the screams had become a natural soundtrack to daily life, but that didn't mean she accepted them without an explanation.

Her search for answers was met with the same frustration as her claims of innocence. They were nothing more than her mind's way of keeping reality at a distance, Dr. Aslinn said. Suspicion about Taunton Hospital and its patients was Avery's way of dividing herself from the rest of the community. In her mind, she was normal, and everyone else was crazy. The staff included.

"The first step to recovery is admitting there's a chance,

just a chance, that everything you believe is wrong," he said. "Could you do that for me?"

"I guess . . . ." Avery's back was nearly as hunched as Violet's when she whispered, " . . . there's a chance."

Dr. Aslinn celebrated her progress, but she couldn't manage to conjure the same excitement. Admitting the possibility that she was a murderer when she didn't believe it confused and disturbed her, which worsened as time passed. Every so often she wouldn't be able to fake it; the confusion would bubble up in her and she'd beat her fists on the couch and scream at Dr. Aslinn until sweat rolled down her face.

The Taunton staff had elegant ways of subduing the patients verbally, but when talk failed, vitamins got the job done. What the nurses called "vitamins" were administered daily in pill form, but in urgent cases came in sharp flushes of liquid to the neck, the arm, or any vein that appeared in a pinch. Avery had taken vitamins before, but she'd never heard of vitamin P or M, and especially not vitamin LB. It took her months to confirm that the vitamins were drugs, but it didn't matter in the long run. The nurses weren't breaking any rules in deceiving the girls. Once Avery knew, she waged a monthlong war of anger and indignation with her medication schedule. But when she gave up the fight, she gave it up forever. She grew to appreciate and even crave the vitamins. Those moments of darkness provided more luster than her dreary day-to-day life in Taunton as she awaited her trial.

Letters from Faye arrived every week, counting down to her next visit. But every time the visitation day arrived, Avery received a call stating something else had taken precedence. Officially, she viewed it as a positive; why in the world would she want the woman who'd ruined her life to visit? But the broken promises piled up, heavy on an already tender heart. With Natalie, and now Faye refusing to visit, along with Dr. Aslinn's increasing pressure to admit her guilt, Avery had begun to question everything she believed to be true about herself. She spent hours reflecting on her life, running through reams of memories and wondering if she could trust them. Time was all she had now, and she filled it with anything she could to distract her from staff and patients gossiping about the gruesome *Martha's Vineyard Massacre*. The mere mention of the murders in passing made her extremely edgy, bordering on irate. She did her best to ignore it, but there came a day when it was impossible to ignore.

With Faye's tearful testimony about Avery's emotional issues and violent blackouts, and Dr. Aslinn's professional opinion about the young girl's tenuous mental state, Avery's defense came off like the ramblings of a diseased mind. Accusing Faye of murder made matters worse, especially with the woman's willing admission of guilt in the concealment of her daughter's early crimes. The jury needed little else, even much deliberation, to condemn Avery Norton. Within an hour, they delivered a guilty verdict that would commit the girl to the juvenile ward at Taunton State Lunatic Asylum until her eighteenth birthday.

They sentenced Faye Hayworth to serve up to two years in Framingham State Prison. She served less than one.

For a week after the trial, Avery wore black. She'd resigned herself to a lengthy stay in the hospital, but she hadn't imagined losing her entire adolescence to a life at war, torn between believing her innocence and accepting her guilt.

With each day, the latter felt more logical. As she withdrew into her sorrow, she lost herself in doubt and troubling thoughts that further eroded her sanity. But no matter how close she inched to the edge, Flint pulled her back. While Avery bonded with most everyone in the ward, she and Flint formed a friendship to rival the one she'd had with Paul. They shared everything with each other. They grew up, blossomed, and learned with each other, and when they sat in their group therapy session and Flint said unwaveringly, "No, I did not know my brother was in there when I set the fire," Avery knew she was lying.

"We haven't heard from you in a few weeks, Avery." Nurse Meredith tapped a pen on her chin. "Do you have anything to share with the group?"

She swallowed dryly as she looked around the circle of yawning patients. "Not today."

"You shouldn't avoid what's happening to you. You shouldn't bottle up your feelings."

"I'm not," she said. "I'm angry. I'm sad and disappointed and lonely. I haven't kept any of that bottled up."

"You were happy last month."

"Last month I had a chance of getting out of here. Last month I had a shot at a normal life."

"The work we do here ensures you have a normal life when you get out."

"Then why is Pam back? She got out—we all saw her—but here she sits. Shouldn't all her work have prepared her better? So she wouldn't have had to come back?"

"We're not talking about Pam. We're talking about you. People are different. They have different ailments, different paths."

Avery grunted. "It seems like our work is more about you than us. If we look normal to you, we're cured. But how do we know *you're* normal?"

The group tittered, and Nurse Meredith scoffed.

"Oh Avery. You don't think that's an original thought, do you? It's . . . " She twiddled her fingers as her gaze sailed the circle of patients. "Let's just say it's appropriate for the *common* room. The truth is, as long as you insist upon battling the people trying to help you, you cannot be helped. You need to let go of your anger, let go of your fear, and let go of your refusal to accept recovery."

"It doesn't matter. I'm out when I turn eighteen."

"You're out of this ward when you turn eighteen," she

said. "Your doctors and nurses decide whether you'll be discharged at that time or moved to an adult ward. The law put you here, but only we can deem you ready for release. And if that happens," she said, turning the page in her notebook, "the law's taking you right back."

Avery clamped her mouth shut and lowered her head. For the rest of the session, she zoned out on the other patients. It wasn't until Brianne complained about a girl purposefully tripping Tyler that something broke Avery's trance.

Someone was screaming outside. Someone was screaming her name.

She thought it was in her mind, but when the other patients perked in their seats and looked around, Avery galloped across the room and threw herself against the bars of the window. The others clustered behind her, including Nurse Day, who squinted through the light and hissed, "Who is that?"

Paul Dillon ran left and right in front of Taunton Hospital, yelling so loud his voice already sounded strained. Avery cried his name, but he didn't hear her. So Flint shouted his name too. So did Sheila and Frankie. Before long, the entire group was calling Paul to the window, and he looked up with a grateful smile.

Panting, he ran closer and waved to Avery. "There you are! Oh my God, Avery, are you all right?"

"What are you doing here?"

"We're visiting my grandfather in Boston, and I begged my mom to bring me here. But the people up front wouldn't let me in. I'm on some sort of list."

"A list?"

"Tell me you're okay," he said. "I've been so worried about you."

"I'm fine, all things considered. But I miss you so much," she said, rousing a mix of genuine and sarcastic sympathy from the patients.

"I miss you too. I still can't believe this is happening. It's not fair. You're innocent."

She shook her head. "I used to think so."

"Keep thinking it. You *are* innocent! Do you hear me?" Paul shouted it to the patients, to the building, to the sky. "Avery Norton is innocent! Say it, Avery! You're innocent!"

Nurse Meredith ordered the patients to disperse, but many stayed close, orbiting like eavesdropping satellites. Clamping her hand to Avery's shoulder, the nurse whispered, "You need to let go, my dear. It's the only way you'll get better. The future is ahead of you. Your recovery is ahead of you. The past will only drag you down."

"But . . . " Her voice creaked out meekly. "But he's the only one who believes me."

"Of course he is. He cares about you. He wants to protect you."

"What's wrong with that?"

"It's the same thing your mother did when you were young, when this whole terrible thing started. You need to take ownership of your sickness, and if you allow him to stand in the way, you'll never get well."

"You're innocent!" Paul bellowed. "Say it!"

"Why can't it be true?" she whimpered. "Why can't I be innocent?"

"Because no one is," the nurse replied. "Not you. Not even him. He might be able to help you someday, but right now all he can do is hurt you. You need to surround yourself with the truth, and he only tells you what you want to hear."

Three guards rushed outside and cornered Paul. He slipped out of their grasp at first, but they eventually caught him and started dragging him away.

"Avery!"

"Let go," Nurse Meredith whispered again.

"Please say it, Avery! I need to hear you say it!" Paul shouted.

She gazed down at him, jaw trembling. Even at his distance she saw the sorrow welling in his eyes.

Together, Paul and Nurse Meredith demanded, "Say it, Avery."

Leaning against the bars, she closed her eyes. Even when she opened her mouth to speak, she didn't know which one she'd appease until she whispered two devastating words: "Goodbye, Paul."

The guards hauled him away, but Avery couldn't tear herself from the window. Long after he was gone, she stood staring out, stunned by her decision. What had she done? How could she have let him go? He'd come so far, fought so hard, and she'd given him up so easily. Exhausted with sorrow and self-loathing, she trudged to her room and flopped onto the bed.

Frankie curled his head around the doorframe. "You okay?"

"Yes. No. I don't know," she replied, her arm draped over her face. "I don't know how 'okay' is supposed to feel anymore."

"Flint and I were thinking of a late-night game, something to take our minds off things. Truth or Dare, maybe? Violet's gone, so we can use her room."

"Where did she go?"

He shrugged. "Where does she ever go?"

"It could be fun," Flint said. She skipped into the room, unaware she'd acquired a small shadow named Brianne, who slunk in behind her with a chirp.

"What could be fun?" she asked.

Flint and Frankie groaned. "If we tell you, you can't tell anyone else. Not even Tyler."

"Fine. That's easy."

"We're playing Truth or Dare tonight in Violet's room," Frankie said.

The girl clasped her hands in prayer and whined. "Can I play? Please?"

"Okay, but remember your promise. No one. Not even Tyler."

"I don't have to tell Tyler. He's been standing here the whole time." She grinned, then jumped in the air as if someone stuck her with a pin. "Ouch, Tyler! Watch your horns!"

CHAPTER ELEVEN

AFTER LIGHTS OUT, Avery, Flint, Frankie, Sheila, Brianne, and Rachel gathered in Violet's room, jittery with excitement.

"Where's Pam?" Avery asked as she joined the circle on the floor.

"She swallowed her vitamin T by accident," Rachel said, scratching at the bandages under her sleeves.

Frankie smacked his head in disbelief, and Flint snarled.

"Damn, I was hoping I'd finally get to ask her how she ended up in here."

"Oh please." Frankie snorted. "You know she would've avoided that question like the plague. I bet she would've only picked dare."

Leaning toward Rachel, Avery whispered, "What does that mean?"

The girl furrowed her brow. "Do you not know how to play Truth or Dare?"

She shook her head, and five sets of eyes turned to her in shock.

"You've never played Truth or Dare? How is that possible?" Rachel said.

She shrugged. "I mostly played with boys back home. Or it was just me and Paul." Avery's voice caught when she said his name, and she dropped her chin to her chest to regain control of her breath.

"What are you saying?" Frankie said. "Truth or Dare isn't manly enough for boys to play?" He puffed out his chest, and Sheila chortled.

"Who are you kidding?" She waved at Avery. "Don't worry. It's easy."

"And Sheila knows all about being easy," Frankie said.

She crinkled her nose, punched the boy in the arm, and began again. "Really, Avery. It's simple."

"And Sheila knows all about—"

The girl reeled back her fist. "Do you want another one?"

Massaging his arm, he puckered his lips and made a prolonged kissing noise.

"All you have to do is pick truth or dare," Flint said. "If you pick truth, you *have to* tell the truth—and if you choose dare, you *have to* do whatever the person tells you."

"What if I don't want to do it?"

"It doesn't matter. You have to do it. It's the rules." Frankie crossed his arms over his chest. "Watch. I'll go first. Flint: truth or dare?"

"Dare."

"Rachel, give me your matches," he said, and Flint's eyes lit up. "I dare you to sit with these matches in front of you for five full minutes without touching them."

Her face crumpled, and she mewled. "Oh come on!"

"You said dare! You have to do it!"

Rachel set a book of matches on the floor, and Flint grumbled. When she closed her eyes, several of the kids whined in protest.

"That's cheating," Frankie said. "You have to look at them."

Flint curled her lip and focused on the matches. "You'd better start praying I don't think of something for you, or you're in big trouble, pal." Her fingers twitched more than normal, and beads of sweat jeweled on her forehead. When Frankie called "time," she snatched up the matches and hugged them to her chest.

"Ahem." Rachel snapped her fingers, and Flint begrudgingly tossed the matches to her.

Many of the dares were like the first one: torturous

tasks that tested the limits of one's ailments. Even though Avery didn't think she had any to test, she chose truth every time. But sometimes the truths were harder to stomach. When Sheila asked her about the blackouts, she told the truth—she didn't have blackouts—and their eruptions of doubt made her want to burst into tears. She crumpled in on herself and stared at the floor; no one picked her much after that, but she paid attention to it all. Like when Rachel admitted she was happier when she was cutting, and later when she did a topless handstand. Or when she dared Frankie and Sheila to make out, and Brianne tearfully confessed she didn't miss anyone in her family. But when Sheila disclosed that she'd gone all the way with every boy she'd kissed, Flint's knee jostled against Avery's. Lifting her head, she watched a smirk twist Flint's face, and she knew her friend had found her mode of revenge.

When Flint's turn rolled around again, she called Frankie's name with sing-song malice and squealed with delight when he answered, "Dare."

"I dare you to go to my and Avery's room with Sheila, and . . . " She sucked on her bottom lip in anticipation. " . . . how did you put it, Sheila? Go all the way?"

Frankie scoffed. "You have to be joking."

"Oh, but I'm not," she said, folding her arms.

"I'm not doing that."

"You have to. It's the rules," Flint said.

"Besides," Rachel added, "you wouldn't want to make Sheila break her kissing-and-doing-it streak, would you?"

Frankie snarled, and Flint snarled back. "You used fire. You had this coming."

"That's completely different. You *want* to touch fire."

"Hey!" Sheila squealed. "I'm not excited about this arrangement either, you know."

Grumbling, Frankie stood and extended his hand. "Let's just get this over with."

"Golly, thanks." She refused his help and dashed to the

door. Peeking out of the room, she gave the all-clear, and they hurried through the ward to room eight.

Flint trilled, "Have fun!" and Brianne giggled as she scratched Tyler's floppy ears.

"If any of you think they're really going to do it, you're crazy," Rachel said, then pointed at the girl stroking empty air.

"Truth or dare, Brianne?"

She whispered into Tyler's ear, paused, and replied, "Truth."

"Finish your story. What happened on the day you were sent here?"

"Oh, wow!" Brianne howled. "Now *that* was an awful day. Ridiculously awful. Actually, the beginning of the day wasn't so terrible. Although, I did burn myself with my mom's hot rollers. Have you ever done that? It really hurts, and you get a big ugly scab from it. It's funny because I did it the week of school pictures, so I had my picture taken with a big scab on my forehead, but not a minute after they took the picture, I rubbed my forehead, and the scab came right off. It didn't even leave a mark. I felt so dumb. If only I'd rubbed my forehead before the picture was taken . . . "

She went on for a while with Flint and Rachel interjecting groans and remarks to "Finish the fucking story, Brianne," and was in the middle of her twentieth tangent when the door to Violet's room opened.

Frankie slunk in like a stray cat from a rainstorm with Sheila on his heels, but they split apart as soon as they could, slumping silently to the floor.

"So, how was it?" Rachel asked.

Sheila shrugged. "I've had better, I've had worse."

"No way," Avery said. "You didn't really—"

"Yes, we did," Frankie said, every muscle tense. "Let's move on."

Flint scrunched her nose. "What's wrong? It wasn't good for you?"

"Get bent, Francine." With a grunt, he stood, and stormed out of the room.

After a long, agitated silence, Avery hummed. "So . . . this is Truth or Dare."

"Yeah, I guess this is why we don't play much," Rachel said.

As they tidied up, Flint's hands shook like she was trying to flick something off her fingers, and it only got worse when they returned to their room. She paced and pounded her thighs and peered suspiciously at her bed.

"Where do you think they did it? Frankie and Sheila."

Avery, already halfway under the covers, froze in terror. "I don't know. I'm not sure I want to know."

"Do you think he'll forgive me?" The girl crawled into bed and pulled the covers to her chin as if fearful of a monster lurking in the shadows.

Avery turned onto her side, and Flint faced her, eyes glittering in the dark.

"Yes, I do."

"How can you be sure?"

"What else is there to do in here? If no one forgave each other, life would be all that much worse for all of us."

Flint's hands steadied as she tucked them under her pillow, and with a yawn, she said, "It's not so bad."

"I was starting to think so . . . before today."

"You mean before Paul."

Avery sighed and flipped onto her back. Staring up at the ceiling, trying to imagine herself atop the Wooden Valentine, she whispered, "There was nothing before Paul."

When Avery made her way to the common room the next morning, she found Violet sitting at the window. But she looked even more haggard than usual. Her head was tilted back and jaw slack, but her eyes were peeled in fright. And they didn't lazily follow Avery's movements like usual. Her focus remained fixed on the window in a dead stare while her body was a glob of melting wax. It was a disturbing sight made more so by the fact that she was slumped over in the wrong-colored chair. The new wound on her freshly shaven scalp claimed responsibility for it all, but no one said it aloud. Avery didn't know why anyone else stayed silent, but she didn't speak about the hospital's barbaric therapies for fear that acknowledging them would make her the next patient under the knife.

CHAPTER TWELVE

MADHOUSE MONTHS PASSED in frightening time. In late February of the following year, a young orphan named Bethany arrived at Taunton. Unlike Violet, Bethany never stopped talking, especially to people who weren't there. She didn't stick around more than a week or two, but the flu she'd brought in stuck around for nearly a month. Most of the girls in the ward got sick—coughing, sneezing, running fevers—but Sheila had the worst of it. Even when she woke up feeling better than the day before, nausea snuck up on her. And because she often got sick before reaching the lavatory, she started a chain reaction in the other ill girls. The custodial staff had their hands full in late February.

That May, Pam turned eighteen. Following a few emotional days, she moved to the women's ward on the other side of the sun bridge. As the adult patients had fewer restrictions and more access to the gardens and paths winding between the hospital buildings, Avery could look outside and see Pam amidst the women of Taunton. It terrified her seeing how easily Pam assimilated with people who'd been confined to Taunton for only God knew how long. But she seemed content with them, happier than she'd been in the juvenile ward. She was still stuck in the asylum, but her rage in captivity registered less each day.

Thinking of the small comforts she'd found in the ward, and how she spent fewer hours each day obsessing over what she'd lost, Avery feared how captivity would continue to change her. She told Dr. Aslinn her fears, but his consolations always came back to placing every ounce of trust in *his* process, *his* assessment of her progress, and *his* ability to reverse her core dysfunctions. She did try to trust him; for a few months after she let go of Paul, she let go of the notion that everyone in Taunton—and maybe the world—was against her. But his answers were always the same, and while he congratulated her on the great strides she'd met during their private sessions, she didn't feel any healthier, or any closer to trusting what everyone said about her. On the contrary, the more progress Dr. Aslinn claimed she made, the more she felt the knots of sanity loosen.

All things considered, she thought she was handling her wrongful incarceration with patience and grace. While the staff worked tirelessly to convince her she was a psychological menace, she clung to friendships as she'd never had on the island. They were loud and messy—the kind Faye would've nipped in the bud immediately—and they got her through the toughest times. When Dr. Aslinn forced her to say she was a murderer, or Nurse Day instructed her to stop blaming her mother for her problems, and she felt like it would be easier to be the violent creature they wanted of her, she would turn to Flint. The girl would calm her with poetry about bonfires and candlelight, which would sometimes stir Flint into a frenzy that Avery, in turn, would quiet.

But it didn't always work, and the agony of Avery's imprisonment would overwhelm her. She imagined her mother locked up less than an hour away and knew, without a doubt, without a scrap of proof, that Faye did not suffer as she did. Rage, like ants through earth, burrowed into her, colonized and excavated her, until she felt like there was nothing of the sweet little Vineyarder left. That's when the nurses increased her vitamin dosage or sentenced her to a stint in the ice bath to cool off. She hated both, but the scars pinching Violet's scalp reminded her how lucky she'd been to have such lenient punishments.

She was still shivering from one such penance a day in early September as she watched Brianne play a riotous game of Hide and Seek with Tyler. The girl in pink pajamas darted up and down the hall, jumping from couch to couch, and bursting into other girls' rooms in search of her elusive friend.

She crept up to room five, pressed herself to the door, and grinned. "I hear your hooves clicking," she sang out. "I hear you panting."

Sheila growled. "Tyler's not in here, so shut up, and get away from my door."

But Brianne was unconvinced. She knew her invisible friend was hiding somewhere in room five, so she threw the door open and leapt onto Sheila's bed. She ripped off the sheets and pushed Sheila aside to see if Tyler was crouched behind her, but Sheila pushed back, throwing Brianne to the floor. With a huff, she continued looking for Tyler behind the boxes under Sheila's bed, but she didn't get far once Sheila seized her by the ankle. She dragged the girl out and grabbed one of her braids when she tried to scuttle back under the bed. Flipping her over, Sheila pummeled Brianne, drawing blood from her lip and nose before the nurses broke through the spectators in the doorway and pulled her off. Brianne wailed as bruises blossomed in her skin and Patrick the orderly scooped her up, but she quieted before they exited the room, pointing weakly at the bed. "There he is! I knew it, I knew he was in there."

It didn't matter how many times Avery saw the nurses subdue someone, it seldom failed to entertain. And because everyone eventually had their turn wrestling with the staff, no one minded the audience. In fact, she thought it might be an unspoken rule among the patients to make sedation as entertaining as possible. After years behind the same bars, eating the same bland food, hearing the same insane stories and useless solutions, the kids craved the violent displays with the same fervor as the rare excursions outside. But that day, as Sheila slackened under Nurse

Radcliffe's needle and they carted her out of the ward, the patients' bloodlust didn't rise with the same intensity. Sheila didn't lash out often, and Avery couldn't recall a single person who'd attacked Brianne before that, so after the initial shock of the altercation wore off, confusion settled over the ward like a noxious fog, and they awaited Sheila's return with morbid curiosity.

For the rest of the day, Avery sat on the couch in the common room, her concentration darted from the television to Violet to the ward doors and back. Each time she heard wheels on the linoleum, she whipped around expecting to see a nurse pushing Sheila down the hall, but after a full day with no sign of the girl, Nurse Mathis forced her to retire to her room for the night.

A few hours later, Avery jolted out of a dream. She wasn't sure what roused her—a scream, she thought, or a high-pitched snore—but the ward was quiet when she sat up in bed, so after a few minutes, she allowed herself to drift back to sleep.

The next day, Sheila's closed door unsettled the patients. Nurse Moore confirmed they'd brought her back to the ward early that morning, though, so the kids spent much of the early afternoon debating whether to knock.

"I think I hear her," Frankie said, ear pressed to the door. "She sounds like she's talking to someone."

"Uh oh. I know Bethany gave us her bug, but I didn't know her hallucinations were contagious, too."

"It sounds like someone else is in there," he said.

Listening in beside him, Flint whispered. "Oh my God, it does. Do you think she has a guy in there?"

"How the heck would she pull that off?" Avery asked.

Frankie sneered. "You know Sheila and pulling things off."

"No, but we know *you* do," Rachel snickered, and he gagged on a fake laugh as Avery took his place at the door.

Clearing her throat, she tapped lightly. "Sheila, are you all right?"

When there was no response, she clenched her jaw, and eased the door open. As the ward lights sliced through the dark, the bed caught Avery's attention. Except for a large shadow splashed across the sheets, the mattress was bare, but when she ventured further into the room, the shadow acquired color and texture. Avery recoiled from the massive bloodstain with a yelp, quickly followed by another when someone cooed softly from the other side of the room. Clutching her heart and peering through the gloom, Avery spotted Sheila huddled in the closet with a bundled towel in her arms. She lifted her face, white as snow save for crimson speckles and smudges, and when she clutched the bundle tighter, the cooing came again . . . and not from her.

"What's going on? Is she okay or not?" Flint asked.

"Shut the door. And don't let anyone else in," Avery said, grabbing a clean blanket from a chair and wrapping it around Sheila's shoulders. "Are you hurt? Are you okay?"

Sheila whispered, "Yes," then "No," and pulled back the towel.

It was the smallest baby Avery had ever seen. Its wrinkled face was slathered in blood and viscera, but she saw shapes of Sheila in every animated expression, especially when she puckered her little red lips. Avery realized at that moment it was the first time she'd seen Sheila without a full face of makeup. Her hair was a mess, her face was ashen and damp, but she looked so beautiful cuddling the little version of her.

Closing the door on the others, Flint joined Avery at the closet, and her jaw dropped. "Holy shit, Sheila."

"Be quiet," she hissed. "I don't want Meredith to hear."

"Are you talking to me, or the baby?" Flint asked. "Because I can do that for you, but I don't think it's going to do the same."

Gazing down at her tiny blood-drenched daughter, Sheila said, "*She*, not *it*."

"Fine. When did *she* happen?"

She shook her head. "I wasn't feeling well, haven't been for a while, and then Brianne came in and made a racket, and I couldn't take it. I feel bad for that, I do, I just lost it. But you get it, don't you, Avery?"

"No, I don't," she replied flatly.

The baby warbled, and her mother shushed her. "I know, I don't believe her either, sweetheart. Anyway, the last thing I remember is Radcliffe knocking me out, and when I woke up I was in here, already bleeding. The pain started soon after that, and it got worse and worse until . . . she was here."

"Did you know?"

She sucked on her lip, and her nostrils flared as she stared at the little girl. "Not completely. But . . . I thought . . . maybe."

"But how?" Flint asked. "I haven't seen any of your boyfriends here since last summer."

Sheila's eyes narrowed. "Do you want the truth? Or would you prefer a *dare*?"

When Flint's face paled, her freckles looked like they could be blood spatters too. She backed away and sat against the bed, her jaw loose and trembling.

"I'm so sorry, Sheila."

"You want me to forgive you? Fine," she said. "Help me clean the room. Help me clean her. Then leave me alone, and keep your damn mouths shut."

Touching her arm, Avery pouted. "Sheila, she needs medical attention. So do you. You have to tell someone."

"No, no, I can't. I know what they do with babies born in here. I've seen it, and so have you, Flint." Sheila's chin dimpled with sorrow, and her voice wavered. "They'll take her away. I'll never see her again."

"Sheila, please—"

She grabbed Avery's wrist and yanked her close. "No one can know. *No one.* Do you understand?"

The jostled baby turned beet red, and her face crinkled as she released a piercing scream. Sheila frantically tried to quiet her child, but the more she rocked and bounced her, the louder she cried. She held her daughter close and wept just as loudly as the floor of the room shook from the approach of nurses and orderlies.

Avery and Flint stepped aside as the staff members flew into the room and crowded around the closet. Sheila screamed and kicked and did her damnedest to claw the faces off anyone who tried to take her baby. But the nurses had claws too, and theirs were full of tranquilizers.

"For the love of God, just give her some time!" Flint shouted at them, and Nurse Meredith spun to the girls flattened against the back wall.

Looking down her nose, eyebrows arched, she replied. "We did give her time. If not for her outburst yesterday, she might've had more. Sadly . . . " She waved to Nurse Moore, who advanced on the frantic mother in the closet.

When the glint of Moore's claws captured Sheila's attention, the orderlies grabbed her arms, and Nurse Radcliffe wrenched her baby away. The time between separation and the syringe was minimal, but Sheila filled those few seconds with the most horrific, gut-wrenching bellow Avery had ever heard.

Even as the sedative flooded her veins, Sheila thrashed and screeched as she reached for her daughter, and Avery watched in horror as the girl's fight died. She wilted to the floor, but her focus remained on the infant in Radcliffe's arms, clinging to those last moments before fate ripped them apart forever.

Avery wept as she ran from the room, her heart breaking for the new mother, and for the first time in nearly year, her heart longing for her own. Absurd as it was, she wanted Faye to hold her and rock her and fight for her. She wanted her to say that the terrible sight, along with every other terrible sight in Taunton, was just part of a long, bad dream.

Once Flint fell asleep that night, she opened her diary for the first time since it arrived, and a photo of her and

Paul slipped out between the pages. Gritting her teeth, she tore out a page and wrote. Her mom was still on her mind, but her thoughts ventured further than that, beyond what she knew to what she *could* know. She'd envisioned having a baby one day, with someone she loved, with *the one* she loved. With Paul, she hoped. She was still so young—too young for such intense devotion—but she couldn't help how she felt. She loved him. And she missed him so much it felt like the symphony of her world was missing its most important instrument. Yet she'd been so cruel to him, to *the one*.

She had to make amends. Whether he accepted it or not, she had to try.

Dear Paul,

I would understand if you throw away this letter the moment you realize it's from me. I would understand if you curse every word I write and tear them into a thousand pieces. I don't deserve kindness after how I treated you. There isn't a day that passes I don't regret it.

But I wouldn't change it. The way things are now, your life will be better without me.

You should know, though, I do still dream of you, and being a part of your life. I still hope. Even as I push you away, I hope.

But I'm so lonely, so scared. I question every thought and every memory. I question my innocence. There are even days I really believe I'm guilty. There are days I believe I'm insane. There are days I want to die, and I feel like I deserve it.

But then there are days when all I can think about is you and how you used to look at me, and I can't imagine I was ever as bad as they say. I think of Natalie and wish she would forgive me. I wish she would visit me. Or anyone. Even my mom. She says she will, but she never does. I guess I can't blame anyone for wanting to stay away.

Sometimes I feel bad for what I've put her through. I actually forget that she did this to me, and I feel bad for her. I want to hate her, but there are days I'd do anything, admit anything, just so I don't have to hate anyone. I don't want anything in me that could poison my love for you.

This is the only letter I will write you from this place, and I don't expect a response. I just wanted you to know how much I love you, Paul. You will always have a place in my heart, even if there's no place for me in yours.

Yours Always,
Avery

Avery mourned the love she'd lost with Paul. But she'd done that many times since coming to Taunton. That night, she mourned everything else: her first real job, off-island trips with her sister, going to college, having a family, having a future, every wonderful and harrowing and stupidly common thing experienced by the world outside Taunton Asylum.

She was honest in her letter—she did still have hope. But possibility and hope were different animals, sometimes allies, sometimes predator and prey. And as the weary custodial staff began cleaning the blood from Sheila's room, Avery could guess which way possibility and hope would go for her.

She didn't know if her letter would reach Paul or how he would react, but she dreamt he would read her words and come back to her, that he'd storm the hospital with guns blazing and save her from a life in agony.

But as the years rolled by, Avery Norton grew less and less hopeful that anyone, let alone her childhood boyfriend, would come to her rescue.

CHAPTER THIRTEEN

THE NEW ARABIAN was a bit skittish. Two potential riders had already passed it by, and it stamped in its stall, hanging its head in dejection. When Natalie approached, it issued a sad little whinny that tugged her heartstrings, and she opened the door to its stall. She held out a handful of oats, and though it shied away at first, it soon trotted out and buried its muzzle in her palm.

As she tacked up the stallion, she hummed to herself to drown out the people whispering nearby. Sometimes it worked, allowing her to go about her day without strangers picking her apart. But not today. She heard every word, every insinuation.

Natalie had taken her mother up on the offer to change her last name to Hayworth, but people still referred to her as "the Norton girl." Though she'd managed to avoid much of the spotlight during the trial, she remained a macabre celebrity to locals. But she refused to turn tail. When it came time to research universities, Faye suggested west coast schools that would distance her from the shame of Avery's crimes, but she wasn't interested. She was a New Englander and wanted to remain one, public scrutiny or not. Plus, despite all her complaints about Dana Hall in the past, she'd found peace there in her later years. Riding calmed her when the trial was at its peak, and when her entire immediate family was behind bars. The stables at Dana Hall gave her more than the stares and whispers stole, so she continued to visit after graduation, as her schedule at Northeastern allowed.

She'd become fond of Northeastern too. The environment suited her, and after a period of sheepish wading in coed waters, she took a large breath and swam straight to the deep end. When her mother visited, Natalie swore up and down that the boys didn't interest her; she was in school to learn. But it was difficult to support the charade once Faye's good behavior aided in reduction of her sentence and an early release. With each trip, her daughter's bad behavior must've become more apparent, because Faye's appearances at Northwestern increased. She dropped in a few times a month, claiming to be in the neighborhood following a visit with Avery—despite being hundreds of neighborhoods apart. Frustrating as it was, it was the only way she got updates about her little sister, who she missed desperately. It broke her heart knowing Avery didn't want to see her, and she always hoped Faye would come with news that Avery had changed her mind.

"I know, I know," Faye would say through a heavy sigh. "But she still doesn't want anything to do with you, honey. It's enough of struggle trying to calm her down for my visits, but I keep going anyway, whether she wants me there or not." She patted her daughter's hand. "I'm her mother. Let me worry about her."

"I wish no one had to worry. I wish—"

"Natalie, that's enough. Must we spend this entire visit drudging up unpleasantness?"

She hated how her mom shrugged off her enduring concern for her sister. Sure, she hadn't lived with them for a few years, so she couldn't know exactly how bad things had gotten on the island, but she also couldn't wrap her head around Avery committing murder. She couldn't imagine anyone was capable of such things, though. Even Faye.

But she did blame her mother when the story broke. She thought the whole thing was a lie then; she didn't know about the evidence, or Avery's presence at the crime scene the previous night, or her confession about killing rabbits.

Nor did she know about Avery's blackouts. She didn't remember her sister being prone to strange spells and fits of violence, but she might've been too caught up in her own life to notice. That's how Faye explained it, anyway, and Natalie knew herself well enough to surrender to the suggestion.

She wasn't completely convinced, though. While Faye vehemently denied the "gardening lessons" Avery claimed she used to encourage her to murder rabbits, she'd used the same biblical metaphors when she gave Natalie the garden. Violence never entered the picture, but she also resigned from gardening duties two days later, when she had her first date with Tom.

That part perplexed her, too. Tom had fallen out of touch after Faye shipped her to Dana Hall. Natalie didn't blame him—Faye put the fear of God in both when she caught them together—so she figured he'd never talk to her again even if they both stayed on the island. But it turned out Tom's mother had reacted similarly to the news and sent her shameful son away. Or so Natalie had heard.

She didn't expect the next time she heard his name it would be listed amongst murder victims found in the basement of her childhood home. Or that her sister would be named as his killer.

She told the police everything she knew. The jury, too. But after all the stressful days and sleepless nights talking to police and lawyers, they deemed Natalie useless as a witness. Plus, after all the interrogations and testimonies, she was no closer to understanding what had happened in that house.

Not that it mattered. Once Avery was officially sentenced to Taunton and Faye was locked up in Framingham, any further discussion of the crimes would've been fueled by speculation alone, and she had plenty of that going on in her own brain. So she took it all in, knotted it up, and buried it in a hidden place she seldom unlocked. It wasn't the healthiest way to live, but it paved the road for her to enjoy whatever twisted version of happiness her family baggage allowed.

Faye sent Natalie to a strict boarding school to curb her youthful abandon, but university life allowed it to come trickling, then flooding back. She hid as many of her liaisons as possible from her mother, but knowing Faye wouldn't believe she'd stopped dating entirely, she told her about the few relationships that lasted longer than a month. Those were never the boys her mother encountered when she showed up unannounced, but most of the guys were cool enough to fudge their names and exit quickly in those instances.

She hated the constant lies, but she knew what would happen if she was honest with her mother about the kind of woman she'd become. No more school. No more living off-island. Faye paid for everything—even from prison, she didn't miss a beat—and she forbade Natalie from getting a job.

She had briefly, working as a waitress in a local restaurant. But once news got back to her mother—Natalie still didn't know how—she found herself suddenly and unexplainably out of a job. It was the start of a dark spiral that consumed Natalie at the start of her freshman year. Getting fired, feeling like her mother was always looking over her shoulder despite being behind bars, walking a razor's edge of morality so she wouldn't "mysteriously" lose Northeastern too filled her with such an overwhelming feeling of helplessness, she did what she always fantasized about when she was riding: she ran away. She'd known Billy for less than two weeks when she broke her east coast rule and took off for California in the 1958 cherry red Corvette he'd borrowed from his father. She didn't know he hadn't asked for permission, or how the police found out and tracked them down before Billy's father knew about the theft, but impossible as it seemed, Natalie knew Faye was behind it.

That's when she knew she was stuck. Less than Avery,

but still stuck. It didn't matter what last name she had, or how many lies she told to keep her mother cordial, Faye would always keep her eldest daughter on an inexorably short leash.

With the frequency of her mother's visits steadily increasing, she decided to abstain from the freshman mixer at the start of her junior year. It was customary for upper class students, boys and girls alike, to prey on incoming freshmen during the kick-off party, and as much as Natalie looked forward to it each year, she'd made too many mistakes and gotten far too lucky already. That's what brought her to Dana Hall that day, attempting to hum the gossipy whispers away. But, as it often did, gossip became accusations that destroyed the placidity of the stables.

She was nearly ready to ride when three spritely students, two of which were identical except for the cleanliness of their riding pants, appeared next to her stall.

"Hey, aren't you the Norton girl?" asked the cleanlier student.

Natalie stopped humming but didn't turn. "No, I'm the Hayworth girl."

"But you used to be the *Norton* girl, right? Your sister killed all those people?"

"I don't know. I wasn't there."

Stepping forward with a frosted pink grin, the third girl smacked her leg with a riding crop. "Oh, come on! Of course she did it. She's locked up in Taunton Asylum, isn't she?"

"That doesn't mean she's guilty."

"Who are you? Her lawyer?"

"I bet you're as crazy as her," the third girl said. "I heard your mom's in jail, too."

Natalie shook her head. "I don't have anything to do with that."

"You're related to them!" the twins squealed.

The girl with the riding crop pointed it at Natalie and said, "It's part of you, like an old song. What's that old song again, ladies?"

The girls giggled and sang in a taunting pitch.

Little Avery Norton,
With her hair done up in curls,
Got bored one day, and so she killed
A hundred boys and girls!

"She doesn't even have curls," Natalie grumbled, and the girls sneered.

"What are you doing here, anyway? Didn't you graduate a while ago?"

"I'm allowed to visit the stables," Natalie said, trying to lead the stallion out of the stall.

The twin with the dirtier pants rolled her eyes. "Didn't it occur to you that the school was glad to see you go? You can't be doing anything for its reputation."

"Wait," the cleaner girl said, eyebrows raised. "Didn't your sister kill animals, too? God, what if it really does run in the family? They shouldn't let you around the horses."

The girls clung to each other in theatrical fear that broke into cackling laughter. Natalie had endured every insult and judgment before, but repetition didn't lessen the agony. Her head was down, so she wasn't sure which girl commanded her to leave. Not that it mattered; the desire to banish the Norton girl from their presence was in everything about the trio. And with passersby stopping to watch the scene, the entire campus might as well have shouted for her to leave.

Regretfully, she returned the horse to its stall, tacked up with nowhere to go, and trudged, under the weight of continuing derisions, to her car. She turned the key and saw her future. Two cocktails would become ten, a stranger would become more than a friend, and everything she hated about herself would feel doubled come morning, but it was better than feeling it at that moment. And there was always a chance she wouldn't fall into old patterns.

But Natalie was never good at games of chance. The

ridicule at the stables drove her to drink heavily at the party, drowning her sorrows as she sat in the corner. She was into her third cocktail, grumbling to herself, when the music changed. Lifting her head to "Sleep Walk," she shook off the heaviness saddled on her by the trip to Dana Hall and scanned the room for a dance partner.

It didn't take long. The dark-haired boy rising from his chair had been staring at her for some time. She was wary, though. In her experience, when someone stared at her like that, it was because they were trying to figure out if she was "the Norton girl." But the boy across the room gazed at her in a wholly unique way.

His eyes ignited something in her as he glided over. Taking her hand and easing her from the chair, he stirred her desire. Her head swam from the grandeur of the stranger plucking her from the shadows and drawing her into the light, and when he linked his arms around her back, she rested her head on his shoulder and felt safe.

She still felt safe in the morning, but she couldn't remember if she'd acted safely. When she woke up with the handsome stranger in her bed, broken scenes from the previous night flashed through her mind, and not a one involved them stopping to use protection. Natalie slipped out of bed and searched the floor and wastebaskets for the prophylactic or its wrapper but didn't find anything. She hoped it was lost in the sheets somewhere. Looking to the bed, she found the boy with dark hair staring down at her. His eyes were even bluer now that she was sober.

"Good morning," he said, his arms begging for an embrace.

Though panic still wrenched her heart, she couldn't resist the stranger's sweetness. With a gust of nervous breath, she climbed back into bed. He nuzzled her neck and kissed her shoulders, but she couldn't relinquish her fear enough to enjoy it.

"Is everything all right?" he said, stroking her hair. "I didn't do anything wrong, did I?"

Before Natalie could divine a subtle way of asking him if they'd used protection, someone knocked on her dorm room door. The shock knocked Natalie out of bed, and she threw on a robe.

"Who is it?" she asked.

"It's Mom." Faye's voice chimed in a minor key. "I was in the neighborhood."

"Shit!" Natalie tossed the boy's clothes at him and screamed in a whisper, "It's my mother. Get dressed!"

"Oh my God." He sounded more amused than worried as he pulled on his clothes, all the while watching Natalie repeat quiet, frantic expletives as she straightened her dress and hair. Satisfied by her appearance, she then grasped the boy's hands and bit her lip. "Can you do me a big favor? Can you pretend to be my boyfriend?"

"What?"

Faye knocked again. "Honey, what's taking so long?"

"I'm just straightening up!" Gazing deep into the boy's piercing eyes, she whispered, "Please, I'll never ask you for anything else ever again. And you can leave right after I introduce you."

His lips curled up the side of his face. "If I'm going to be your boyfriend, don't you think I should know your name?"

"Oh, right." Her face flushed pink. "It's Natalie Hayworth."

He shook her hand. "Nice to meet you, Natalie Hayworth. I'm Paul."

"Nice to meet you, Paul. Thank you for this." With a long exhalation, Natalie whispered a prayer, and flung open the door.

Faye was smiling, but the warm expression fled the instant she laid eyes on the boy in her daughter's room. Natalie glanced over her shoulder at her fake boyfriend, whose face drained to white as he squeaked.

"Mrs. Norton?"

"Paul Dillon," Faye hissed. Sauntering into the room,

she looked him up and down. "You've certainly grown up. But what on earth are you doing here?"

Natalie blinked in confusion. "Am I missing something? How do you two know each other?"

Faye gaped at her daughter. "Are you telling me you don't recognize your sister's childhood friend, Paul?"

"You're *that* Natalie?" he screeched. "You said your last name was Hayworth."

"Hold on," Faye said, massaging one temple. "You two don't know each other? Then why is he in your room at 9 a.m., Natalie?"

"I—we—"

Faye's face blanched. "Oh, dear Lord! You had sex with *him*?!"

"I didn't know who he was!"

"That's even worse! Oh God, I'm going to be sick." Faye wilted to the couch like she might pass out, but she had full control over the glare she beamed at Paul. "You're two for two now, aren't you? Destroying Avery's life wasn't enough?"

"Me? You're the one who destroyed Avery," Paul shouted. "You're the reason she's locked up in that madhouse."

"Please. Everyone knows it was you who drove her off the deep end," Faye said. "Yes, I was guilty of hiding her crimes, but you led her on. You let her believe she was sane and that you cared for her."

"I loved her," Paul snarled at Faye. "I still love her. Not a day goes by that I don't think of her."

"Were you thinking of her while you were in bed with my eldest?" Faye's voice wavered, and her face crumpled as she gulped, like she was swallowing bile. "You disgust me. Both of you."

"What are you two talking about?" Natalie asked. "How did my mother destroy Avery?"

Faye shot him a fiery warning, but he lifted his chin with a sneer. "I'm not a kid anymore, Mrs. Norton. You don't scare me. Avery made me stay out of this for my family's sake, but I've been silent long enough."

Rising from the sofa, Faye wrapped her arm around Natalie. "Don't listen to him, dear. He's trying to hurt me because Avery had to be sent away. He's always blamed me."

"You deserve the blame!" Paul roared. "You've been lying to Avery—and *about* her—for years, and I wouldn't be surprised if you've been lying to Natalie too."

She pulled free from her mother and stamped her foot. "Will someone please explain what's going on?"

"Avery isn't a murderer," Paul said. "And she's not crazy. Everything she said was true. Five years ago, Avery and I stowed away in the back of your mother's car and saw her put two dead bodies in her trunk."

Faye huffed. "This is ridiculous."

"Why would I lie? What would I have to gain?"

"I'm sure I don't know, but you obviously feel like I should be punished for something. Well, if you think this thing between you two isn't painful enough, you're wrong. And not just for me. It's going to break poor Avery's heart. She was just telling me today how much she still cares for you, Paul."

"That's bullshit. You haven't visited more than once."

Natalie shook her head. "My mom sees Avery all the time."

"No, she doesn't. Avery wrote me a letter four years ago saying Faye never visits. She said she was scared and lonely, and that she missed you terribly, Natalie. She really wishes you'd visit her."

Natalie's throat tightened. "She what?" Wheeling around, she screamed at her mother. "You told me she didn't want to see me!"

"And she told Avery *you* didn't want to see *her*," Paul said. "More lies and manipulation courtesy of your mother. Unfortunately, I didn't know any of this until recently. I only got the letter this year. If it was up to my parents, I wouldn't have gotten it at all."

Natalie withered to her bed with a whimper. "I don't know what to believe anymore."

Paul sat beside her, his voice calm. "Natalie, I have no reason to lie to you."

"No?" Faye said icily. "If she takes your side, you're more apt to get another night in her bed. And let's face it, that's all this is about. That's all it's ever been about."

"You couldn't be more wrong, Mrs. Norton."

"Hayworth," she snarled.

"Both of you, stop," Natalie barked as she hurried across the room. "I need to see Avery. I need to hear her side of this."

Faye groaned. "You're wasting your time. I told you, she doesn't want to see you."

"Paul says she does. And honestly, Mom, I do have more reason to trust him than you."

"You're confused, honey. You need time to think." Faye's frown softened and the corners curled upward. "Why don't you take a little break from school? You can come home with me."

"I'm not going anywhere with you."

"Natalie, please be reasonable. You're not actually going to go see her. Not you. Not in a place like that."

"If it's good enough for Avery, it's good enough for me." After a pensive pause, she straightened her back and said resolutely, "But you're right about one thing, Mom. I do need time to think. You should leave."

"Are you sure?"

"About this, yes. I need to be alone."

Faye sneered at Paul. "Why does he get to stay?"

"He's leaving too, but you're leaving first."

Natalie held open the door for her mother, but Faye didn't move. Anger locked her joints and tightened her fists. But when she finally moved toward the exit, her face was soft, even amiable. She kissed her daughter's cheek and smudged away a lipstick print.

"If you need help figuring things out, I'm always here

for you." She said goodbye to both of them, but she glowered at Paul, teeth bared, before pulling the door shut.

He shuddered and rubbed his bristled arms. "Do you mind if I stay here for a bit? I keep picturing your mother waiting around a corner to bash my brains in with a hammer." He chuckled, but his eyes glimmered with genuine fear.

"You don't really think she killed those people, do you? My mom's nuts, but I don't know if she's capable of murder."

"And Avery is? Some of those people were twice her size."

"She's always been strong. Athletic."

"So that makes her capable of killing innocent people?"

"Physically."

"I'm not talking about that. Think of her, think of everything you know about her, everything you love about her, and tell me you really think she could kill those people."

Natalie collapsed onto the couch and massaged her temples.

"I think I need to be alone," she said, and he nodded, tossing his jacket over his arm. "But before you go, I need to know something about last night."

His cheeks flushed, and his mouth twisted up his cheek. "It was great, if memory serves."

"Yes, it was, but that's not what I was going to ask. It's just—I can't remember if we used anything. Protection, I mean."

"Oh. That."

The shame in his hushed voice gave Natalie her answer, and her heart sank.

"I'm sorry, I was nervous and excited and—I know it's not an excuse, but I guess I forgot. I don't have anything bad you need to worry about, though." The blush darkened and spread when he added, "You were my first."

"Oh," she said, hit with a mix of shock and pride.

"I swear I didn't know who you were, but I am glad this happened with you, Natalie. With someone I care about. Still . . . it can't happen again."

"I know. If Avery found out—"

"She can't. I don't want to hurt her. There's no reason this whole thing can't be our little secret."

Natalie chuckled bitterly. "Yeah. A secret between you, me, and my crazy mom."

"We'll just keep our distance from each other for a while. Then she won't feel threatened by . . . whatever this is."

"That's a good idea," she said, drumming her fingers on the dresser. "That could work."

"For what it's worth, I'm sorry I didn't recognize you. I should have. We spent enough time together as kids, didn't we?"

"Sure, but you were always looking at Avery." She smiled, and he swallowed hard.

"Right. Goodbye, Natalie."

"Bye, Paul."

They did a fair job avoiding each other. There were no rumors on campus, no jibes from Faye; they barely crossed paths over the next several weeks. But the day before Natalie planned to visit her sister in Taunton, she felt fluish and made an appointment at the campus clinic.

Less than two months after the freshman mixer, Natalie and Paul's little secret had grown too large to keep. Staring down the barrel of a positive pregnancy test, Natalie Hayworth sat silent in the doctor's office, too angry to cry. She knew her options, and she'd heard enough horror stories about one of them to take it off the table completely. When it came down to it, she was going to have a baby.

They were going to have a baby.

Paul massaged his neck as he paced her dorm room. "I can't believe this. I really can't believe this. What are we going to do?"

"Have it," she said, her voice strained.

"What about school? What about Avery?"

"I'll go see her. I'll talk to her. Maybe she'll understand." She exhaled shakily. "And don't worry, you don't have to do anything. I can handle this on my own. I know you didn't mean for this to happen."

Paul stopped pacing and stared at her. "Neither did you. So no, you're not doing this on your own." Chest puffed, jaw clenched, he dropped to one knee.

"What are you doing?"

"The right thing." Taking her hands in his, he said, "Natalie Hayworth, will you marry me?"

She laughed, and his brow crinkled. "I'm sorry, but you're kidding, right? Don't you think the baby is bad enough?"

"It's the sensible thing to do, Nat. My parents will help us. We can get through this, make a life."

"But we're not in love. Do you really want to be in a loveless marriage?" She stopped. "Actually, there *is* love. Between you and my little sister."

"I haven't seen Avery in years."

"You said yourself you still loved her, right in this room, the day after—" She gestured to her belly with a grunt. "This."

Paul gently pressed his and Natalie's hands to her stomach. "It won't be loveless. Because of *this*."

Staring into his glacial eyes, she asked firmly, "Are you sure?"

He raised his eyebrows. "Is that a yes?"

"Yes, it's a yes."

She wept as he embraced her, but Paul knew her tears weren't those of a joyful bride-to-be. He couldn't blame her, but he'd also never tell her that the face of a different Norton sister flashed through his mind the moment his knee hit the floor.

CHAPTER FOURTEEN

" **A VERY, YOU HAVE** a visitor."

She popped up from the couch and gawked at Nurse Wilkens in disbelief. "You did say 'Avery,' didn't you?"

"Why are you so surprised, dear? Didn't you just have a birthday?"

"I didn't have visitors on thirteen through sixteen, so I don't see why I'd expect one for seventeen."

"Well, you've got one now. A determined one, at that," Nurse Wilkens said. "Wait in your room, and we'll let her through."

Avery ran to her room in such unbridled excitement she didn't feel her feet touch the floor. Sitting on her bed, her knees jumping and fingers twitching as bad as Flint's near a box of matches, she stared at the doorway. She had no expectations, but her hopes were high, spinning her mind with thankful, long-lost faces that inched her to the edge of the bed.

When the visitor burst into room eight, Avery's heart sank. Faye wrapped her arms around her daughter, singing, "Happy birthday to you, Happy birthday to you . . . "

Avery was glad for the contact, but her body stiffened at the embrace, which Faye noticed immediately.

Pouting her bottom lip, Faye tilted her head. "What's wrong, honey?"

Breaking free of her mother, Avery crossed the room to Flint's bed. "Where would you like me to start?"

"You're right," she said, rubbing her palms on her lap. "That's a silly question. Forget I said anything." From her purse, she removed a small blue box with a silky bow and held it out to Avery. "Happy birthday, sweetheart."

She approached cautiously and squinted at the gift. "I wasn't expecting anything."

"It's just a trifle. Actually, it was yours to begin with, and it's time it went back to you."

Avery pulled the ribbon, opened the box, and gasped at the brass ring nestled in a cloud of cotton. Tears filled her eyes, and her quaking voice stuck in her throat. "Why? After five years, why are you doing this now?"

Faye huffed through flared nostrils, her focus dropping to her lap. "I suppose the ring was a symbol of what I thought was being taken from me—of Paul Dillon taking you away from me. You're my last baby, Avery. My most precious. I wanted to protect you. It was wrong of me, I know, and I've paid a deep price for it. But you'll understand when you have children one day." Faye stood and ran her hand down the girl's jet-black hair. "But none of that matters anymore. You're all grown up now, and so is he. He's moved on."

Faye's statement walloped Avery in the face. Her expression drooped, and her shoulders slumped, but she clenched her jaw to force a small smile.

"Oh? I hadn't heard."

Her mother's eyes batted wildly. "Really? I thought one of them would've told you by now."

"One of who?"

"Paul and Natalie, of course." Faye's lips curled. "They're madly in love."

Avery retreated. "I don't believe you."

"It's true. I attended the wedding myself."

"The *wedding*?"

"If you could call it that, of course, exchanging vows at the courthouse. I was disappointed they couldn't wait to have the ceremony in the church, but when two people love each other as much as Natalie and Paul, you can't stand in their way for the sake of tradition."

She turned her back on her mother and stared out the window. Wringing the bars, she watched Pam and the older female patients walk the path around the campus, and her words came low and cold. "Why did you come here today?"

"I wanted to wish you a happy birthday in person," Faye said. "And to say I'm sorry I didn't come sooner. I really thought you'd be happy to see me."

"Why would you think that?"

"Because you said so in the letter you wrote Paul four years ago."

Avery glared over her shoulder, panting.

"You see? I'm not making it up. Paul's part of our family now. He's your brother-in-law."

Avery laughed spitefully. "And you wanted to gloat. You wanted to torture me." Facing her mother, she wiped the tears from her cheeks. "When is this going to end, Mom? When will I have suffered enough for you?"

"My darling, I do wish you'd stop thinking I'm out to get you. I came here with the best intentions. I've missed so many of your birthdays—"

"You missed this one, too. You're a month late."

"And it's high time I started making up for it," Faye said. "You need me now, Avery. More than ever."

She wrapped her arms around her daughter and petted her hair. Again, Avery took a moment to savor the long-absent sensation, but memory and loathing soon followed, and she wriggled out of her mother's arms.

"If Paul really is with Natalie, I doubt you're as happy about it as you're acting."

That's when it hit her. Shaking her head in pity, she said, "That's why you're here. You're mad at Natalie for being with Paul, and you knew I'd be mad too, so you figured we could be mad at her together. Sorry to disappoint you, Mom, but if you thought you could turn me against her, you're sadly mistaken."

"It's not just her. Paul has betrayed you too. The letter

you sent—he didn't just tell us about it. He was mocking it, ridiculing your words of love." She cradled Avery's face in sympathy. "He's not the boy you remember. He's changed."

"But you let Natalie marry him? You're so full of shit."

Faye responded with a swift smack across Avery's cheek and stuck her finger in her face. "Do not make the mistake of thinking I'm here out of weakness. If I wanted to stop the wedding, I could have. But why, when it helped set so many wonderful things in motion."

Avery clutched her burning face. "Get out."

"Oh honey, I'm sorry. I don't want to fight. Come on, let's just try to enjoy the day together."

In the doorway, Flint cleared her throat, and Faye turned to see the fiery teenager and a slender boy standing akimbo. "Mrs. Norton," she said. "We've heard so much about you."

"All good, I hope." Faye chuckled nervously, but Flint and Frankie's expressions were clear enough to make her grab her purse. "Maybe I should get going. But I'd like to see you again, Avery. Soon. We can't let so much time pass between visits."

"That's never been up to me," she said.

"I know, and I'm going to be a much better mother to you from here on out. We need each other more than ever."

"I told you to get out."

Faye clenched her jaw in surrender, and Flint and Frankie entered the room as she walked out. But she stopped in the doorway and turned, a vicious scowl pinching her face.

"You want me to be the bad guy? You want to believe I don't care about you? Go ahead. But I do, deeply." She sniffled and tapped her chest lightly as if trying to coax a beat from her broken heart. "All I ever wanted was to have a good, loving family, and I've met opposition every step of the way—from you, from Natalie, from Jason. It is your moral failing that casts me as the villain, and I'll play the part if you want. In fact," she said, zeroing in on Flint and Frankie, "I wouldn't be surprised if your parents feel the same way. It's no wonder they don't visit."

Avery watched in horror as her friends' backs hunched and chins tilted to the floor.

"Don't listen to her," she said. "Your parents don't visit because they're scared. They're not trying to punish you for being different. She's the only one who thinks like that."

"How could a child know what a parent thinks? Your parents don't visit because you blame them, because you embarrass them, because you refuse to be normal. They don't visit because they've given up on you," Faye said. "But unlike them, I will not give up on my child. Some people ignore the problem, but not me. I endure, I study, I evolve. I learn how to correct the problem. That Jack Graham fellow knew something about fixing people, and I've learned too."

Faye took stock of every cherubic face paling, every gaze drooping in shame, then disappeared from room eight with glorious strides. The silence that fell over them seemed to solidify in her absence. It encased the young patients in agitated misery and populated their minds with scores of doubt echoed in lined expressions. Avery didn't know what to say to comfort her friends. As they shuffled out, heads bowed, she sat on her bed and opened her fist. She'd been squeezing the brass ring so hard it left an aching purple indentation in her palm. Part of her wanted to keep squeezing it. She wanted to clutch it so tight it worked its way into her flesh, maybe even grow into the bone. Then she'd never have to worry about losing it again.

Instead, she pried up the floor tile atop the secret hole where she kept her diary, dropped the brass ring inside, and slammed the tile back into place. With that, Avery decided she would banish all thoughts of her past. She had to look toward the future, and if she was ever going to have a good one, she needed to do whatever it took to get out. Even if that meant believing she was a killer.

Lying down, Avery stared up at the ceiling, searching the emptiness for visions of her future. But only one pale image appeared in the teal paint, and no matter how she tried, she couldn't shake the sight of Paul Dillon gazing up at her from the Taunton grounds, whimpering as she ordered him away.

She made him run. She made everybody run.

Avery tried to put her mind to bed, but it became more talkative as the minutes clicked by—a miserable reminder that time healed no wounds in Taunton Asylum.

Time was also an enemy to Natalie Hayworth, but for vastly different reasons. She'd managed to keep her pregnancy a secret from her mother for a few months, but Faye eventually weaseled it out of her. She'd done the same thing with the engagement, which she insisted the couple keep brief to minimize the fallout once Natalie revealed her condition.

Sucking in her stomach as much as possible, the young bride tried to focus on her future husband as she recited her vows, but her attention inevitably slipped away, over Paul's shoulder, to the best man.

Noah looked so beautiful in a suit, and the bluebell in his lapel brought out the clover tints in his eyes. She'd only known him for two months, but they'd been the most enlightening two months of her life. Maybe it was her raging hormones, or how she was losing interest in the man she'd agreed to marry with each day counting down to their nuptials, but Natalie's body ached to be in Noah's arms. As Paul's best friend, he'd fought his blossoming feelings for her just as powerfully, but the night before the wedding, their emotions got the better of them and they surrendered to their desires.

Entangled, their bodies speckled with cooling sweat, Noah ran his fingers over Natalie's round belly.

"I'm sorry," he whispered, and she laid her hand atop his.

"Please don't be. I'm not. I can't be, not even for *her* sake," she said tapping her stomach.

"Her?"

"I think it's a her," she said, blushing. "And if she were in my spot, I wouldn't want her to ignore love either. Because I do love you, Noah. It's crazy and stupid and dangerous, but I do."

He kissed her forehead and nose and lips. "I love you too, Nat. I've never felt this way about anyone. I want to be with you."

"Me too." She sat up, cradling her stomach and sniffling. "But we have to be careful. If my mom found out—"

"You mean, if *Paul* found out. He's the one I don't want to hurt."

"Neither do I. But Paul would forgive us. If my mom found out, she might . . . I don't know . . . do something."

Sitting up, he crinkled his forehead at her. "What?"

"It's hard to explain. I just don't know what she's capable of. Or . . . maybe I do, and that's why I'm so afraid of her. Paul said—"

"Your own mother?"

She buried her face in the crook of his arm. "I've been so frightened, Noah," she whimpered. "I'm scared if I screw this up, she'll try to take the baby."

"You're a grown woman. This is your child, and she can't just take it—*her*—away."

"You don't understand. She knows things. She can do things. And if Paul or I try to cut her out of this child's life, she'll pursue us even harder."

"You kept her from attending the wedding, right?"

"She only cares about us marrying because of the baby. It's not about me anymore, or about Paul. It's all about her. I can feel it. She wants the baby."

He squeezed her tight and kissed the top of her head. "I would never let that happen, and neither would Paul."

"You don't have a choice. Not when it comes to her. At least, that's what it feels like to me." She grumbled in frustration. "I wish I knew the truth. I wish I knew whether

I had to worry." She wiped away her tears and chuckled. "But I'd probably worry either way. This is a perfect mess I've gotten myself into, and believe me, I've had some whoppers."

"If it counts for anything, you pull off 'perfect mess' with absolute grace."

She giggled, then frowned. "But for how long? How long can I endure all this fear with a smile? How long can I tell Paul I love him when my heart belongs to you?"

"Are you sure Paul's heart belongs to *you*?"

"I already know it doesn't." She caressed her stomach tenderly. "This is the only heart that's truly mine."

"Not the only one. I'm yours, Natalie," Noah said as he kissed her fingers and the belly beneath. "I'm hers too." Kissing his way up her body, he gazed into her eyes and whispered, "Till death do us part."

That night, Natalie's marital bed saw more passion and romance than it did on the night of her wedding. Although Paul kissed her body with the same technical tenderness as Noah, there was a distinct disconnection. At their most intimate, Natalie and Paul felt miles away from each other. And Faye, in her car outside their apartment, drummed her fingers on the wheel and counted the minutes until her daughter would run to her, begging for comfort.

But Natalie never considered running to her mother for consolation. As the months passed, she remained tightlipped about her waning affection for Paul and her growing love for Noah. And it wasn't easy. She did want to run. She longed for familiar arms to enfold her, to make her feel strong again, like the big fish on the small island instead of the drowning skunk she'd become. It seemed a lifetime since they'd shared an ounce of affection for one another, but Natalie needed to know if it was still possible. She needed to see her sister.

CHAPTER FIFTEEN

PAUL HAD INFORMED Natalie of Taunton's visitor list, which kept undesirables out of the hospital.

Figuring her mother had added her ages ago, she gave the name Anne Elliot at the front desk.

Avery was lighting a cigarette when Nurse Radcliffe called her name. Her smoky exhalation blocked the approaching visitor's face, and she waved the smoke away, but she still didn't believe what she saw. Entering the common room of Taunton Asylum, Natalie pulled her trench coat tight, and the cigarette tumbled from Avery's lips.

Flint dashed to retrieve it, but Nurse Moore got it first and stubbed it out.

"Natalie?" Avery's throat went dry, and she gulped. "What are you doing here?"

Natalie could hardly believe the woman standing before her. She'd still thought of Avery as the skinny little girl with jet black hair she played patty-cake with, the rambunctious creature she'd loved, envied, and tried to shield from their mother's lessons. From her mother's odd tutelage to their father's abrupt departure, Natalie had fought to suppress so many things about her childhood. But at that moment, gazing upon Avery, a young woman with years of sorrow entrenched in her expression, they all came streaming back. It was more train wreck than stroll down memory lane, and it piled more anguish onto the weight already crushing Natalie's shoulders. She wanted to crumple to the ground and cry, but instead, she flung herself forward and wrapped her arms around her little sister.

She whispered, "I'm sorry," but Avery was too stunned to respond. "I'm sorry for a lot of things. But mostly, I'm sorry for not trusting you."

Avery pushed herself out of the hug. "So you trust me now? That's lovely." She sneered. "But how do you expect *me* to trust *you*? You've never defended me. You've never visited me. And you married the only boy I've ever loved."

Natalie's face flamed with humiliation. "You know about me and Paul?"

"Mom was here a few months ago. She told me."

"I guess I'm not surprised," she said. "I wanted to tell you. I've been wanting to come here for a while, but there were . . . complications."

"Yes, I imagine planning a wedding, even a courthouse wedding, is a complicated job. But I wouldn't know anything about that, would I? There aren't many eligible bachelors in a madhouse. And who'd want to marry a killer, anyway?"

"I know you're not a killer, Avery. That's why I'm here. I wanted to talk to you, to see you. I wanted—"

"Forgiveness? Is that it, Nat?" She scoffed. "You people only come here for one thing: to feel better about yourself, to surround yourself with crazies so you feel normal."

"I don't think you're crazy."

Grief propelled a stiff chuckle from her throat. "That's even worse. You don't think I'm crazy, but you let me rot in here for the past five years?"

The question struck Natalie silent, and tears rolled down her cheeks as she scanned the room of strangers hanging on their every word.

"Well?" Avery said. "If you want to talk, let's talk. Take off your coat and stay a while. You came all this way."

"I wish I'd come sooner. I should have."

"Yes, you should have. But you're here now, and no matter how furious I am, I have to appreciate that."

Natalie clenched her jaw and said, "I hope that's true." Removing her coat, she revealed her large, round belly. "I'm sorry about this, too."

Avery gasped, and the common room erupted with a cacophony of intrigue.

"Is it Paul's?"

She nodded, her chin quivering, and Avery shook her head wildly as she stormed away from her sister.

"It's not what you think," Natalie, said chasing after. She latched onto Avery's arm, and the girl spun with a growl.

"She was right about you," Avery said. "Mom was right about everything."

"No, Avery. Whatever she told you, it's not true. It was a complete accident that Paul and I met and—" She ran her hand over her belly. "We didn't recognize each other until after it happened, and then . . . it was too late. It's the only reason we got married."

Her lungs emptied, and dizziness swelled over her. "Wait. Are you saying you don't love him?"

Patients had gathered around the pair, their faces begging for Natalie's answer as hungrily as her sister.

Glancing around anxiously, she whispered. "Can we go to your room?"

Avery led the way and closed the door on the mob, aware they'd likely stay close. "Go on. Say what you need to say."

"I don't know how," Natalie started, but detecting no sympathy from her sister, she continued soberly. "I'm in love, Avery."

"I'm not sure I want to hear this anymore."

"No, not with Paul. I don't love him. I never did."

"You married him."

"I didn't want to, and I wish I hadn't. I wouldn't be surprised if Paul thinks the same thing." Sitting on the bed and looking up at her little sister, she said, "He still loves you."

Her throat tightened. "You don't know that."

"Yes, I do. And what's more, I feel it in everything he does. I feel it as strongly as my love for another man."

"Who?"

Her face warmed in affection. "His name is Noah. He's amazing, and he loves me. My baby too."

"And Paul's baby," she added.

Natalie sucked on her cheek and blinked back tears. "I know you must hate me. I can only imagine all the things Mom's told you about me, but I need you to know that I've wanted to visit a million times. Right after you were brought here, I wanted to come, but Mom said you wouldn't see me."

"She told me *you* didn't wouldn't see *me*. She said you were disgusted by me."

"I know. Paul told me everything. And Avery . . . " Natalie met her sister's eyes, her chin trembling when she spoke. " . . . He told me about the party up-island, and what you both saw that night."

Avery's eyes welled, and she gripped her sister's hand. "It was real? I didn't imagine it?"

"He said he saw Mom put two bodies in her trunk, and you told him to keep it a secret."

"I didn't know what she'd do if I let him speak out. I thought she might hurt him. But after all this time, after everything they've told me, I'd started believing I imagined the whole thing. The jury said I was guilty. The doctors said I was guilty. Even people in here, my only friends in the world, say I'm guilty. How could I not be guilty if everyone's so sure of it?"

"I can't pretend to know the truth of everything that's happened. But I know this: I might not be in love with my husband, but I do trust him, and he never once thought you did those things."

Avery threw herself into Natalie's arms, bumping her big sister's belly. She laughed, but it turned sad quickly. Natalie placed Avery's hand on her stomach, and a strange, lovely fluttering wiped her sorrow clean. She and Natalie shared a smile that comforted her in a way she nearly forgotten. She couldn't hold onto it, though. Comfort was wonderful, but there'd be plenty of time for that when she was free.

Stepping back, Avery crossed her arms over her chest and raised her chin. "What now, Nat? How are you going to get me out of here?"

"After the baby's born, we'll appeal your case. Paul will tell the world what really happened that night, and Mom will go down for all of it. We'll fix this, I promise. Soon, Taunton will be a distant memory." Natalie squeezed her sister again and lightly rubbed her back. "I'm so sorry you had to go through this. I can't imagine how it's been for you."

"Sometimes it's not so bad. I talk to people. I drift away. I lose myself in simple comforts. But then I think of everything I've missed by being here. So many years, so many opportunities, vanished like smoke in the wind. Not that I've felt a good gust of wind in years." She sat on the edge of her bed, her head cradled in her hands. "I killed the rabbits in the garden, and I was punished for it. More than five years separated from everything I knew and loved. Five years of my youth crushed beyond repair. And for what? Some stupid bunnies?" She stopped, then lifted her head. "No, not for them. And the law didn't punish me, either. It was *her*. Mom punished me because she couldn't control me, because I wouldn't stay locked away with her."

"We can't let her win."

"She *did* win. That damn garden. Those damn rabbits. She got exactly what she wanted. I'm locked away, unable to touch anything that makes life worth living, now and forever. Whether I get out of here or not, I will always be *Little Avery Norton*."

"We'll fix it. Years from now, no one will think of you like that."

"Of course they will. How are strangers supposed to see

the truth when my own sister couldn't? I needed you, Nat. At the trial. Here."

"I was scared. I'm still scared," she whimpered, but Avery offered no compassion. Quite the opposite. She drew close with her teeth clenched instead and spat enraged words across her sister's face.

"You're married to my boyfriend, you're carrying his child, and you're in love with another man. You haven't earned the right to be scared. Not until you've been in here. Not until you've been locked up and drugged and treated like a wild animal."

While Natalie wept, Avery breezed past and peered out her barred window.

"When I was little, I swore I could see avenues of possibility opening before me, more and more over the years, waiting for me to be grown, to be ready. I didn't know where they would lead me, or when, but they were there. Now that I'm grown and ready, all I see are dead ends. Gates, padlocks, crumbling cliffs. My future is empty."

"No," Natalie said. "Paul is there. I'm there."

"Ah yes, the newlyweds, and what a lovely sight they are."

"Paul knows about Noah and me," she said. "We told him after the wedding, and he took the news a lot better than we expected. And after we decided how to get you out, we came to an arrangement. Avery, when all this is over, Paul's yours. And you'll have a niece or nephew to love." Natalie strolled to her sister, her body ablaze in the striped afternoon light. "Just because the past five years have been hell doesn't mean the future has to be." She took Avery's hands in hers, and the girl broke down in tears.

"Then why does it feel like it?"

"Because you're still in here. Because although you can see stars from your window, the bars of your cage won't let you see them all. After so many years of looking up at a broken sky, you think the stars don't shine on you anymore. But it's not true," Natalie said. "You deserve as much starlight as anyone. You deserve sunshine and rain and beaches covered in seaweed. And I'm going to make sure you get it. I promise you, everything's going to be better soon. And for as long as I live, I won't let you feel alone again."

Avery had imagined this moment so many times she had to convince herself it wasn't another daydream, that when her sister's arms enfolded her, they would hold her instead of fading away. She thought nothing else in the world could top that feeling, until Natalie cradled her little sister's face and said the four most beautiful words:

"I believe in you."

When they broke apart, Avery kissed her palm and tenderly placed it against her sister's stomach, hopeful. Even through the long years of staring out the window, praying that every jumping shadow might be Paul coming to rescue her again, she never thought her release was possible. She just had to withstand imprisonment a little longer, like the niece or nephew in her sister's womb, and avenues of possibility would appear for them both.

As the baby fluttered under her hand, Avery said, "I promise she won't ever feel alone, either."

"She?"

With a smile, Avery shrugged and embraced her sister again, tighter, longer.

She carried the joy from Natalie's visit close to her heart through the chaotic sadness of the next couple of months. Rachel transferred to McLean Hospital, where the staff had sent Sheila sent after giving birth, and Frankie, no longer allowed to break the gender segregation rule when he turned eighteen, moved to the men's ward. Avery was so grateful she still had Flint, but that wouldn't last much longer either. Even if Natalie and Paul weren't working on her release, Flint's eighteenth birthday was just around the corner. Her heart ached at the thought, but she knew everything would be all right. She had already started musing about plots to get Flint out of Taunton once she was a free woman herself.

Once she was free . . .

God, there'd be nothing she couldn't do. Imagining Paul, Natalie, and Flint by her side, Avery felt a bit of her old verve. The triumphs, the missteps, all those beautiful leaps other people didn't appreciate because they'd always been free enough to take them: they were all waiting on the outside, nearly within reach. Her stallion was nearing the sweet spot of the carousel. The music was swelling, her arm outstretched, and as her hooked fingers neared the steel ring hanging out of the dispenser, she wasn't discouraged. The brass ring was just behind it, she could feel it.

CHAPTER SIXTEEN

SOPHIE MARIE DILLON alerted her mother she was ready for her world debut just after two o'clock in the afternoon while her father was working a double shift at the Union Oyster House. Luckily, though not surprisingly, Noah was with Natalie when she went into labor, and he rushed her to the hospital with plenty of time for Faye to scold her for not getting there sooner.

Since the week before Natalie's due date, Faye had been staying off-island so she'd be close when the call came. She beamed with joy the entire drive to Massachusetts General, but the fair-haired stranger holding her daughter's hand when she entered Natalie's hospital room dashed all bliss from the grandmother-to-be. It was bad enough Natalie had slept with Paul, and bad enough she'd gotten pregnant, but if she was also messing around with another boy, something might have to be done.

"Don't worry, Ms. Hayworth. She's doing fine," Noah said, shaking Faye's hand. "I sure am glad you're here, though."

"And you are?"

"Noah Hanson. Paul's friend? We met at the wedding. I was the best man."

"Of course. Forgive me," Faye said. "I was more focused on my daughter that day. As I should be now."

She pushed past Noah to shower attention on Natalie, but through no fault of her own, her thoughts frequently drifted to the stranger holding her pregnant daughter's hand. He was cradling it too tenderly, and Natalie was staring up at him too intensely. The intimacy between them made Faye's skin crawl, and when a nurse asked if Noah was Natalie's husband and she replied despondently, "No, just a friend," she knew for certain.

Natalie was at it again.

Soon after Paul arrived, it was time for Natalie to push, and the nurses escorted them all from the room. But Paul didn't go far. He paced the hall outside her door while Faye and Noah sat opposite each other in the waiting room.

He smiled at her, unaware of his impending doom, and Faye smiled right back, savoring the eerie calm before her storm.

She cleared her throat, and his eyes lifted to her. "You're Paul's best friend, right?

"Yes, ma'am."

"So you tell him everything?"

"Everything."

"Like how you're sleeping with his wife?"

He sputtered. "Excuse me?"

She gesticulated casually, dismissive of his shock. "Maybe I shouldn't assume the baby is Paul's. It could be anyone's, I suppose."

"I don't know what you're talking about, Ms. Hayworth. Natalie's a good girl, and Paul is definitely the father of her baby. She would never—"

"Never what, sleep around? Why not? She's been doing it for years. She thinks I'm stupid, but I'm not. Not when it comes to my children."

"Natalie told me you were a bit intense," he said, and Faye chuckled.

"What a lovely euphemism."

"Ms. Hayworth, I care very deeply for Natalie, and I won't allow you to insult her."

"How gallant you are," she said. "I'm sure it didn't take you long at all to worm your way into her bed."

Noah snarled. "What's wrong with you? You don't even know me."

"But I've known plenty of men like you," she said, as she squinted at him. "You're the kind of man who would cheat and steal and feign love to get what you want. The kind of man who leads a woman on and showers her with affection until you meet the next lovely young thing without kids or responsibilities. Do you know what happens to men like that, Noah? Do you know what happens to men who can't keep their pants on and priorities straight? Do you know the punishment for poisoning the garden?"

"It's a girl!" Paul ran down the hall and burst into the waiting room. "I have a daughter!"

Faye clapped her hands and leapt from the chair. "May we see her?"

Paul beckoned them to follow, but once he disappeared through the doors, Faye wheeled around and hissed at Noah.

"Break it off with her. I don't care how. Just break it off."

"Ms. Hayworth, I love your daughter, and she loves me. I won't break anything off unless she wants it." Puffing up his chest, he added, "I don't know who you think you are, but you don't scare me."

An eye-crinkling smile spread over her face. "Thank you, dear."

"For what?"

"For making this even easier." With a chuckle, she pushed through the doors, leaving her daughter's lover in stunned silence.

Little Sophie was perfect in every way. But as Faye beheld her granddaughter, she also saw all the ways life could spoil that perfection, just as it had spoiled both of her daughters. Sophie's glittering stare seemed to mock her, and with each blink, Faye saw her failures reflected in ice-blue eyes.

But she would not fail Sophie.

Oh, how she longed to let the old ways rise. It had been

so long since she'd last tended the garden. After Avery's arrest and her own incarceration, she had to alter the frequency of her gardening trips, as well as her methods. Though she preferred numbing people and drawing out their poison with God-given brutality, she had to be careful. If the police found someone mutilated in the same fashion as Avery's victims, there would be questions for which Faye would have to provide answers, and she'd rather avoid that situation altogether.

The ingenuity of Jack Gilbert Graham spurred her toward a more effective gardening technique. Though it required more effort and a great deal of research, acquiring the components proved easier than she'd anticipated. She worked her talents well—persuading the right man, making the right promise—and procured everything she needed to set her trap. The hardest part was getting in and out of Noah Hanson's apartment without someone spotting her.

Faye followed him home from work a few weeks later, staying three car lengths behind until he parked at his high-rise apartment. She stealthily tailed his ascent to the seventh floor, her mind beautifully aflame with purpose. Even if Noah was a better match for Natalie than Paul, she couldn't permit her daughter to fly around doing as she pleased, jumping from one man's bed to another without consequence. Faye had to teach her a lesson, and when the authorities found the charred remains of her lover, Natalie would never forget: what Mother says, Mother means.

Once Noah disappeared into apartment seventy-three, Faye scuttled down the hall and pressed her ear to the door. For a while, she heard running water, Noah stacking dishes, and an occasional whistling melody. She flattened herself against the door when the apartment fell silent, and nearly fell backward when the doorknob twisted. Retreating down the hallway, she rounded the corner and peeked out at Noah emerging from his apartment. He locked the door and dropped his keys in his coat pocket, and then, with a cautious look to the right and left, he placed a single key under his doormat.

Faye couldn't believe her luck. She felt as though every saint she worshipped was so wholeheartedly endorsing her plan, they were demolishing every roadblock in her path. After Noah's car vanished down the road, she retrieved her paisley gardening bag from the backseat, and rushed back up to the seventh floor. She kicked aside Noah's doormat, and the key winked at her, almost elated for its part in her plot. Eagerness shook Faye's hand, and the key jumped the keyhole a few times before she could unlock the door.

Entering, she thought the kid had a nice place. Too nice for a home wrecker.

The apartment was tidy—frantically so—and Faye realized why when she flung open the closet door. It was loaded with the junk Noah had hastily swept from the surfaces of the living room and kitchen. Having raised two daughters, Faye knew the look of a quickly-yet-shoddily cleaned room. She shook her head, pitying his sloppiness, but smiled when she realized it was the perfect place to stow her bag. She placed the gardening tools in the back of the closet behind a stack of magazines, and grudgingly used a familiar sweater to cover it all. Faye had lovingly knitted the garment for Natalie with her own two hands, in her precious free time, and her thoughtless daughter had left it in her lover's apartment to be treated like any other piece of filth.

Outside, as she gazed up the face of the apartment building, Faye's heart pumped with the adrenaline she'd missed for so long. The bag would ignite in four hours— surely enough time for him to return and get comfortable on his couch before Faye's newest lesson burned through him. Even if the initial ignition wasn't enough, the closet kindling would help it along nicely.

The deed wasn't done, but with her tools stowed and timer set, Noah Hanson was as good as dead, and her heart soared with delight. She didn't have the usual gardening grime on her hands, but it only took a moment to conjure dozens of sensory memories. Crimson sludge caked under her nails, her slippery fingers tacking together as they dried, the coppery smell of success like God's own breath— they were the ideal intoxication. But as Faye drove away from Noah's apartment, she thought she could learn to love the smell of smoke.

Excitement still jittered through her hours later as she stood outside Natalie and Paul's apartment across town, until she heard Sophie's cries on the other side of the door. The infant's caterwauling tugged at her heart. The new parents must've felt so lost whenever Faye wasn't around to guide them. They were still so young, so undisciplined. How could Sophie ever become a strong, levelheaded, morally centered young lady in such an environment? Children needed order and stability. They needed a house and a garden, and the kind of life Natalie and Paul couldn't provide.

But Faye could.

The unplanned pregnancy still disappointed her daily, but it also gave her the opportunity to correct the mistakes she'd made. She would ensure Sophie didn't fall victim to the same headstrong streak as her mother and aunt, and that she would learn to love working alongside her grandmother in the great days to come.

Faye had felt like a failure for years, even before Avery's arrest. She'd tried so hard to raise good girls, but it seemed the harder she tried, the more impetuous they became. It wasn't her fault. She thought it was for a long time, but after a lot of long sleepless nights in Framingham, she realized it was Jason's. He was around just long enough to put that nasty, defiant streak in them. He poisoned the garden, and he deserved the blame for anything that bloomed rotten.

She did miss him, though. She missed going to the cellar and knowing right away which withered corpse was his. Staring in his empty eyes and laughing in his pit of a face, she loved knowing that despite all the wickedness he'd inflicted on her, she'd won. And she told him often, inches from his shriveled brown lips, inhaling his cloying perfume as she whispered, "I won, you cheating bastard."

Along with freedom, his death gave Faye the means to groom bigger and more tangled gardens. Being a doctor's wife supplied her with certain perks, but as a doctor's widow, she had money, sympathy, and access to enough men with medical supplies to heal even the sickest flora and fauna. Jason Norton proved more useful dead in the cellar than he'd ever been walking the earth.

When the authorities confiscated her corpses, Faye felt like they'd stolen pieces of her soul, her tutelage and faith. It still pained her sometimes, but Sophie helped. The baby was an adorable ball of clay in her hands, smiling up at her in a way that said, "Take me away from this place, Gramma. I'm always happier when I'm with you."

Faye gave the apartment door a little rap before letting herself in. She entered with her arms outstretched to take the crying baby from Paul, which he hesitantly allowed. Sophie quieted after a few bounces, and Faye grinned. "Where's Natalie?"

"Class," he said wearily. "You know I don't like it when you burst in here like that, Faye."

"Why not? Afraid I might stuff you into a trunk?"

His nostrils flared. "That would be funny if it weren't true."

"You know, it's wild imaginations like yours that lead people into situations like these. You would've been better off if you didn't have to be such a little rebel," she said, and gave Sophie an Eskimo kiss. "Not just you, of course. Lots of people would be better off if they followed the rules."

"Like Avery and Natalie? And your husband? Oh, and Natalie's ex-boyfriend? Not to mention the countless others you murdered in cold blood."

"If you really believe that, why haven't you thrown me out of your home? Why haven't you ripped your child away from me?"

"Because Natalie has asked me to, and I respect her wishes. Just as I respected Avery's when she asked me to stay quiet about what I saw. If you had any respect for either of your daughters, you'd get out of their lives as quickly as possible."

"I'm willing to, if that's what Natalie really wants. But you should know, there are lots of little secrets that could come to light in my absence. Secrets about her. Secrets about you. And I doubt the authorities would be keen to allow a baby to stay in the care of someone with so many dirty little secrets." She crinkled her nose and waved dismissively. "But that'll never happen. Because I'm here to protect all of you. Even from yourselves."

"You're delusional."

"The jury didn't think so. They seemed to think the people accusing me of murder were the crazy ones." Faye patted Sophie's back, and she cooed gleefully. "Maybe you don't have to be so far away from Avery after all, Paul. Taunton Hospital has a men's ward."

He snorted, his eyes glinting with malice. "I guess we'll see."

Her face shrank to a pale point. "You're bluffing. You don't have the guts to reopen this wound."

"Believe what you want, but there might come a time when you have no choice but to own the truth—the *real* truth—about what actually happened that night on the island. And when that happens, Faye, it might not matter if I have the guts or not. Because it'll be Natalie who brings it all crashing down."

Faye slithered toward Paul like a cobra preparing to strike, but the phone rang, and he spun around to answer it.

"Hello? Hey, Martin, how are you?" Almost instantly, his jaw slackened, and his face faded to sickly gray. "What? Is he . . . "

Setting Sophie in the bassinet, Faye bit down on her smile and tried to contain the excitement in her voice. "Is something wrong, Paul?"

"I'll be right there." He slammed down the phone, exhaled a shuddering breath, then zoomed to the coat rack.

"Paul, what is it?"

"There was an accident at Noah's apartment. A fire. No, an explosion." He shook his head, fumbling with his jacket buttons. "I don't know what it was. I just have to get over there."

"Oh my goodness, Paul, I'm so sorry. Wait, Noah was your best man, wasn't he?" Faye clutched her face in theatrical shock. "I hope he's okay."

"I don't know. It sounds bad." His voice trembled as he searched for his keys. Finding them in a bowl of plastic fruit, he pointed one at Faye. "Can you watch Sophie? I don't know how long I'll be gone."

"Of course. That's what I'm here for."

Sophie giggled when Gramma Faye squeezed her toes, and when Paul left the apartment, she indulged in a giggle of her own.

She waited in giddy anticipation for Natalie to come home from class, hoping she'd get to be the one to tell her about Noah's accident. She stared at the door intensely, at the lock, at the knob, unaware how tense her body had gotten until the phone rang. She flinched, pulling a muscle in her back as she jumped up. She considered it slightly rude to answer another person's telephone, but thinking it might be Natalie with an explanation for her tardiness, she broke her rule.

"Hello?"

The voice on the other end was barely audible. "You better get over here, Faye."

"Paul?"

"501 Lakewood Avenue. Leave Sophie with the Greens next door."

"Paul, what's going on?"

"Get here as soon as possible," he said, and the line went dead.

It felt like her brain was sweating and leaking out of

her skull as she reflected on her time in Noah's apartment. Had she left anything at the scene of the crime that would've survived the fire? Had she passed anyone who could identify her? Maybe she hadn't been as careful as possible, but she was certain she'd covered her tracks.

Reluctantly, she left Sophie with the next-door neighbors and drove to Lakewood Avenue. Billows of gray smoke stained the sky, visible from several blocks away. The cacophony of sirens began soon after the plumes appeared, and though Faye's nerves persisted, excitement bubbled hot beneath her anxiety. She hadn't expected to see her handiwork, and it was more amazing than she'd imagined. There was divinity in the destruction, scorched and scattered across the apartment block. Everywhere Faye looked, people were in distress. Most, she assumed, deserved to be.

The firefighters had doused the flames, leaving Noah Hanson's apartment little more than a charred void in the high-rise. Paul was speaking with the police when Faye pulled in, and the moment she stepped out of her car, an officer marched over.

"This is just awful," she said, her heart racing in elation.

"Yes, ma'am, it is."

"That poor boy." She thought she would bury her face in her hands and sob to cement the charade, then she noticed the ambulance drivers wheeling side-by-side gurneys from the building.

"Oh dear. How many people were injured?"

"A dozen injured," the policeman answered. "Two killed."

A jagged lump formed in her throat. "Two?" Her heart was still racing, but the delight was gone.

"Yes, Faye. Two," Paul said. His face said it all, eyes bloodshot and skin glazed in sweat as he trudged toward her.

"No . . . " Faye's tears came fast, like hot wax scalding

tracks in her cheeks as she released a plaintive moan. "No, it can't be her!" She flung herself at Paul. "How can you be sure? How do you know it's her?"

"Her car," he replied, fatigued. "It's right over there."

Faye turned to see her daughter's Dodge Coronet, and her knees turned to rubber, buckling and slamming the ground as she wailed. Pressing her forehead to the ground, she clawed the pavement. "Oh God, Natalie. How could this happen?"

"They don't know yet. Bad wiring, maybe."

"What was she doing here? She wasn't supposed to be here. You said she was in class."

"We should talk about this later."

"About what? Did you know she was here?"

"Yes. Natalie and I had an arrangement."

She sat up on her knees and sniffled. "Arrangement?"

"Natalie and Noah were . . . together, and I allowed it."

Faye stood, trembling as she locked her knees and glared at her son-in-law. Sorrow still affected her voice, but a dangerous rage overwhelmed it as she hissed, "You're telling me you knew your wife was having an affair with your best friend, and you didn't feel compelled to do anything about it?"

"Why would I? I didn't love her. At least, not like a husband *should* love his wife. I loved her enough to wish her happiness. Noah made her happy, and I understood her love for him just as she understood my love for Avery."

Faye snarled, spraying spittle in his face as she spoke. "You are pathetic. Is your life so empty that you have to cling to fleeting childhood lust?"

"I wouldn't expect you to understand."

"I understand perfectly," Faye said. "I understand that this is all your fault. You knew she was here. You lied for her. You lied to me." Her chin quivered as she choked back a sob. "And now my daughter is dead."

She hadn't felt such unbridled devastation since childhood. With her stomach twisted in nausea and a knot in her throat she couldn't swallow, she hovered somewhere between awake and asleep as ambulance workers explained where they would take her daughter's body. She noted their words but absorbed none. It wasn't until a policeman was rattling off the next steps in the investigation that something broke through the haze. From beneath the sludge of sorrow, a note of happiness bloomed in Faye when she realized she'd put an end to whatever Paul and Natalie had been planning.

CHAPTER SEVENTEEN

AVERY REELED WITH joy over the birth of her niece. If people were given reasons to rejoice in Taunton, they held onto them for dear life. Even though Avery hadn't met Sophie, the good news could keep her going for months—especially with her court appeal on the horizon. While she waited for Natalie and Paul's impending visit to discuss the strategy of her release, no amount of Taunton's tedium or torture could steal the smile from her face.

Nurse Mathis tapped on the window of the nurses' station. "Avery Norton, phone call!"

Skipping from her bed, Avery hopped into the shallow wooden cubby and pressed the phone to her ear. "Hey, Natalie, that you?"

Someone choked out a sob and sniffled.

"Hello?"

"Avery, it's Mom," she said, voice thin and trembling. "I'm afraid I have some bad news."

Knowing her mother's definitions of good and bad differed greatly from her own, Avery replied apathetically. "Yeah? What is it?"

"It's Natalie. She had an accident."

A bolt of pain struck Avery's chest, and her heart twisted amidst the bone. "What kind of accident?" She dropped her voice low. "What did you do to her?"

"Me? Why would you think I had anything to do with it?"

"Because you always do."

"It was an accident, Avery. An explosion. A faulty gas line and bad wiring."

"What are you saying?"

"She's dead. Natalie's dead. Oh God, my baby."

"No!" Avery wailed, and Flint ran to the bank of phones. "It's not true!"

"There was an explosion at her friend's apartment, and she died. Him too. I'm so sorry, honey, but it's true."

"What about Paul? Is he okay?"

"What's wrong with you? I just told you that your sister is dead, and all you can think about is your childhood boyfriend? I really don't understand you kids. Affairs and arrangements and fickle lust? It's enough to make me sick."

"Arrangements?" Avery's lungs deflated. "You knew, didn't you? You knew about Natalie and Noah."

"How do *you* know about it?"

"Because she told me. She came to see me a few months ago and told me everything. I mean *everything*, Mom. I know what I saw that night was real. Paul remembers it, too."

"Of course he does. He remembers it for you, to make you feel like you're normal, but he's wrong to deceive you like that." Faye heaved a musical sigh. "His lies won't make you better any sooner, sweetheart."

"Why are you still playing this game, Mom? You've already lost. Paul and Natalie spoke to a lawyer."

"Not yet they hadn't." Avery heard the smile in her mother's voice when she said, "So you see, I do still have cards to play."

"You bitch."

Flint touched her knee in concern.

"Say one more word and I won't let you come to her funeral." When Avery didn't respond, she chuckled softly. "It's tomorrow at Sacred Heart. I've already spoken with your doctors, and they've agreed to let you out for the day— under the supervision of a policeman and an orderly."

"You mean in handcuffs."

"You are a criminal. But as Natalie's sister, I thought you'd endure anything to see her one last time, even to bury her." Faye's voice hushed to a hostile tone. "But if you do anything, if you say anything . . ."

Her chest aching, she whimpered. "I won't."

"Good. I'll see you tomorrow then."

"Wait, will Paul be there?"

The only response was the deafening click of Faye severing the connection, and Avery dropped the phone as she slumped against the wall, howling in grief.

CHAPTER EIGHTEEN

THE NEXT MORNING was appropriately wet and gray. Wearing an ill-fitting sheath dress Flint had lent her, Avery pressed her wrists together and allowed the cold metal to close around them.

"It's not too uncomfortable, is it?" Patrick asked.

"Would it make any difference if I said 'yes'?"

He blinked but didn't answer. Instead, he said, "It's chilly," and draped a wool coat over her shoulders.

She thanked him, knowing it would probably be the only kindness she'd receive that day. Between vitamins, batons, and pistols, both the orderly and the officer assigned to escort Avery Norton to the Vineyard were armed—excessively, she thought, considering Meredith had coaxed her into taking two doses of vitamin T before leaving the ward. The pills knocked her out as soon as Patrick strapped her into the car. She woke up during the ferry ride to the island, the smell of diesel smacking her hard, but the rocking of the ocean quickly carried her away again, to a place she hoped the reality of the day couldn't touch.

In her dream, she was coming home under happier circumstances. A summer vacation, maybe. Yes, a vacation was exactly what she needed: to be wild and free and scale the rooftops of Gingerbread Houses with youthful exuberance. Not alone, of course. Paul was with her, his body bronzed by the July sun and a smile blazing as he helped her onto the roof. While her memory had preserved his beauty as she'd known it, her imagination granted him an appealing glow of maturity.

Atop the Wooden Valentine, they gazed out at the campgrounds, but the Tabernacle and ornate houses and the park beyond Wesleyan Grove had disappeared. Instead, the garden behind the Norton home stretched out to sea, and strolling between rows of daylilies, Natalie waved to her sister. As sunlight haloed her head, the breeze carried soft music that embraced and entranced her, causing her to dance wildly through the garden, unaware of the ghastly shadows creeping up behind her.

Avery shouted warnings, but the music drowned her out. Natalie couldn't even hear the crying child, whose desperate shrieks grew louder with each melodic swell. The sea swelled too, rising and churning until its frothy caps doused the sun, and the only light left in the world encircled Natalie's face. She remained serene as shadows oozed through the garden's veins, bloating the stalks with disease and withering the blooms to noxious sludge. She didn't notice when the polluted plants bulged immense behind her, slurrying into a gargantuan rabbit with blister-red eyes, or when its immense fangs curled over her head, and the baby wailed its voice to a raw wheeze. Avery didn't know where the baby was, but she knew it was her niece; even if Natalie didn't recognize it, she knew.

Except, the crying didn't affect Paul either. He was as absentminded as Natalie, staring peacefully into the distance as their world destroyed itself.

Only the rabbit gave Avery its attention. Its red eyes smiling, it lowered its wet, black mouth, and with a snap, its jaw slammed closed on Natalie Norton, extinguishing her light forever. As Avery screamed in agony, the beast crashed to the ground, and the garden became a swirling ebony pit. Its whirlpool force tore the elegant trim from the Wooden Valentine as Avery clung for dear life. But as shingles and planks flew past her, Paul strolled toward the hungry black vortex. Avery tried to grab him, begging for him to turn around, but he looked back only once—a hint of a smile on his face—before opening his arms to the dark.

The spiraling zephyr plucked Paul from the roof and sucked him into the garden pit, where he vanished into nothingness.

Avery was all alone now—except for the crying child now sitting on the apex of the house. When she squealed, her aunt screeched, "Sophie!" and dug her nails into the shingles as she pulled herself toward the baby. Sophie gurgled in glee, her chubby fingers extended. But when Avery was only inches away, the garden's vacuum drastically increased and ripped her from the roof.

As the maelstrom carried her aching body into oblivion, Sophie cried louder than ever before, but it wasn't because Avery was gone, or because the garden was consuming the rest of the world. She was crying because of the woman now standing beside her—lifting her up, kissing her, cradling her as if she were her own. The last thing Avery heard before the darkness devoured her was the woman's hushed voice.

"No more tears, Sophie," she said. "I'm giving you the garden."

Avery awoke with a shriek that caused Officer Hanley to reach for his club, but Patrick gestured for him to put it away.

"Where are we?" she asked woozily. As she lifted her head, the car passed the Portuguese-American Club, and she knew they were close to Sacred Heart Cemetery.

Sleep had rumpled her dress and hiked it up too high, and since she couldn't fix it with her hands cuffed, she had to ask Patrick to pull it down before she got out of the car. Kind as he'd always been, it was an extra smack of vulnerability she didn't need that day.

The weather hadn't improved. Fog rolled thick through the cemetery, obstructing not only the gravesite but the faces of the mourners as well. As she walked the path flanked by armed men, she thought she might still be dreaming, especially when she heard a baby crying. But there were other voices, too, sharing cruel tidbits of gossip regarding the gruesome celebrity attending the funeral that day.

"I can't believe they're letting her come."

"Can you imagine riding on that ferry with her?"

"With any luck, someone gave her a nudge overboard."

Avery stopped in her tracks, sick to her stomach. The officer and orderly exchanged glances, and Patrick touched her shoulder.

"Do you want to leave?"

It wasn't a horrible idea. What difference would it make if she left? No one needed her there. No one wanted her there. Maybe even Natalie would've been disgusted by her presence, stealing focus from her tragic death.

But then the fog shifted, and a man stepped through the haze wearing an expression that pulled Avery forward. It was a look of warring anguish and adoration which she'd seen twice before in her life. Both times, it belonged to Paul Dillon.

She picked up her pace to meet him, but Officer Hanley seized her arm and stopped her. Paul eagerly closed the distance between them, not once looking at the officer or the orderly as he said, "Hello Avery."

It sounded like a sigh of relief. When she whispered his name in reply, Paul closed his eyes as if trying to better absorb it, and the sight fluttered her heart as she hadn't felt in years.

He looked just how she'd pictured him. He was still the tall, trim boy she remembered, but he'd acquired more than a few stylish charms; his hair was longer, his face more angular. But his eyes were also puffy and dark, and he moved differently, slower. But perhaps the child in his arms had something to do with that. Avery's worship drifted from Paul's ice-blue eyes to his daughter's, gazing up at her from a pink blanket.

She gasped, instantly enamored, and reached out to touch her. Even if the handcuffs hadn't stopped her, Patrick and Hanley were right there to pull her away. With one hand on each shoulder, they held her back, and she bowed her head in shame as derisive whispers rose from the graveyard haze.

"You can stand by me," Paul said.

"We'll say where she can stand," Officer Hanley replied, and pushed Avery through the fog to the grave.

Her handlers found a space for her among the other mourners, albeit several feet away, and without the luxury of moving about. She didn't recognize many faces in the crowd, or maybe she wasn't used to those people looking at her with such disdain. Her gaze swept around the circle of attendees, settling on the most disdainful of all.

A black lace veil hung over Faye Norton's eyes, but her glare penetrated it when she took her place next to Paul at the grave and lifted her head to Avery. Sophie was crying, and Avery didn't blame her; at that moment, she wanted to scream her head off, too. Instead, she gritted her teeth and strove to keep her mouth clamped shut. But as the service began, her lips eventually trembled open and caught the falling tears. She couldn't hear most of what the priest said, partly because of her distance, but also because her myriad thoughts were too rampant to allow his words any purchase.

She did note, however, that his pronouncement of "ashes to ashes and dust to dust" was too evocative for comfort.

"Would anyone like to say a few words?" he asked.

"I would." Faye pressed a tissue to the corners of her eyes and stood at the head of the coffin. "I never imagined I'd see this day. Even with all a mother's worry, all the scenarios that fly through your head when your children go off on their own, I never pictured this. But we must try to take what comfort we can from it. We're together. I'm sorry that it took this to bring us together, but we're all here, all loving Natalie, all missing her terribly. Today is for her. It's for her young daughter who will never know the kind of woman she was." She exhaled a shuddering breath and clutched her hand to her breast. "She was a strong woman, but she was a sad woman. By Holy Mary, Mother of God, I hope she's happy now. I tried to be an example for both of my daughters, and obviously, that didn't work out the way I planned. All I can hope for now is that they take the lessons from this life and use them well in the next. I believe she will," Faye said, a quivering smile crossing her face as she looked to the murky sky. "I know that Natalie sees us now. I know that she's watching, and I hope she knows I'm still watching her. We all are."

The mourners bobbed their heads, but Avery and Paul didn't move a muscle.

"I only have one more thing to say. I know it's not exactly the best time, but I feel like it might be the only time." Faye withdrew a piece of paper from her dress coat. "This is a letter Natalie wrote to me before her death. Before Sophie was born, actually. There are things in it that shame me as her mother, but I'm not here to judge. That's God's job. I'm here to honor her wishes, which she disclosed to me in this letter."

She inhaled deeply, shakily. To everyone else, it was the epitome of the sorrowful mother preparing to delve deeper into her grief, but Avery and Paul exchanged loaded glances, knowing better.

"Dear Mom," she started, "Two months to go! Part of me can't wait until it's all over, and the other part wishes it would never end. I don't know how you did it twice, but I'm glad you're around to help me through it. It's been eye-opening, that's for sure.

"Because of that, I feel like I need to be honest with you about something. It's something you're probably not going to like, so believe me, if I could keep it hidden forever, I would. But things have gotten a little scary, and I don't know what to do anymore." Faye cleared her throat and stole a glance at Paul before dropping to the letter again. "The truth is . . . I'm in love with another man, and I've been seeing him behind Paul's back."

A collective gasp arose from the circle, and all eyes shot to Paul, who tried his best not to make contact with any of them.

"Paul knows all about it," Faye continued, twisting the gasp to a murmur. "I couldn't bear to hide it anymore, so I told him everything. He did not react well. I can't blame him for being angry, but it just keeps getting worse. He yells at me all the time. He threatens me. He threatens the life of our child. And now, he's started hitting me—"

Paul lurched forward with a growl. "What are you doing, Faye?"

"I'm just telling the truth. Natalie wanted me to know these things, and I want the world to know them."

"But they're lies! Natalie didn't write that!" Finally acknowledging the policeman, he shouted, "She's lying!"

"I'd actually like to hear the rest of the letter," Hanley said, his hand resting on his club.

"Thank you, Officer," Faye chirped. "I'm glad you're here, and I'm glad the others will be here soon too."

"What others?" Paul said, and Faye licked her lips before continuing.

"I'm afraid, Mom. I'm afraid he might do something to Noah and me. He talks about it sometimes, and there are times I think he's joking, but sometimes I think he could go through with it. If he wanted to, I think he could just blow us up, and no one would ever know he did it."

"You're unbelievable," Paul said. "You're sick!"

"If something happens to me, please take care of my baby. Please keep her safe," Faye continued, but Paul rushed at her and ripped the letter from her hands.

Officer Hanley and Patrick barreled at him. Taking Sophie out of Paul's arms, the orderly whisked her away while the policeman struck his shoulder with a club. The people shrieked and scattered, but Avery stood frozen, staring at her mother's satisfied expression when three police cars pulled up to the cemetery.

"Right on time," she whispered.

The police ran up the hill, and while they wrestled Paul

to the ground and cuffed his hands behind his back, Patrick handed the crying child to Faye.

Seeing Sophie in Faye's arms promptly melted Avery's shock and pushed her forward. She lunged, reaching for her throat, but she was only able to grab a handful of hair before Patrick wrenched her away.

"I'm only doing what's best for Sophie," Faye said, her voice like a weeping wound. "I wish you could understand. It's what Natalie wanted."

"Bullshit!" Avery howled. "You're a liar and a murderer. You're the last person who should have custody of her. You're the one who did this to us. You're the one who deserves to die!"

Patrick tried to cover her mouth, but she chomped down on his hand and wriggled free. She didn't get far, though—just a few steps before the distinctive pinch of a needle penetrated her neck. Vitamin P charged through her veins like fire, and the world became a dizzy pool of pale color as she sank to the ground. With her cheek planted against the soil heaped to cover her sister's coffin, she saw Paul, still pinned to the earth. Their shared gaze lasted only moments, but it would stay with her for eternity.

"Thank you," he said. "Thank you for trying."

The police pulled him to his feet, and as they led him to a squad car his daughter's cries turned shrill, and Faye clutched her tighter. The sedative made it difficult for Avery to lift her head, but she fought the powerful desire to sleep and focused on her mother. Faye only smiled, but to Avery, she was howling with laughter. She was slapping her knee and pointing at the fools she'd conquered so easily.

As Patrick scooped her up, he said, "Not smart, Avery. Really, not smart," but the words rolled out in Faye Norton's voice.

Before she lost consciousness, she opened her eyes as wide as possible and glared at her mother. While Paul's gratitude repeated in her mind, and the curtain fell, Avery hissed at Faye: "I will never stop trying."

CHAPTER NINETEEN

A **STRANGE SMELL** crept through the tiny holes in Avery's oblivion and found its way into her dreams. There were many facets to the odor, but its two strongest contradicted one another. The first was a sharp, clean smell, and the other was savagely raw and smoky like a cinder that had jumped the hearth. The odor grew stronger as her consciousness returned, and when she beheld her surroundings—the equipment, the padded table—a justifiable panic consumed her. She'd never seen the room firsthand, but she'd heard enough stories to know exactly where she was.

Nurse Meredith frowned as she unbuckled the table straps. "Assault, Avery? After we allowed you to leave hospital grounds? That's something we just can't tolerate."

"I didn't mean to hurt Patrick," she whispered, woozily sitting up in the wheelchair. "I don't want to hurt anyone but my mom."

"That's a horrible thing to say. That poor woman has been to hell and back these past few years."

"She made that hell herself. She caused all of this. She should be the one in here, not me."

"I really thought you were progressing," Meredith said sadly. "We all did. We thought you stood a chance of getting better without us having to resort to this."

Avery whimpered. "What are you going to do to me?"

Nurse Meredith stared at the girl, her lips clamped and nostrils flared as she exhaled heavily. She didn't speak. She simply nodded to orderlies Verger and Thomas.

They pulled her from the wheelchair. She felt like she was fighting them, thrashing and kicking, but she was still so weak from the sedative she hardly moved an inch. They laid her out on the table, and Thomas pinned her with his gargantuan hand while Verger strapped her down. She grunted as he pulled the straps tight, and when Meredith rolled a cart stacked with strange electronic equipment toward the table, her grunts turned to insistent sobs.

"I didn't kill those people, Nurse Meredith, and nothing will ever change that. Please don't do this to me. I'm innocent."

After years of begging and bargaining in that room, the staff had learned to tune out the tears. Their hands moved quickly with the equipment and electrodes as they prepped Avery for treatment. The screaming and pleading were just another part of the process, maybe even a perk of the job.

She thought it might be that way for Verger when he held up a rubber mouthpiece with a head strap and trilled, "Bite down, darling." Despite her best efforts, he forced it between her clenched teeth, and Orderly Thomas buckled the strap so tight she thought it might tear the corners of her mouth. Once they dropped her head to the pillow, she didn't try to lift it again.

Equipment whirred all around her; people turned dials and flipped switches, but she didn't crane to see them. Despite her fearful curiosity, she figured it was best not to look at the gun before it blew her brains out.

The isopropyl alcohol sent cold shivers through her body as Thomas wiped it over her temples, but the same thing happened when he attached the electrodes, and when Meredith leaned over her and chirped, "Ready?"

Avery whined, and the orderlies grunted. She squeezed her eyes shut, clamped down on the mouthpiece, and hoped for a quick death.

The current obeyed the nurse's hand at first, but once it reached the cerebral playground inside a lump of flesh named Avery Norton, it ran wild and free. It burnt her up, it broke her apart, it caused her to convulse madly on the table, and it didn't give its glorious destruction a second thought. While every step of the current's impassioned dance solidified its purpose for being, it stole a piece of Avery's being away until the lights of her mind flickered in malfunction.

She wasn't sure what fixed it, but the lights were steady when she looked around again. And so was she, standing at the center of a small room with a high ceiling and walls plastered with small sheets of paper.

"Hello, Avery." A gentle voice called to her from all sides and plucked her heart with excitement.

When her mother appeared to her with arms extended, Avery gleefully glided into them. Faye kissed the top of her head and her cheeks, and Avery giggled as she squirmed in her mother's embrace.

Then she remembered.

She pulled free, eyes narrowed. "This isn't right. Don't I hate you?"

"Not here," Faye said, pinching her daughter's cheek. "This place was built before our hatred, deep in the earth, deep in the ocean, where angels plot in their sleep and children wait to be chosen. It is beautiful, isn't it? Except . . . " She frowned, tapping her chin with a tapered finger. "It's much too cluttered. We need to make some room."

Faye scanned the walls and selected a particular piece of paper. When she ripped it away, a beam of light shone into the room.

"There. Isn't that better?"

"What is that?" Avery asked, pointing to the paper.

She inspected it apathetically. "Learning to ride a bike." When the page ignited in a blaze, Faye grinned, then whooped as it disappeared in a puff of smoke. Turning to the wall again, she joyously ripped the papers away. With every ray of light that burst through, Faye cheered, each new charred hole in her daughter's brain a victory.

"Fractions!" Faye exclaimed as pages turned to smoke.

"Losing your last baby tooth! Having chicken pox with your sister!"

Avery felt like her brain was emptying, but the weight on her shoulders increased with every loss, and she crashed to her knees. She gripped her head and moaned. "What's happening to me?"

"Tap dancing! Piano lessons! The color blue!" Faye boomed louder with each exclamation as the papers sailed down like ribbons of flame, until there was only one piece of paper left.

Plucking the final page, her thunderous voice shook the room. "Paul Dillon!"

When the last beam of light shone in, the pressure of emptiness forced Avery to her stomach. It was so intense, the shadow that stretched over her felt like the biggest relief of her life.

"All right, Avery. You can hate me again."

Confused, she looked up at the strange woman whose shadow cooled her pain.

"How can I hate you?" she asked. "I don't even know who you are."

CHAPTER TWENTY

SHE AWOKE TO a new world. The sting of sunlight drove her back under the covers in dread, but scrunching up in the darkness didn't help. Pain stabbed her right shoulder, and when she found she couldn't move her arm. Forcing herself up, she puzzled over why it was in a sling and she was on a bed that felt like a sack of broken boulders. As she took stock of her surroundings, every muscle in her body ached, culminating in a steady throb that hammered her brain. The other bed in the room was empty, along with the open drawers of the dresser beside it. The only thing that indicated anyone else had ever existed in the room was a piece of paper tucked in the back of the bottom drawer. A farewell note, it seemed, to someone named Avery.

It said: *Dear Avery, I guess we won't see each other after all, but I didn't want to leave without saying goodbye. You've been a loyal and loving friend to me, and I'll be eternally grateful for that because I know I'll never have it again. You are a good person, and you deserve happiness. But even though I'll miss you terribly, there's a part of me that's happy I'll never see you again. If I don't see you, it means you're free. And I am too, you know. I always have been. Try not to worry about me, and I'll try not to worry about you. Just, please, don't forget me. Your friend always, Flint a.k.a Francine.*

Slipping the letter back into the drawer, she didn't know who Avery or Flint/Francine were, but they sounded like good friends. Too good to have lived in such a stark room with barred windows. Then again, she was in that room too, so what kind of person did that make her?

She was peering between the bars, wondering why she wished someone would run out onto the lawn and scream her name if she didn't *know* her name, when a nurse opened the door.

"How are we today?" she asked, pencil primed on a clipboard.

Pressing her back against the bars, she panted. "Who are you? Where am I?"

The woman crinkled her nose and made a check mark. "That answers my question, thank you. How are you feeling otherwise? You've been in and out for a few days, but this is the first time I've seen you up and about." When she squeezed ointment onto a cotton ball and approached, Avery shrank in fear. "Don't worry. It'll help your burns."

The girl didn't realize she had burns, but when the nurse dabbed the ointment onto her temples, she recoiled at the sting.

"The electrodes must've been damp," the nurse said, tacking on a murmured apology. "We don't want your burns to get infected, do we? Let me help you. How's your arm?"

Pain rocketed through her shoulder when she moved. "It's in a sling."

"Well, you remember the word 'sling.' That's something. And you're welcome for the medical care."

"Where am I? What am I doing here?"

"Don't worry, dear. It'll come back in time." Gesturing to the door, she arched an eyebrow. "Would you like to look out the window? Violet seems to enjoy it."

"Who's Violet?"

The nurse hummed and urged her into a wheelchair. It felt good to collapse into it, and to be pushed out, from one strange room into another, until a multitude of eyes clamped onto the girl with the burnt temples. She didn't know them, but many gestured at her in recognition, even sympathy, and her stomach clenched.

"How long have I been here?" she asked, and the nurse's face crinkled as she placed a pill in the girl's hand.

"Take this."

"What is it?"

"A vitamin. It's good for you. Take it."

She didn't want to swallow the pill, but the expressions of every nurse around her suggested she didn't have much of a choice. Even the eyes that seemed to know her, maybe even cared about her, were otherwise wreathed in shades of surrender.

Gulping the pill, she allowed the nurse to steer her to the window with a cheerful air that thinned the moment they neared. The girl sitting in the purple chair looked half-dead, and a sinister scar twisted the flesh on her forehead. Her eyes were unfocused and her face slack, but when the nurse rolled Avery up beside her, the girl's focus shifted slightly to the right.

The nurse said, "If you need anything . . . " but her voice trailed off within the first steps of her departure. Neither girl was listening, anyway. The bluebird flitting from branch to branch had already captivated them. When it flew away, the girl in the purple chair kept staring ahead while her visitor turned.

She said, "Hi," but the girl said nothing. "That's a nice color." She pointed at her seat. "All of the other chairs are orange. You must be the lucky one."

The girl swiveled her head with unnatural fluidity and stared at her in a way that made her feel feeble, naked, and alone. She cleared her throat, mostly to remind herself she still had a voice, which sounded like an antique squeezebox when she finally spoke.

"Why are you in here?"

The girl in the purple chair wheezed a chuckle. "Wouldn't you rather know why *you're* in here?"

The girls in the lounge gasped in shock, shooting up from their seats.

"She talked!" one exclaimed. "Did you hear that, Tyler? Violet talked!"

With her gaze glued to the window again, Violet shushed them and whispered, "The nurses ordered them not to speak to you, not to tell you who you are, but they gave me no such order. I'm not much of a talker, anyway."

"Why not?"

"What's there to talk about? Nothing I could say would save me, just like your protests can't save you. I have no stories to tell because I have no memory. Moments like this happen less and less. New vitamins are made every day, and someone has to be the guinea pig. So I just look outside. There are lovelier things beyond the prison bars. The birds, the trees, the rabbits . . . "

Faint light illuminated a corner of Avery's mind. "What did you say?"

"Rabbits."

The word felt important, but she didn't know why. Then, piece by piece, an image entered her mind. A white rabbit with a blue dot on its belly. It confounded her at first, but clarity came fast, filling her brain with a celestial burst of light.

"The rabbits . . . the garden . . . "

Memories careened through her brain with frenetic energy. Whirling out of the wheelchair, Avery threw her good arm around Violet's neck and thanked her for rescuing her from oblivion. But the girl in the purple chair was as slack and vacant as ever. Even the common room was empty. And though the world was bright as heaven moments before, shadows now oozed toward Avery from all directions. The sun was down, and the ward was quiet, but her mind was a big band of frenzied thoughts. As more memories streamed back, she retraced her mental steps until she found the last event she remembered clearly: the orderly sticking electrodes to her temples.

Avery touched the raw flesh and winced. Her brain backtracked from there. She was given electroshock treatment because she bit Patrick. She had bitten Patrick because he tried to hold her back from attacking her mother. She attacked her mother because Faye lied about Paul and took Sophie. Faye lied and took Sophie because Natalie wasn't there to stop her. Natalie wasn't there to stop her because . . .

Tears burned her eyes.

The funeral. Natalie's funeral.

Although the slightest movement fired missiles of pain through Avery's shoulder, she hugged her body tight and sobbed. Her sister was dead. Natalie . . . Natalie . . . Norton . . .

Avery's heart ached so sharply she couldn't swallow. What was Natalie's middle name? She could recall her dead sister's birthday but not her middle name. Scanning her mind, she knew that she loved Paul, but she couldn't remember their first kiss. Had they even had one?

While much of her memory had returned, scorched holes still riddled her mind. Some spots were too insignificant to trouble her, but with monstrous bites taken from its core and structure, her brain felt unstable, liable to topple and spill things that could never be replaced. She hugged herself harder, hoping it would hold her sanity together as she whimpered, "What did you people do to me?" Sniffing hard, she tilted her face to the ceiling and boomed. *"What did you people do to me!"*

Radcliffe rushed out of the Nurses' Station with her syringe ready, but Avery dodged her and ran down the hall. She got so close to the exit she didn't care whether it was locked or not, but just as her fingers wrapped around the handle, Patrick emerged from the shadows and latched onto her injured arm. He twisted it, and Avery screamed as she sank to the floor. When Patrick plunged the syringe into her neck, she noticed the bite mark on his hand—as well as the satisfaction on his face before vitamin P dispatched a numbing haze throughout her body. But the agony in her heart remained, following her into the dark.

She expected to wake up in the electroshock room again, but when her vision cleared, she realized the walls were moving. A full-body swell of nausea suddenly changed her perspective, though. *She* was the one moving. In a wheelchair pushed by Orderly Thomas, Avery sped through the sun bridge, away from the juvenile ward.

Her tongue felt both hollow and heavy, but she was able to mumble out a few questions Thomas ignored. His jaw remained clenched throughout the journey across the hospital, and his eyes didn't drop once to acknowledge her. Two unfamiliar orderlies opened a series of double doors for them, the last set putting Avery face-to-face with a cramped room of imposing figures. Eight doctors and nurses, including Meredith and Aslinn, sat at a long table littered with charts and folders, their faces warm with welcome as the orderly locked the wheelchair in place.

Nurse Meredith folded her hands on the table and scrunched her nose. "Good morning, Avery. How are you feeling today?"

Avery scanned the adults with pen tips hovering over their journals. Most appeared wound tight as drums while a few doctors were slumped, their eyes ringed with exhaustion.

"I'm confused," Avery whispered.

"That's to be expected."

"I'm confused as to why I'm still here."

The colleagues exchanged looks and murmured comments but gave her no answer.

"My mom killed my sister," she continued. "She stole her baby."

Nurse Meredith waved her hand dismissively. "No, Avery. None of that happened."

"It did. I saw it."

"You're mistaken."

Avery's face flamed with rage, but her voice wavered when she said, "How would you know? You weren't there. None of you were. You don't know anything!"

Dr. Aslinn slammed his palm on the table. "Be quiet!"

She jumped, then sobbed softly. "I don't understand this. You're not even trying to find the real killer."

"That's not our job. Our job is to get you well, and . . . " He pinched his lips and flexed his fingers against the tabletop. " . . . Well, I'm sad to say we've failed. You're no better than you were the day you arrived. I'm at my wit's end with you, Miss Norton, and I'm afraid there's nothing else I can do to help you. But I believe Dr. Yingling can."

He gestured to his neighbor, a sturdy man with small, round glasses who lifted his chin in pride.

"Thank you, Doctor." Yingling readjusted his spectacles, casting crescent-shaped shadows over his chiseled cheeks. "Yes, I believe I can help you, Avery. After reading your file and discussing with your former doctors, I think you're an especially mature young woman. Would you say that's correct?"

She bobbed her head, and her arms prickled with cold gooseflesh.

"I thought so. That's why I expect you'll do much better among adults. After all, you're not a child anymore, are you?"

Her breath caught like ice in her throat. "You're moving me to the adult ward? But you can't. My review isn't supposed to be until my eighteenth birthday."

"Considering the recent events, the board was inclined to bump it up a few months."

"That's not fair!"

Aslinn pointed at Avery and huffed. "Neither is your refusal to cooperate with us. Everything we did was in your best interest, and you fought us every step of the way."

"To be fair," Nurse Meredith started, "she was receptive for a while. She was making progress before this whole messy business with her sister."

"My mother killed her!" Avery bellowed, rocking the chair from side to side. "She killed her! Her own daughter! And Paul's best friend! Please, Paul's in danger now, too, you have to believe me."

Orderly Thomas squeezed the back of her neck. His fingers pushed into her windpipe, and she promptly calmed. She held up her hands in supplication, and he released her.

"Outbursts aside, I believe she can still be rehabilitated," Dr. Aslinn said. "We made a few strides together. She had started to admit the possibility of her guilt."

"I'm not guilty," Avery said.

The committee groaned, shaking their heads and jotting in their journals with furrowed brows.

"This continued delusion is why we can't allow you to stay in the juvenile ward anymore, Miss Norton," Yingling said. "It's not safe for the other patients, the ones who *do* want to get better and leave someday."

"I want to leave, too."

Yingling leaned forward, the corners of his mouth lined with subtle wrinkles. "Show me. Or you're not going anywhere."

Her toes curled in her slippers, and pain rang through her ribcage. She gripped her chest and folded forward onto the table with a moan.

"It's not all bad, is it?" Nurse Meredith said. "You'll get to see some of your friends again."

Avery snapped up from the table, her teeth bared and her voice a raspy warning. "I'm not crazy, and I'm not guilty, but I've been locked up for almost six years for being both. My body's been frozen, my brain has been fried. I've been drugged up and told I'm a bad person on a daily basis, but I'm not. I don't deserve any of this. Do you really think some 'friends' are going to make me feel better?" She beat her fists against the arms of the wheelchair. "I was supposed to get out of here! Natalie and Paul were going to help me."

Dr. Yingling paged through his journal. "Paul Dillon, yes? The man who was accused of killing your sister?"

"My mother killed her," she said, panting. "Natalie and Noah. She killed them for custody of Sophie. I know it."

"Do you have proof?"

172

"No, but—"

"But?"

"She's done it before. Not like this. She never blew anything up before, but she *did* murder people. And now she's trying to steal Sophie."

"Avery, your mother doesn't have custody of Sophie Dillon," Dr. Aslinn said.

Her mouth fell open. "But I saw the police give Sophie to my mom at the funeral."

"Only to care for while Mr. Dillon was being questioned," Yingling replied. "She's with her father now, and your mother is home on Martha's Vineyard."

"How do you know that?"

"She called for you a few days ago, but you were still recovering from treatment. We thought it was best to wait."

"*She* told you?" Avery screeched, her heart racing. "Don't you see? She could be lying! Paul could be in jail right now. She could still have Sophie."

"She doesn't, Miss Norton," a silver-haired nurse said gently. "Your niece is safe and sound with her father in Boston."

"For now, maybe, but my mother won't give up that easy. She won't stop until Sophie is hers. You didn't hear that fake letter she wrote. She's ruthless. She's crazy. She'll do whatever it takes to have her way." Avery raved as she leapt out of the wheelchair, appealing to the doctors with desperate shrieks. "Why are you just sitting there? We need to warn Paul. She could be in Boston right now."

An orderly wrestled her into the wheelchair, but when he withdrew a syringe, Dr. Yingling instructed him to put it away.

"That's not how we're going to deal with her anymore," he said. "Do you understand what I'm saying, Avery? I won't allow you to sleep through your psychosis. You are a murderer, and under my care, you *will* acknowledge it. You will make a concerted effort toward recovery, or so help me God, you will experience things I can't even begin to describe. If you think the last six years have been hell, Miss Norton, get ready for one doozy of an aftershock." Dr. Yingling's eyes were soft, almost smiling, but his angular face was rigid and cold when he said, "Do we understand each other?"

Tears streamed down Avery's cheeks. When she nodded, they fell to her knees, to her slippers, to the linoleum. She couldn't help wondering how many tears had fallen on that floor, how many hearts and spirits broken in that room.

"Your belongings will be packed for you and delivered to the new ward," Dr. Yingling said. "Nurse Day will take you there now."

Meredith's face puckered when she approached the wheelchair. "Do you want to walk?"

Avery shook her head. "I'm dizzy."

Meredith grunted in annoyance as she unlocked the wheelchair. Firing her a wink before the nurse turned her about, Dr. Yingling said, "I'll see you soon, Miss Norton."

CHAPTER TWENTY-ONE

MORE THAN TWO dozen eyes latched onto Avery Norton as Nurse Meredith rolled her into the ward, interrupting a group therapy session. Several patients clearly didn't appreciate the disruption and glared at her in disgust. Others wore expressions of intrigue, some looks bordering on voracious, and a small remainder of patients waved to her in youthful recognition—Flint and Pam, notably.

"Everyone, this is Avery," the nurse said. "She's not quite eighteen, but I'm sure you'll make her feel like one of the group."

Avery looked to the nurse for something more, a note of sympathy, a gesture of fond farewell, perhaps, but Meredith Day promptly turned on her heel and marched out of Avery's life forever.

A slim raven-haired nurse in the circle of chairs stood and beckoned Avery forward. "Welcome to the group. I'm Nurse Foster," she said in a British accent that barely escaped between her large, clenched teeth. "We've been expecting you."

"Thanks . . . I guess." Avery cautiously avoided the other women on her way to an empty chair in the circle, but one of the patients deliberately stuck out her foot and tripped her. When she pitched forward, a friendly pair of arms caught her, and she met Flint's eyes with a grateful sigh, causing a portly woman nearby to make kissing noises at them.

Nurse Foster snapped her fingers, and all eyes

returned to her. "We were in the middle of Karen's story. Please continue, Karen."

A slight woman with frizzy hair and a crooked nose sat up in her chair. "Sure, well, like I was saying, my mother was always scared of the basement. All her life, she was scared of basements, so I guess she figured I would be, too. So, when I was bad or doing something she *thought* was bad, she'd lock me in the basement. But she'd forget about me, or maybe she just didn't care enough to let me out until right before my father got home. Either way, I'd be locked in the basement for hours, sometimes all day, and I guess I got pretty lonely. So, I'd talk to people, people I made up to get me through it." She picked at her lip, tearing a translucent strip of skin free and flicking it at the floor. "But when I moved out of my parents' house, the people didn't go away. Every time I felt sad or lonely or rejected, one of the basement people would pop in and try to cheer me up. I tried to explain it to my friends and coworkers, but no one understood. I had to quit my job, and I stopped going out entirely. Then I was all alone in my house, and the basement people were all I had."

"You understood they weren't real, though," the nurse said.

"Yes, but I couldn't make them go away. I tried confronting my mother about it. I thought maybe some kind of closure would get rid of them, but she just called me crazy and made me come here. She's the reason I'm like this, and all she could do was call me crazy and sweep me under the rug. God, I hate her. She's the world's worst mother."

Before she could stop herself, Avery scoffed loudly.

"Do you have something to contribute?" Nurse Foster asked, squinting at her.

Avery shook her head, which felt like a cinderblock on her shoulders. She sank lower in her chair, her mother's face blazing in her burdened mind.

"Wait! I know who you are now!" A woman with a

moon-shaped face pointed a stubby finger at Avery. "You're that girl who killed all those people. The Martha's Vineyard Massacre, right?" The woman laughed, propelling her foul breath across the circle. "Wow. I bet you think you're hot shit, dontcha?"

She didn't lift her gaze from her knees as she mumbled, "Not at all."

"I gotta know. What made you kill those people?"

Her head still drooped, she scanned the ring of women. "I didn't, since you asked." Met with scorn and doubt, she cleared her throat. "I don't feel like talking about it right now."

"Come on," the woman urged. "Enlighten us, Little Avery Norton. What drives a kid to chop up a dozen people?"

Flint bared her teeth and hissed. "Back off, Meg."

"Shut up, firebug." With a sneer, Meg spat at Flint's feet, and the girl launched into an artistic thread of obscenities.

Nurse Foster raised her hands and barked, "Quiet, both of you." Her face was a knotted threat until Flint and Meg settled back into their chairs. Then, folding her hands calmly in her lap, a smile brightened her face. "The group wants to know, Avery, and you will have to tell us something eventually. But since it's your first day, we'll let it slide."

"Thank you."

"Enjoy it, dear, if that's important to you. You won't get so lucky next time," she said through a sneer. "This session is adjourned."

As the rest of the group pushed their chairs against the walls and returned the common room furniture to its usual spots, Avery remained seated, her head bowed and heart speeding.

A woman kicked her chair, shouting, "Up!" and jolted Avery out of her seat.

Her pulse speeding, she drifted over to Flint. "What is wrong with these people?"

"Did you think the patients were any less crazy over here? You're still in an asylum, Avery."

"I know that." After a second, she shrugged. "All right. Maybe I thought adults would act more mature and at least *seem* less crazy."

"The opposite, actually." Pam strolled to the pair with her chin high. "Adults acting like kids are way more annoying than kids acting like kids." Slapping Avery on the back, she added, "How's life, Lizzie?"

It had been years since Avery and Pam were in the same ward, but at that moment, any animosity she'd felt toward the girl—now a grown woman—faded. Like it or not, Pam was one of her only allies in the new ward. The trio retired to Flint's room, but when Pam tried to close the door, a curvy blonde nurse in a loose uniform scuttled up and stopped her.

"Not with that one," she said, pointing at Avery.

"Cool it, Nurse Charles. I know how to handle her."

Avery scrunched her nose. "Handle me?"

When the nurse raised her eyebrows, Pam grunted. "Fine. I'll leave it open," she said, and Nurse Charles strutted back to the station, satisfied.

Flint led Avery to the bed, where she hunched in misery. "What happened? When you weren't back before my birthday, I thought you'd gotten out."

"My mom tried to take Sophie, just like my sister thought she would." Her voice trembled, and she wrung her hands as she struggled to speak. "At the funeral, she read a letter Natalie supposedly wrote when she was pregnant. It made Paul sound angry and abusive, and it claimed Natalie wanted our mom to take care of the baby if anything happened to her."

"Which it obviously did," Pam said.

Avery's chin dimpled, and sorrow dammed her throat. "I guess I didn't react well."

"They gave you shocks, didn't they?"

"How did you know?" she said, wiping fresh tears from her cheeks.

"Busted arm, sizzled forehead, a vague Violetish

expression—you're a walking, talking member of the electroshock club. Hell, you're lucky to be walking and talking at all," Pam said. "Then again, it always surprised me when you could."

"What's that supposed to mean?"

"Darian, you're up," Nurse Charles announced from the station. As a patient with golden-brown skin and thick curls sashayed out of her room and pranced down the hall, the nurse added, "Avery Norton, you're next."

She hung her head out of Flint's room. "Next for what?"

"You need to see Dr. Yingling," Flint said, pulling her back in.

"Oh," she grunted. "I've seen enough."

Pam snickered. "He's got a lot more to show you, I guarantee." Glancing at the clock, she twitched her nose. "But you've got a while before then. Darian always makes the most of her time. It's easier that way."

Avery wasn't sure what Pam meant, but she feared she'd find out soon enough. While she waited for her turn with Dr. Yingling, Flint and Pam gave her a tour of the adult ward. The layout wasn't much different than the previous ward, except for an extra lounge and significantly more bedrooms to accommodate all the patients. No one offered her a kind word outside of her former juvenile captives, and after a dozen icy glares from the others, hearing her name from the nurses' station inspired a twinge of relief.

"Dr. Yingling is ready for you, Avery."

"That was quicker than expected," Pam said, gnawing on her thumb. "I guess Darian was his first of the day. He never lasts long on the first."

"What do you mean?" Avery asked.

Flint wrapped a reassuring arm around her shoulder. "Try not to worry. You don't have to do anything."

"But you should if you want to be treated well," Pam added, and spat out a jagged hunk of fingernail.

"Now, Avery," the nurse said sternly. "Up the hall, through the second door on your right, then the first on your left. You can't miss it."

"Alone?"

Meg whined mockingly as she passed. "Aww, does the baby need someone to hold her hand?"

Avery's first instinct was to hang her head and shuffle away, but an ember of Faye Norton still burned in her mind. Her mother wouldn't cower or slither off in fear. She would stand tall and focus all her energy on her opposition, right or wrong.

The ember flared and caught, and Avery felt like she grew taller as she glared at Meg. Within seconds, the glower forced the patient into a sulky retreat, and Avery's heart leapt in unexpected glee. She grinned in her triumph and strode down the hall, following the nurse's instructions with rekindled confidence.

"Dr. Stephen Yingling Ph.D." greeted Avery with large gold letters on frosted glass, kicking up a new cyclone of anxiety. But she exhaled it, and her hand was steady when she turned the doorknob.

It was locked.

"Just a moment," someone said hurriedly from the other side.

When the door popped open, Darian walked out with a cigarette clenched in her teeth, trailed by a ribbon of smoke.

"He's all yours," she said, bumping Avery as she walked past.

"Come in, Miss Norton." Dr. Yingling stubbed out his cigarette and tucked a brass Zippo lighter in his shirt pocket. "Have a seat, please."

The couch was the same as the one in Dr. Aslinn's office, but Yingling's felt more worn, the cushions less springy. As Avery sank in, her focus danced across the gilded degrees and paintings around her. While the majority were beautiful landscapes, mountain ranges and deserts, an oil painting of two young women in a skiff captivated Avery most. She'd never been to the mountains; she didn't care for the desert. But the ocean . . .

She wondered if she'd ever see that clear teal water again. Would she walk the stony beaches or feel the sea spray on her face as she inhaled a brisk island night? Would she ever again share it with Paul?

When Avery's focus returned to Dr. Yingling, he was staring at her. A lopsided smile creased his face as he said, "I take it you like my office."

"Dr. Aslinn had a secretary. Why don't you?"

"I don't like having anyone but trained therapists within earshot. How's your shoulder?

"Better. A little sore, but better."

"Enough to lose the sling?"

"I think so." Avery began sliding it off, but when she winced, Dr. Yingling stepped in to help her remove it.

"You were lucky to have only dislocated your shoulder. Some people end up with broken bones."

"Lucky me."

He tossed the sling onto his desk and leaned against the edge. "I understand why you don't like me. If I were in your situation, I probably wouldn't like me either. But you have to understand that I'm here to help you."

Her lip curled bitterly. "Does everyone in this place follow the same script? If you people wanted to help me, you would've released me ages ago."

"We'll release you when you're healthy."

"You mean when I accept the guilt for my mother's crimes."

He pursed his lips. "It's a little more complicated than that, but in essence . . . " Yingling crossed his arms over his chest. "Yes, we believe the recovery process can't even begin until the patient admits recovery is needed."

"The only recovery I'll need will be after I'm out of here, something to help me heal from the tortures of this place."

"Our intention isn't to torture you. We—"

Avery snarled. "If you say you 'only want to help me' one more time, I'm going to scream."

A smile crept up Dr. Yingling's cheek. "Go ahead. I'm used to it." He sat on the arm of the sofa, his shadow falling over her like oil. "What is it you hate so much about the hospital, Avery? What is it about the outside you think you're missing? I guarantee you're happier and healthier in here than you could ever be out there."

She scooted farther down the couch, offended. "You think I'm happy?"

"I think you could be, if you allowed yourself. But if you keep thinking of yourself as unjustly imprisoned, you'll never be happy. A stubborn mind doesn't evolve, my dear, which means it has no need for hope, nor love. Don't you see? Even people in bondage sing songs of freedom, but every song you sing is a requiem. You're addicted to your sorrow." Dr. Yingling moved from the sofa's edge to the cushion beside her. "I can give you comfort, Avery, or whatever you think you're missing. I can help you remember how it feels to be happy."

He leaned in so subtly she didn't notice how close he was until his face was inches away from hers.

"What are you doing?"

"Do you miss being touched? I often find that's what female patients miss most about the outside." Stroking her cheek, he whispered, "Do you miss the closeness, the tenderness? Do you miss the warmth of a man?"

Avery started to answer, but Dr. Yingling silenced her with a forceful kiss.

At first, she was too shocked to process what was happening, but when his lips tried to part hers, Avery pushed the doctor away and slapped him across the face.

"How dare you! You're disgusting!" she shrieked and scrambled to the door while Yingling rubbed his cheek.

Crooking an eyebrow at her, he said, "But it made you feel alive, didn't it?"

"It made me feel sick! How could you do that? You're a doctor, for God's sake!"

"Exactly. I'm a doctor. *Your* doctor. I say whether you're sane or insane, whether you stay or you go." He smiled as her jaw dropped. "So I'll ask you again: do we understand each other, Miss Norton?"

She shook her head, heavy with rage. "You can't be serious."

"My ward has the highest success rate in the hospital. You can win your freedom, but you have to play by my rules."

"What would I have to do?" she asked meekly, as her skin attempted to crawl off her bones.

"Everything I ask of you. And you don't have to worry if you don't know how to do something. I'm a good teacher."

A burning stream of bile crept up her throat and she gagged against the door.

"If you want, you can think about it and let me know your decision during our next appointment. Ask around if you have to. I'm certain your friends will recommend you play along."

"You mean you've done this with Flint? And Pam?"

"Pam, yes. Francine is indecisive like you, but she hasn't been here for long. She'll come around, just as I'm certain you will. You're a smart girl, Avery. Make the smart choice." He rose from the sofa, sat down at his desk, and folded his hands in front of him. "That's all for today."

She stared at him in stunned silence. When Dr. Yingling opened a folder and sifted through paperwork, she walked rigidly out of his office. Disoriented by shock and disgust, she took a wrong turn and ended up at a door marked "No Admittance." Curious, she opened it and faced a storage closet packed to the nines with large amber bottles. Hoping for something more interesting, she closed the door and started back to the ward with far less verve than she'd left it.

Back among her sour-faced peers, Avery felt more alone than ever. A nurse with a large ink stain on her uniform shuffled by, barely acknowledging Avery when she asked the location of her room. The nurse pointed her to room fourteen, which seemed as dismal as the others until she entered and found it more so. Her new roommate Darian was splayed out on one of the beds, her full lips curling into a fake smile.

"Well, if it isn't Miss Sloppy Seconds," she said in a sing-song snarl, then pointed to Avery's belongings on the other bed. "Your stuff's here."

"I don't know what you're talking about, but thanks, I guess," Avery murmured as she transferred her clothes to the dresser.

"Oh that's right," her new roommate continued. "You prefer being called Lizzie, don't you?"

Avery spun around to find Darian inches away, daring Avery to channel Faye again. And she was more than willing to comply. Though they stood eye to eye, she grew taller with her increasing anger until she felt like the tallest tree in an otherwise withered forest. The back of her head pounded, but her fury squeezed it into a tiny ball of flame that could spread and devour any woodland—starting with the insignificant tree wavering before her. Glaring at Darian, Avery snapped, "Back the fuck off," and the woman's head shriveled between her shoulders as she slunk out of the room.

When the pain in her skull softened to pleasure, Avery relished her victory. It disgusted her a bit, recalling her mother to scare someone into submission, but by God, it worked like a charm.

Flint entered, her head cocked as she confronted Avery's blank stare. "Are you all right?"

"No. No, I don't think I am."

Sitting together, it only took a moment of Flint's consoling for Avery's resolve to crack, and she collapsed against her shoulder.

"Did you—" Flint exhaled heavily. "Did Dr. Yingling—"

"No." She lifted her head and wiped away her tears. "But I have to, right?"

"You don't have to. I haven't."

"I know. He told me."

Flint's face screwed up to one side. "Isn't there supposed to be confidentiality between doctors and patients?"

"If there is, I doubt it's Dr. Yingling's highest priority." Dabbing tears from her cheeks, she exhaled heavily. "Are you going to do it?"

She swallowed hard. "I don't know yet."

"But you've never done it before, right? With another person, I mean."

"No. I've never done it before."

"Do you think you could do it with Dr. Yingling?"

Flint bounced off the bed and peered out the barred window. "I don't know. Could you?"

"No," Avery said resolutely. "But it's the only way I'm getting out of here, right?"

Looking over her shoulder, her eyes glittered at her friend. "It's not the only way."

"Flint, be serious. These people are never going to let me out."

"Unless . . ."

"Unless what?"

She turned around, her face serene. "I think you know."

Avery slid off the bed, her brow creased with doubt. "Unless I take the blame for the murders. Unless I let myself be 'rehabilitated.' Is that what you're thinking?"

Flint shrugged. "It doesn't have to be true. People used to do it all the time. I read about it. A long time ago, the King of England made everyone sign a contract saying they'd changed religions, but not everybody really changed. They just said it so he wouldn't banish or execute them. He could never take away their true beliefs."

"This isn't about beliefs. This is the truth. I'm innocent, and I refuse to lie about that." She raked her fingers across her scalp so hard, her nails created rows of fire that felt like they burned through her skull and blistered the surface of her brain. She could've sworn she exhaled a smoke when she said, "But I can't sleep with Dr. Yingling, either. I just can't."

Flint's focus returned to the window. "I guess we're lifers, huh?"

Avery spat, "To hell with that. I'm sane, and I don't deserve to be treated like this. Neither do you."

Her friend's face sagged to an expression of lament Avery hadn't seen before, and when she tried to comfort her, Flint pulled away.

"I'm not like you," she whispered. "I deserve to be here."

"That's not true. You've been my best friend for almost six years. I can't think of a time when anything you did made me feel unsafe."

She bit her lip. "I appreciate that. But how I act isn't how I think. It's an everyday struggle for me. And that's what it is, an act. The fire has a hold on me, and sometimes, I can't help myself. I only hope that when I turn down Dr. Yingling, he won't skimp on the treatment I need."

"How can you say that? You don't belong here."

"Yes, I do. I'm sick, and I knew it long before I was sent here," she said. "But I'm not crazy enough to think you should suffer through the same shit as me."

"Then help me," Avery said, grasping her friend's hand. "I need to get out. If what they said was true and Paul is back in Boston with Sophie, my mother will be coming for them. I know it."

She tried to pull away, but her friend gripped her tighter. "Avery, stop. You're scaring me."

"You can't be nearly as scared as I am. I've already lost my sister. I can't bear to lose Paul, too."

"I'm sorry, but if you won't lie, and if you won't sleep with Dr. Yingling, there's not much else you can do."

"There has to be a way. I can't stand another day in here."

"You have to."

"I won't!"

She released her friend so forcefully that Flint flew across the room, crashing against the other bed. Wilting to the floor, she stared up fearfully as Avery advanced on her.

"Tell me there's a chance. Tell me you'll help me if I find it."

Her chin trembling, Flint blinked. "Yes, of course I will."

Avery smiled and squeezed Flint's shoulder in gratitude. "Thank you. I promise you, Flint, I'll find a way. Then we can go anywhere. You, me, and Paul. We can start a new life somewhere no one knows us."

As Avery helped her stand, it appeared Flint had a response at the ready, but she didn't speak. She simply bowed her head and started out of the room.

"I'll think of something," Avery called after. "I'll get us out of here."

Flint stopped in her tracks and leaned against the doorframe. "I didn't believe you were a good person when you first came to Taunton," she said, turning slightly. "I admit it. I didn't believe you were innocent."

"It's all right."

"No, it's not. I assumed you were just as bad as the news said, as bad as the nurses warned us. But you assumed I was good from the beginning, and with everything you've learned about me, you still do. You were the only one who ever did that, and not just with me. You treat all the patients like they're in your situation: good people left to rot in this horrible place. For that kindness alone, I owe you." With her back to Avery again, she added, "This is the least I can do," and walked out.

Avery's brain sloshed with exhaustion. She crawled onto her new bed and stretched, aching for the stupor of sleep, but her mind sped with speculative plots, and her heart fluttered with the fantasy of freedom. She could nearly smell the sea, the crisp, obliging sea that would carry her away from the sorrows of her past. But somewhere beneath the salty aroma, the familiar scent of daylilies crept into Avery's brain. The ocean silt surrendered to the sky, the rabbits battled in hunger, and deep within, a garden grew in the dark.

CHAPTER TWENTY-TWO

AVERY TRIED TO maintain an air of confidence when Nurse Phillips summoned her for her next appointment with Dr. Yingling, but her legs turned rubbery on the march to his office. When the wobbles didn't desist, she clenched her jaw and focused on steadying each step as she repeated to herself, "I can't do it. I *won't* do it."

The ominous scent of cigarette smoke wafted down the hall and snaked under his office door as Avery stood in front, her forehead beaded with sweat. Hearing a soft moan, she pressed her ear to the door. When it opened a few moments later, Avery fell forward, but a pair of hands caught her. She was relieved they belonged to Flint instead of Dr. Yingling, but relief twisted to fear when she beheld her friend's splotchy red face. It looked like Flint had been crying, and when Avery saw Dr. Yingling sitting on the edge of his desk smoking a cigarette, she was afraid she knew why.

"Flint, you didn't . . . !"

She didn't answer. She lifted her chin with a sniffle and strode out of the office as Dr. Yingling crushed his cigarette in the ashtray.

Smiling, he pushed away from his desk. "I must say, you look lovely today, my dear. Like a raven with a broken wing."

"Thanks, I guess."

"Unfortunately, I have to cancel our session," he said, as he threw on a suit jacket. "Something came up, and I have to leave for Mass General. But don't worry, I'll double your time next week."

"You don't have to."

"I insist. Now, if you'll excuse me . . . " He shooed her from the office and pointed her back to the ward.

She obeyed, grateful, but oddly unfulfilled. It took a lot of energy preparing to refuse the doctor's advances, and she wanted it finished. Trudging back into the ward, she aimed for Flint's room.

Avery pressed herself against the door and rapped lightly. "It's me, Flint. May I come in?"

The knob twisted, and the door drifted open. Avery tiptoed in as Flint sat cross-legged on her bed, twisting her sleeves more manically than ever.

"Here, take it." Flint grunted and tossed a brass Zippo at Avery.

"What's this for?"

"Your escape," she said. "Start a big fire, and you'll be able to slip out during the hysteria."

Avery turned the lighter over in her hands, examining the flint and wheel as she shook her head. "I . . . I can't start a fire."

"You goddamn better!" The words resounded like thunder as the girl glared viciously. "After what I did to get that, you better make it worthwhile."

"What did you do?"

"Everything he asked," she whispered, her chin quivering. "But I did it for you."

Avery sat beside her, but Flint abandoned the bed and crossed the room to the window.

"I didn't ask you to do that. I never would."

"I know," she said. "And you also might've never found a way out of here. Just take the lighter and say thank you. It was awful carrying it back here without striking it."

"I do appreciate it, but I could've gotten matches from someone. You didn't need to do that for me."

"Matches go out easy," she said. "Zippos don't."

"I guess you're right."

"Trust me, I'm right."

She pocketed the Zippo, and Flint returned to the bed beside her. They sat in silence for a few moments while Avery's brain reeled with incendiary thoughts of freedom.

"How do I do it?" she finally asked. "What do I set on fire?"

Flint smirked. "I could give you a few suggestions."

The door flew open, and Pam strolled in. "Why do you guys look so serious?" She pushed the pillows off the other bed and flopped down.

"Dammit, Pam!" Flint whined as she collected the pillows. "You know Cheryl's obsessive-compulsive."

"I'm helping her work through her issues," she said with a chuckle. "What are you two talking about?"

"Sorry, Pam. It's a secret."

"So? I'm great at keeping secrets."

Flint tapped her chin and hummed. "That's true. I've never seen anyone keep a secret as long as Pam. We still have no idea why she's in here."

"And you never will," she said, crossing her arms over her chest. "See? I'm a pro."

"I don't know. I think if you want to know our secret, you have to tell us yours," Avery said.

"No way. I've kept it safe this long, and I'm not about to break my streak. Besides," she said, "how would telling you my secret prove what a great secret-keeper I am?"

"She has a point," Flint said, closing the door. "But you have to promise you won't say anything, even if you don't approve."

"Now I'm even more intrigued." Pam sat up straight on the bed, her legs crossed and hands gripping her knees. "All right, I promise."

"Say it like you mean it," Flint said.

"I do mean it! I really promise, okay? Jesus!"

Avery grinned and spoke as if delivering one of her mother's unquestionable sermons. "We're getting out of here. We're breaking out of Taunton."

Pam didn't flinch.

"Did you hear what I said?"

"Did *you* hear it?" she asked, scoffing. "Do you know how many times I've heard people say that since I was brought in? How many of those people do you think succeeded, Avery? Take one guess."

She grunted. "Not many."

"Not *any*. Some of them probably could have, I'll admit, but something held them back, kept them inside. It's the security these walls provide."

"Security?" Avery screeched. "Taunton is a prison!"

"No. It's a refuge," Pam said. "It's a sanctuary for all of us poor wretches with broken minds. It protects us from the judgment of the outside world and protects the outside world from our madness, but it also gives us the chance to live free."

Avery shook her head in disbelief. "What kind of freedom is there behind bars?

"The kind only a lucky few experience," she said. "It's true, we miss a lot of good things that normal people get out there, but we also miss the bad. Our only stresses and labors are internal. As children, we were cared for. We were educated, protected—"

"Frozen, drugged, shocked . . ."

"For our own good," Pam said.

"You can't really believe that. They were horrible to us."

Flint said, "No, Avery," and touched her friend's hand. "They weren't."

She pulled away, her head aching and nauseated stomach sailing up and down like a carousel horse. "How can you say that? Especially after what Dr. Yingling did."

"It was unpleasant," Flint said, "but things will be better for me now. I'll get better care, better treatment."

"You two are crazy!" Avery wailed. "How could you prefer being locked up to being free?"

"You just answered your own question. We're crazy," Pam said. "Just because you think you're not, don't deny us the progress we've made in admitting we are." Her voice was steady, and more sincere than Avery had ever heard it. Arching an eyebrow, she added, "Out of curiosity, how do you plan to escape?"

"A fire."

Pam's focus shot to Flint. "I guess I don't have to ask who came up with that idea. In that case, I can help you."

"There's no need. She can just burn her sheets," Flint said.

"Someone would put that fire out in a minute. You'll need much longer than that."

"What do you suggest?"

"There's a storage room not too far from Dr. Yingling's office. It would be the perfect place to start a fire."

Avery gasped. "I know that room! I found it a few days ago. But how will that help?"

"I'll show you."

"Tonight?"

Pam chortled. "And be caught at the scene of the crime? No thanks. Once was enough for me." She shook her head and slipped from the bed. "I'll show you now. Then you're on your own."

"Do you mind if I stay?" Flint curled up under her covers. "I'm exhausted."

"You've done enough," Avery said, pulling a blanket over her friend. "Get some rest before tonight."

As she and Pam exited Flint's room, Pam muttered, "She won't need it," and closed the door.

"What do you mean by that?"

"Forget it. Let's get this over with."

When they neared the Nurses' Station, Avery whispered, "How do we get past Nurse Phillips?"

"If you were sticking around, I'd say you have a lot to learn," Pam said. "This ward ain't like the last one, Lizzie."

Avery groaned. "You know how much I hate that name."

"Yes. Yes, I do."

Pam slid past Nurse Phillips's desk and through the

exit with shocking ease, beckoning Avery to follow. Once she was through, Pam grabbed her arm and towed her down the hall before the guards in the adjoining corridors could spot them. They dashed down the path to Dr. Yingling's office, breezed past his sanctum, and pushed open the closet door to reveal the towers of amber bottles filling the room.

"It's isopropyl alcohol," Pam said. "Flammable as all get out."

Avery entered, beholding the amber forest ripe for torching and, for a moment, understood Flint's compulsions completely. Facing Pam again, she wrinkled her brow.

"Why are you helping me?"

Pam gnawed on her bottom lip and licked away the resulting blood. "Because I was the Lizzie before you. I was the one who made the papers. What you're accused of doing, I actually did."

"Who did you kill?"

Ignoring her, Pam unscrewed the cap from a bottle of isopropyl alcohol in the back of the left corner row. "It should be good to go by tonight, but I'd ask Flint when you get back. This isn't my area of expertise."

She tried to breeze out of the closet, but Avery latched onto her arm. "Pam, you don't have to stay here. You can come with us."

With a snort, Pam shook her head. "I don't know what kind of sunshine and roses you think awaits you out there, Avery, but we're not the same. We might be in here for a similar reason, but my problems are nothing like the mess you've got going on. Out there, and—" She twiddled her fingers at Avery's head. " . . . in there. Whether this works tonight or not, I wish you the best of luck with all that."

"Are you sure? We could all keep each other safe."

"When you say 'all,' you don't mean Flint, do you?"

"Of course."

"Oh, honey, you're in for a rude awakening."

"She's my best friend, and she's coming with me. If you were smart, you would too."

She rolled her eyes and skittered to the ward entrance, her back flat against the wall. When Avery joined her side, she whispered, "If you were smart, you wouldn't ask us. You'd leave us out of it completely, Lizzie."

She gave the all-clear, and they slipped back into the ward, right under Nurse Phillips's nose.

"You'll see. Flint wants freedom just as much as I do," Avery said.

"And what about everyone else? What about the people who don't know this place is going up in flames tonight?" Pam's voice changed as she walked ahead of her, each word sounding more like Avery's mother.

"You might not be a murderer yet," Faye Norton whispered to her mind, "but you will be before the night ends."

Avery could accept it as a mere hallucination, but it stuck in her like a thorn that had been sweating poison into her brain for years. She imagined the fire rousing patients from sleep—the fear, the chaos—and her gut tightened.

But it was too late to turn back. She didn't *want* to turn back. With each day that Taunton drove her a little madder, it also drove a bigger wedge between Avery and her promise to Natalie. Whatever happened to the other patients, Avery couldn't allow her mother to get to Paul and Sophie.

As she surveyed the ward, she recalled what she could of the last six years. There were obliging holes, moments when she surmised her brain shut down to protect her. The chunks she recalled were torturous enough, anyway. But each memory, distinct or distant, originated with one ghastly accusation. When Faye shifted the blame to Avery, she'd declared war on her daughter. Young and afraid, Avery didn't have the power to do anything about it then, but like Dr. Yingling was so fond of telling her, she wasn't a child anymore. Once Taunton was burning, she would be free, and Faye's luck would run out.

As such terrifying exhilarations percolated in her veins, she found she couldn't stop fidgeting during the group counseling session that day. Her hand lived in her pocket during the meeting, turning the Zippo over and over, delighting in how something so smooth and cold could wreak such irreparable hell.

Flint leaned over and whispered, "If I have to take that away from you, you're not getting it back."

She stopped fidgeting, squeezed the lighter in her fist, and lifted her head to find the circle of patients staring at her.

"Avery, I think it's time for you to share with the group," Nurse Foster said.

She shook her head. "No thanks. I've said everything a million times before."

"Not to us. Maybe if the group knew you better, a lot of the hostile looks you're receiving right now would disappear."

"They can be as hostile as they want; it doesn't bother me anymore. I know what I did and didn't do, and so do the people who really care about me. The rest of you claim to listen, but you never hear a word I say. You won't even entertain the notion that I've been wrongfully convicted. The more I protest my innocence, the crazier I sound."

Meg grunted. "Well, no shit."

"And that's exactly why I don't care. You want to say I'm crazy? Okay, I'm crazy. You want to call me a lifer? Fine, I'm a lifer. I'm done having my story disputed. If listening to your insults and bullshit theories is what passes for progress, to hell with progress."

The nurse sighed. "I'm sorry you feel that way, Avery."

"Don't. Save your pity for someone who really needs it."

"Dr. Yingling will be back on Monday," Foster said, jotting on her notepad, "and I'm going to suggest he schedule an immediate session with you. He should hear everything you're saying."

"It won't make a lick of difference, but go ahead and schedule the appointment if you feel like wasting the ink."

She pointed her pen at Avery and narrowed her gaze. "You need a serious attitude adjustment, missy. Your total disregard for the treatment process—well, it just burns me up!"

Chuckling, she said, "If you think you're burned up now, just wait."

When the group disbanded, Avery returned to her room and lay on her bed, imagining the night to come. Darian followed her in, looking to whip her into an argument, but Avery simply lifted her head from her pillow and glowered the girl into retreat. It was getting easy to do. Maybe too easy.

She knew she had a long night ahead and needed rest, but she couldn't calm her mind enough to sleep. A sweet and sour distillation of excitement and fear sloshed in her skull, sounding like a sea of whispers. The voices eventually blended into comforting white noise that, while still too distracting to coax her into sleep, assured her that she and Paul would be together soon.

Time passed slowly as if mocking her impatience, but when the hour hand crawled to eleven, a smile crept up her face, and she slid out of bed. Exiting the room quietly, she tiptoed across the moon-striped ward to the nurses' station, where she found Flint crouched in the shadows.

Her eyes glinted wild, wet with tears when Avery scooted up beside her.

"How long have you been here?"

"A while," Flint whispered. "I was too excited to sleep."

"I know what you mean."

"No, you don't," she muttered. When Avery shot her a puzzled look, she pulled a tiny smile and crawled for the exit.

They dashed down the dim hallways, ducking office windows and patrolling guards, until they reached the storage closet. When Avery opened the door, a cloud of fumes slapped her and Flint in the face, causing them to recoil with muffled gags.

The shock was brief, however, for the aroma also bore a sweetness that exhilarated the girls for different reasons.

Avery cleared her lungs, dug the lighter out of her pocket and flipped it open. With her finger positioned on the wheel, she looked to Flint, whose cheeks flushed as she stared at the lighter.

Hands clasped in prayer and voice trembling with hope, she whispered, "May I do it?"

She handed over the Zippo, and Flint caressed it like a hunk of gold.

"Are you ready?"

Avery strode into the closet's reeking haze and kicked over one of the bottles of isopropyl. It smashed, flooding the floor and tripling the cloying stench. "I've been ready for six years."

Flint said, "I doubt that was necessary," then smirked. "But I won't scold you for it."

The girls pressed their backs to the opposing wall and, with a grin, Flint flicked the Zippo's thumbwheel. The flame sprung to life, instantly captivating her. Avery whispered her name, and as if saying goodbye to a lifelong friend, Flint sniffled sadly and slid the lighter across the floor into the room.

The puddle instantly caught fire, but Flint didn't move. The growing flames enthralled her so completely Avery had to haul her away from the closet—seconds before it burst into an inferno that swelled out into the corridor.

Avery screamed as she dragged her friend like a ragdoll down the halls, slamming doors shut behind them. She shouted for Flint to move faster, but it felt like her friend was pulling in the opposite direction, trying to slow her down. As they rounded a corner, Patrick the orderly was crossing the hall, and they crashed into him with a shriek.

Face paling, he stammered, "What are you two doing down here?"

"Thank God, you're here! There's a fire near Dr. Yingling's office," Avery squealed.

"You don't really expect me to believe that, do you? If there was a fire, Francine would be running *towards* it, not away." He chortled, but when the fire alarm clanged out an urgent warning, Avery flashed him a vindictive smile.

The alarm echoed in the screams of Taunton patients and employees alike. They soon appeared in the hall, running frantically past the trio.

"Where's the fire?" Patrick asked a fleeing nurse.

"The western wing and spreading fast," the nurse said. "The women's ward is already gone."

Flint grasped Avery's arm. "The whole ward? Avery, all those people . . ."

Avery pretended not to hear her; she zeroed in on a flock of patients bolting down the stairs and wondered how quickly she and Flint could disappear among them.

"Avery, are you listening?"

She didn't answer. She blinked wildly and grabbed the orderly's sleeve. "There could be people trapped in there, Patrick. You have to help them."

"You two go down to the lobby and wait." With that, Patrick leapt into the oncoming river of people and vanished in the smoke.

"Let's go, Flint." Avery grabbed her hand, but Flint shook her off. "What's wrong?"

"The western wards are gone. People we knew are gone, and you just sent Patrick in there. You've spent the past six years trying to prove you're not a murderer, but you just killed so many more people than you were accused of before."

"That's just my mother talking," Avery said.

"What? No, it's not. It's me. It's the person who's had faith in you all these years."

"Flint, this was your idea!"

She shook her head. "A burning bed was my idea. Not this."

"We don't have time to argue right now. We have to move." Avery pulled on Flint again, but the girl wouldn't budge. "Please, we have to go. The fire is close. I can feel it."

"Me too." Her voice dripped with sorrow, but the tone turned blissful when she added, "Isn't it wonderful?"

"Please don't do this," Avery said, wiping sweat from her face. "It's getting so hot."

"I'm sorry, Avery, I can't go with you."

"What do you mean? The fire—"

"The fire is why I'm staying," she said. "But please don't think it's because of you. It was always going to be this way. It's me. I'm sick."

Avery's chest stung with grief, and tears spilled down her cheeks. "No, Flint—*Francine*—please don't do this. You're my best friend. I can't leave you behind."

"You don't have a choice."

The hall was filling with smoke as the fire drew nearer: something that filled one girl with despair and the other with joy.

Flint tightened her jaw. "You have to go now."

"No, I'm not leaving without you."

"I belong here," she said. "Forever."

Flint's smile was so wide, so perfectly steady, that Avery couldn't deny she was looking upon true happiness. As flames poured into the corridor, her bliss increased, and Avery whimpered in surrender. She turned from her friend in fear, but love spun her back around. Throwing herself at Flint, she embraced her tighter than ever.

"You're not crazy," she said. "Not even now." Avery kissed Flint's forehead and whispered, "But I still wish I could save you."

"I'm not the one who needs saving." Glancing back at the approaching flames, she said, "I'm just a girl who wants to know what it's like inside."

"I could guess for you," Avery said.

"And you'd be wrong. Whatever it is to you, it would

be the opposite for me. It's my freedom. It's my future. Yours is still waiting."

Avery kissed her friend again before pulling away in a fit of tears. She hurled herself through the door at the end of the hall, then spun around and pressed her hands against the glass. Their focus connected, and Francine called to her over the roar of the fire.

"I'll speak for you, Avery! I'll tell them why you had to do this! I'll make them understand!"

The flames rolled over Flint like a furious tidal wave, instantly devouring her hair. Her clothes caught fire next, and her flesh soon followed, but she stood all the while with her arms open and a smile the inferno could never burn away.

Smoke ballooned and burned in Avery's lungs as she bolted down the stairs into the lobby, where panicked people clustered near reception. Nurses held their patients close and stroked their hair while the frenzied doctors formulated a plan to rescue the stragglers. There were others, however, who gave the stationary people nary a glance before flying past them and out the front doors. Avery followed suit, slipping through the hordes, and out into the kindled night. She inhaled the air of freedom, but it didn't match the satisfaction she'd imagined. The world she'd once known had a new smell now, worse than the electroshock room. And it was all Avery Norton's fault.

She sprinted from Taunton Hospital, and the screams chased after. Her belly twisted with acrid regret, but she didn't falter. She ran until she reached the outlying gate, stopping first to catch her breath, then to behold her sickening work. Frantic figures appeared between fiery waves on the hospital's upper levels. They howled as they tried to break the glass and squeeze their bodies through the barred windows, keener to jump than burn, but the screeching terror increased abruptly as the blaze took a massive bite out of the building's skeleton and tilted the west wing toward the earth. With a sizzling squeal, the wing collapsed, followed by flaming hunks of wood and bone crashing to the ground like renegade rockets in the night. Avery wailed apologies, but the discordant sound of snapping wood and breaking glass cut her off and called her attention to Taunton's apex, where the fire-engulfed cupola melted through the roof.

Avery shrieked to the people still clustered in the lobby. "Run! The roof is collapsing!"

But they couldn't hear her, and very few budged from the danger zone as the cupola sank lower and lower. She gritted her teeth and ran back to warn them, but she only gained a few meters before the cupola's last supports gave way. Floor by floor, the blazing dome smashed through the hospital's weakened levels and into the lobby with a devastating crash.

Like the hospital itself, Avery's strength thinned to nothing, and she buckled to the ground. Without a second thought, she clamped her hands together and began to pray. It had been many years, but the prayers came to her as effortlessly as they had when she was young, when her mother taught her about God and the Virgin Mary and how they'd blessed Avery more than any other of their children.

Burning flesh was not a blessing. Flint's sacrifice was not a blessing. And yet, as she pleaded to the heavens for forgiveness, gratitude washed over her and doused the flames of remorse. She was well into the Lord's Prayer when a fleeing patient rushed by and knocked her over. Strokes of red and orange lit the fellow escapee's face, twisting her expression into a grimace as she looked down on Avery.

"I hope you're thanking Him," Pam said.

Avery held her fists to her heart and whispered, "I was."

Pam offered a small wave as she dashed away, disappearing into the dark, but her words stayed with Avery. As she collected her strength and continued her flight from Taunton Asylum, as the fire engines drew close and her prison became a dancing red dot in the distance, her mind remained focused on that singular feeling.

All those people—innocent men, women, and children—now dead, because of her. And she was thankful, and so very blessed.

CHAPTER TWENTY-THREE

A VERY SPENT THE night curled up beneath a barberry bush ten miles from Taunton Asylum. She figured the police would be sweeping the area, so she didn't allow herself to slumber too deeply. Every time her mind drifted off, it resurrected the terrified screams of the people she'd sentenced to death, and she snapped back to reality.

But they were there, too. Flint, most of all. Avery's gut ached knowing her truest friend in Taunton had both ignited and nourished the fire that liberated her—liberated them both, she supposed, since Flint had chosen to surrender to her sickness. A sickness Avery always denied.

Flint was right about the way she viewed her: like someone just as unfairly committed. But in the end, Flint deserved to be in the asylum. She *wanted* to be there, and Avery couldn't understand why. She couldn't imagine being so sick she'd want anything the hospital had to offer, or that she'd do something so terrible to keep from leaving.

But what had Avery done to ensure she didn't spend one more day there? Wasn't that sick and terrible, too? Was it her love for Paul or her hate for Faye that made her so ravenous for escape that she left a trail of carnage?

She didn't allow herself to ponder it further. As soon as Paul popped into her head, he stayed there. Even with her severe exhaustion, she reveled in fantasy and ached for the moment he would hold her again. Tighter, deeper, forever.

She waited until the alarms died and all the world went

silent, and as she crawled out from under the barberry bush, the sun rose to greet her.

It was warmer than ever, bathing her in gold as she stretched her body and wriggled her fingers to the sky. She couldn't take the time she wanted to absorb it; it would have to wait until she reached Paul. But once they were together, once she knew Sophie was safe, she would absorb it all. She would worship the sun and stars, the pebble beaches and ocean tides, the way they all deserved. And she'd allow them to worship her in kind.

For now, she had to keep moving.

Avery tidied herself up as best she could. She wiped the ash off her face and smoothed her hair, but her shirt was torn, and rosy abrasions still peppered her body, so she wasn't shocked when cars zipped by without slowing. When a Chevrolet Bel Air Convertible finally pulled over, she scuttled to the vehicle with outpourings of gratitude. But as the young woman behind the wheel absorbed the state of the hitchhiker, her brow wrinkled in regret.

"Are you all right?" she asked.

"I was in an accident," Avery said frantically. "My tire blew, and I ran off the road. Please, if you could drive me into the city, I'd really appreciate it."

"You're not a psycho killer, are you?" Humor flickered across the driver's face, and Avery forced a chuckle.

"Not that I recall."

The young woman bopped her head at the door, and Avery thanked her as she slid into the passenger seat. As she steered back onto the road, she said, "I'm Olive, by the way. Is there somewhere in particular you need to go?"

"I was on my way to surprise my friend Paul. I haven't seen him in years. Actually," Avery said, massaging her aching neck," I don't even know where he lives. I was going to look him up once I got to town."

"What about your car?"

"Once I find him, I'll get a tow truck. But I don't want to think about it for now. I'm too sore."

"Are you sure you don't want me to take you to a hospital?"

"No!" She rolled her shoulder and groaned. "I'm fine, I'm just being dramatic."

"It's all right if you just want to lean back and close your eyes for a bit. It's still about a half hour until we reach Boston."

Avery exhaled in gratitude and Olive turned on the radio.

Elvis Presley's velvety voice washed over Avery as she sank into the vinyl seat. She knew she couldn't let herself fall too hard, but after a few miles of travel, she felt powerless to stop it.

The next thing she knew, she jolted awake. The car was stopped on the side of the road, the radio blaring, and Olive was staring at her with both hands clenched around the handle of a pocketknife.

"What's going on?" Avery asked.

The radio crackled, and the WBZ newscaster continued his broadcast. "She should be considered armed and dangerous. Again, all motorists should be on alert for an eighteen-year-old girl with black hair traveling by foot. It is believed that she is the cause of the fire at Taunton State Hospital that led to the escape of fifteen other patients and the deaths of dozens more. We'll keep you updated as this story progresses."

Olive trembled as she brandished the knife. "Are you her? Avery Norton, the girl who burned down that hospital? The girl who killed all those people on Martha's Vineyard?"

Avery lifted her hands in surrender. "I don't want to hurt you."

"Are you her?"

"Yes, and no."

She swiped the blade at Avery and snarled. "Get out of my car."

"I just need a ride. My name *is* Avery Norton, but I didn't kill anyone. Please, you have to take me to Boston."

"I told you to get out!" Olive barked.

She lunged with the blade again, but Avery dodged it and scrambled out of the car. Discarded on the roadside, her brain pounding and hands in the air, she whimpered.

"I wasn't going to hurt you."

Her intentions didn't matter; there was no appealing to Olive. The young woman was gone before her car pealed out onto the highway.

The city was in sight, and Avery was too. Word was out, a police car would pass before long, and every moment she spent exposed to traffic was another moment that could doom her. She tore a strip of fabric from her sleeve and tied her hair back, but she knew she was fooling herself with any disguise. Her headache spread, chapping every nerve in her body, and making it feel like her bones were splintered and scraping her muscles from the inside out. But thoughts of Paul and Sophie slammed her feet over and over along the highway, through the ditches, down the streets, and into the first diner she saw.

She located the phone directory and scanned for Paul's name.

Dillon, Paul. 1400 East 3rd Street, Apartment #523.

A load of fiery bricks tumbled off Avery's shoulders as she collapsed against the wall with a grateful sob. She had miles to go, but at least she had a destination. Grabbing a coat from the rack by the diner door, she pulled up the hood and rushed down the street. By the time she was climbing the stairs to Paul's apartment, Avery was glazed in sweat and near delirious with exhaustion. Her stomach twisted into quivering knots, and her hand was a wet sponge of anxiety when she knocked on the door to #523.

There were footsteps, soft voices, and with a series of clicks, the door opened.

Avery's excitement crescendoed like music, but at the height of the harmony, a woman answered the door, and it felt like her joy jumped off a cliff into a sea of dread. The woman's face was turned away as she called Paul's name down the hall behind her, but it didn't matter. It didn't even matter that she looked nothing like Faye. In Avery's mind, she was once again too late. Her mother was still three steps ahead of her, destroying any chance her daughter had for happiness.

The young woman turned to the door again, her face soft and warm as an island morning, and Avery clutched her racing heart.

"You're not her," she panted.

The woman at the door flinched. "Can I help you?"

"I'm Av—I'm here to see Paul Dillon. I'm here to—" Avery looked past the woman, down the hall, and saw a man frozen, his blue eyes glittering.

"Avery?" He moved slowly and rigidly, his mystification increasing as he neared. "Avery, is it really you?"

Paul Dillon stood before her as beautiful as ever, lustrous and strong, but the deep pits of disbelief in his eyes chilled Avery to the bone. She didn't move from the doorway, unable to set her filthy feet inside his home without him welcoming her in. She felt like a vampire on the threshold, thinking Paul's doubt would keep her in the hallway forever, but just as she contemplated retreat, he rushed forward and closed his arms around her. He whooped in exultation as he lifted her up and spun her, giving her what felt like a thousand kisses in ten seconds.

"I've been praying you'd come," he said, wiping remnant ash off her forehead. "Ever since I heard what happened."

Despite her grimy appearance, Paul looked at her like she was a flawless gem. The feeling was alien in her heart, swelling and building an undeniable, new longing. She wanted to kiss him passionately, to peel off his shirt and dig her fingernails into his skin, but when the unfamiliar woman closed the door, Avery backed away. She half-expected to earn a dose of vitamins for daring to touch him.

Glancing at the woman, she whispered, "I'm not interrupting anything, am I?"

"Not at all," Paul said. "Avery, this is Anna Mulberry, Sophie's nanny."

Avery extended a filthy hand, and Anna's nose scrunched in disgust as she hesitantly shook it.

"Nice to meet you," she said, covertly wiping her hand on her skirt. "I'm going to put Sophie down, then I'll leave you two alone."

Once Anna shuffled down the hall, Paul embraced Avery again. His arms enfolded her so tight, she could barely catch a full breath, which bothered her less than the fact that she probably stank to high heaven. Burying her face in his neck, she tried to focus on his scent instead. It was sweet and spicy at the same time, with a hint of natural musk that smelled far nicer coming off of him than the pubescent girls of Taunton's juvenile ward, and something pulsated deep inside her. She'd felt it before, but never so intensely, and never knowing she had the freedom to do something about it.

His cheeks were bright red when he released her and turned to the kitchen. "I think I need a drink. Would you like one?"

"Sure."

While he washed two glasses, Avery caught her reflection in a clock face and recoiled at her messy appearance. She combed her bangs with dirty fingernails, improving them in theory only before Paul set a cold bottle of Chablis on the dining table.

"Is wine okay?"

She shrugged. "I think so? I've never—"

He gasped, his hand flying to his mouth. "I'm so sorry. I wasn't thinking."

"It's okay, really."

"I guess there's lots of things you haven't tried," he said, as he poured the wine.

"I guess so." She smiled sheepishly, and the blush in his cheeks spread to the rest of his face, making his eyes blaze even brighter.

Clinking his glass against hers, he said, "To the future."

She whispered it back, but she wanted to shout it. She wanted to sing it out so loud her voice would scour the last few years from everyone's memories. If she could do that, she'd stop lamenting everything she'd missed out on, stop obsessing about the tortures of Taunton and the puzzle pieces she was never able to force into fitting. She'd still go after Faye for what she'd done, but it wouldn't be for her. It would be for Natalie and their dad, and all those poor people who had the misfortune of looking like mismatched rabbits. But she didn't have the volume to shout, nor the energy to sing.

She lifted the glass to her lips. Erasing her own for the next few hours would have to do.

The crisp white wine was more aromatic when it hit her tongue, flooding her senses with sweet yet floral flavors that confused and titillated her. But although it quenched her thirst, the dry aftertaste roused it again. She licked her lips and hummed as another gulp burned cold down her throat.

Paul and Avery didn't speak. As they drank, they savored the silent existence of one another. In all their time apart, he'd never left her heart, but that version of him felt more like a ghost than a real person, haunting her with the fear that the boy she loved didn't exist anymore. Or perhaps he never had. When Dr. Aslinn's therapy had its strongest hold on her, and he'd convinced her she'd hallucinated the good parts of her life to block out the evil she'd done, she believed Paul was a hallucination, too.

As she gazed into his piercing eyes, she knew he wasn't a figment, but he also wasn't the boy she'd fallen in love with all those years ago. The ghost had vanished, leaving behind a living, breathing man she didn't know—a father, a widower—but she wanted to learn as much as possible. Because it *was* possible now, and based on the way they drew closer and closer together, their bodies knew it.

Anna Mulberry strode into the kitchen. "She's asleep. Is there anything else you need?"

"No, thank you, Anna."

She hummed, giving Paul's visitor a curious once-over as she threw on her coat. The moment the door closed, Avery sighed in relief.

"You don't think she'll tell anyone, will she?"

Paul didn't respond. He took the wine glass from Avery's hand and cupped her face. A multitude of fears swarmed her thoughts, but when Paul kissed her hungrily, she melted against him, and her thoughts turned amorous. Even so, when his hand moved up her side and against her breast, she pulled away.

"I'm sorry." Her head dropped in embarrassment. "I don't—this is all new to me."

"Hey," he said, lifting her chin. "I understand completely. We can go slow. I'm in no rush."

"I am," she said, squeezing his thigh. "I don't want to waste any more time. But not like this. I'm all dirty."

"Really? I didn't notice." He kissed her neck, but when she winced in pain, he apologized. "Oh my God, Avery, you're hurt. Are those burns?"

She hitched her shoulders to her ears. "Some."

Sitting back, he clenched his jaw. "Is it true what they're saying? Did you start the fire at the hospital?"

"It wasn't my idea, and I didn't light it, but . . . yes, it started because of me. I needed to get out, and Flint—" Her voice caught in her throat, the words barely squeaking free. "She helped me. She's the reason I'm here right now, with you."

"You don't have to talk about it. Take as much time as you need." He refilled her wine glass, handed it back, and smiled. "I'm going to draw you a bath. Just relax and try not to think about that place."

But the moment Paul left for the bathroom, a thousand memories of Taunton Hospital hijacked her mind. There was little room for anything else; even more than double the years on the island couldn't compete. She barely recalled how her life used to be, when days of happiness and safety didn't seem like a silly fantasy; her early childhood was especially difficult to conjure. Doubt warped the memories of her father and delivered them as crumpled notions peppered with cigarette burns. Natalie was easier to find, but her death tied sandbags of sorrow to her memory, dragging her deeper into her sister's subconscious.

Paul sat on the tub's edge, scissoring his fingers under the running water as Avery approached the bathroom. A warble from the end of the hall caught her attention, and she narrowed her focus on the peach-colored bassinet in the bedroom. When she glanced at Paul, he bopped his head with a smile, urging her on, and her heart thudded as she neared her niece.

Gazing down at Sophie in enchantment, Avery's eyes filled with tears. Her little niece was looking all around, burbling as she kicked and punched the air. Then, her focus found her aunt in the colorful fog of life, and Avery understood with perfect clarity the concept of love at first sight.

But a startling jealousy soon crept into her mind. Sophie had her father's eyes, but Natalie was everywhere else. Avery was glad she could see her there, to remind her every day of her beautiful sister; she couldn't help wondering, though, what Sophie would look like if she were Avery's daughter. While Natalie's influence softened the robust features Paul had given her, she thought hers might've turned the girl to cold, onyx stone. And it might've been true—maybe someday she'd know for sure—but one thing was certain: Avery's features would've saved Sophie from being the perfect likeness of Faye Norton.

Her grandmother had to love the hell out of seeing herself in the baby's face. It was no wonder she wanted to get her hands on her so badly.

"Your bath is ready."

She flinched when he pressed his chest to her back, but by the time he'd slid his hands over her shoulders, down her arms, and folded his fingers between hers, Avery was calm again. She turned slowly, readjusting her grip on his hands as he led her from the bedroom.

Steam wafted into the hall, immersing Avery in a dream-world she'd thought might never come true. But here it was, better than she'd imagined. Here he was, pulling her through the curtain of fog to the clean, warm water. He stood her at the edge of the bathtub, squeezed her hands once more, and said, "Holler if you need anything."

He turned to leave, and she grabbed onto him.

"Please don't go. I can't be—" When her face trembled with rising grief, he uncurled his hand tenderly against her cheek. She exhaled the tightness in her chest and whispered, "I don't want to be alone."

"I'll stay as long as you want," he said.

She smiled and let down her shaggy black hair. First raking her itchy scalp with her nails, she combed out her tangled locks. She tried not to look at her reflection for fear it was worse than she imagined, but not a trace of judgement crossed his face. With her gaze locked to his, Avery lifted her blouse over her head. He watched her in hushed devotion, and once she'd shed her last stitch of clothing, he took her hand gently and helped her into the water.

Her wounds stung as the heat swallowed her body, but she relished the pain. She could've never stretched out like that in Taunton, or enjoyed the feeling of bubbles building a honeycombed dome on her chest.

Dipping her head back, she ran her fingers over her scalp again like she could scrape out every sickening thought. She washed the dirt from her burns like she hadn't set a hospital ablaze. She probably should've acted shier about being naked in front of him, but she didn't see the point; after years of supervised baths, ice and otherwise, she was more bashful about the ECT scabs on her temples than her body. Or maybe it was because he wasn't focusing on her body.

He shook a shampoo bottle. "Want some help?"

Avery splashed the water in delight, and he squeezed the shampoo onto his palm.

"I know why you're here," he said, working it into her hair. "You came to warn me about your mom. You came to protect Sophie. And I respect that. But the police have been by twice already. You took an enormous risk."

"It's already worth the risk," she said. "But I didn't just come here for Sophie. There's another reason."

He leaned her back and washed the shampoo from her hair. "Is it that you love me?"

She popped up, sputtering, wiping the water from her face. "I . . . um . . . well . . . do you love *me*?"

Soap dripped thick down Avery's chin, and Paul thumbed it away with a chuckle. "You're damned right I do."

She grinned as she submerged herself in the bathwater and flexed her toes against the faucet. "This water feels so good, so clean. I always felt dirtier after a bath at Taunton."

"You don't have to talk about that."

"How can I not? It's all I know."

"What about us?" he said. "Just think about you and me running around in the summertime, scaling fences and gingerbread houses and conquering whatever dared stand against us."

Avery glided her fingers over an abrasion on her knee. The scab softened and vanished to a red ribbon adrift in the waves. "Because it makes me obsess over what I've lost and mourn what we could've been by now."

"What if we could start over? You, me, and Sophie," Paul said. "What if we could go somewhere new and give ourselves a second chance?"

Avery sat up in the tub and pulled her legs to her chest. As the water sloshed back and forth, licking her thighs with foam, her heart was a hummingbird. Elation made her feel weightless, like if she let go of her knees she'd float right to the surface.

"I want so badly to believe that's possible. I want so badly to believe I can forget the past."

"Then we will. We'll leave Boston. We'll leave Massachusetts. Hell, we'll leave America if you want."

"How?"

"My parents have a boat on the island. We can sail away and never come back."

Avery shook her head. "We can't go back there. Someone else might recognize me. My mother—"

"You could disguise yourself. I have some of Natalie's clothes . . ."

Avery whimpered and dropped her hands so emphatically she splashed water in Paul's eyes. "No, I couldn't. It's bad enough that I'm here, with you, with her baby . . ."

She folded over her knees, the hummingbird more like one of the sandbags around Natalie's ankles as she tried to steady her clipped breath.

"I'm sorry. I didn't mean to upset you," he said, running his hand over her slippery back. "I'll get you some clothes tomorrow."

She lifted her head. "Why are you being so nice to me? You're acting like nothing's changed. You're acting like I'm here on a weekend getaway."

"Nothing will ever change the way I feel about you. Call me stupid, call me a freak, but I've always known the feelings between us were real. Eternal too. I never gave up on us, Avery, because I've always believed we'd get you out. Actually, *that* was stupid. I should've always known you'd get yourself out."

He leaned in to kiss her, but she dodged his lips and stood up in the tub. Water cascaded down her body, and Paul couldn't resist watching the droplets roll and ride her curves back to the bath. When he met her eyes again, she whispered, "I love you, too, you know. And I want you."

His hands skated up her slick legs and hips and arms as he stood to face her. "Me too. But I wouldn't think of doing anything you're not ready for."

"What makes you think I'm not ready?"

"I don't know. Maybe because I'm not sure *I'm* ready anymore."

Avery was at once very aware of her nudity. She started to cover herself but stopped when he cupped her face with both hands.

"Please don't misunderstand me. I love you, I want you, I'm all yours, but you have to admit, we're basically strangers."

"Good," she said, curling her hands over his and pulling them to her heart. "That's exactly how I want it for our do-over. I want to learn everything about you." When she stepped out of the tub, Paul enfolded her in a towel. Savoring the warmth flowing through them both, she tilted her chin to him, voice strained. "But our pasts will always be there. We can bury what happened—and maybe we'd be so happy we really would forget for a while— but it will still be there, in our souls, poisoning whatever might bloom between us."

He scoffed. "I have to be honest, I'm not loving the gardening metaphors."

"*That*," she said, retreating a few steps and pulling the towel tight. "That's why we'll never be strangers. You'll never be able to look at me and not see a dumb kid duped by her mother, or maybe even a convicted murderer."

He approached cautiously and waited for her to smile in consent before he kissed her collar bone. "Maybe not. But I can promise to try. Can you make the same promise? Do you think you'll ever forgive me for what happened with Natalie?"

"I forgave you both for that long ago." When he arched an eyebrow, she crinkled her nose and bobbed her head from side to side. "Okay, I still feel a little strange about it, but I'm not angry or anything. Natalie insisted it was an accident, that you only married for appearances, and I believed her. I don't hold either of you responsible. And knowing something so beautiful came from it . . . " She tiptoed to the door and looked around the corner to the bassinet. When Paul took her hand, they walked down the hall to Sophie. Looking down on her, breathing her in, Avery said, "How could anyone hold a grudge about the magic that made Sophie? Besides, it's insignificant compared to Faye's crimes against us. After Natalie—and she tried to blame you—"

"We're here, Avery. You, me, and Sophie. We're safe."

"For how long? Faye's still out there, and by now she probably knows I'm out there, too. She could still hurt us both. After what she did to Natalie and Noah, I honestly don't know how far she'd go to shut us up. I think she's just as liable to plot our deaths for weeks as knife us on the street. Then where would Sophie be?"

"I'd actually like to stop talking about it," he said, as he set a stuffed bear by his daughter's arm.

"I'm sorry. I'll stop."

"No—I mean, yes, sometimes, please, but—you came all this way. It's your first day out, and I'm asking you personal questions while you're standing in a towel in my bedroom—"

"Yes. About that . . . "

He apologized as he grabbed a pair of his pajamas from the closet and handed them to Avery. "Whatever you need, help yourself. Don't feel like you need to be polite."

"It's not politeness, Paul. In Taunton, I couldn't grab the book sitting next to me without a nurse thinking she might need to drug me." When she set the folded towel on the bed, Sophie's eyes creaked open, and Avery smiled at her as she buttoned her shirt.

"I'm sorry I didn't testify in your defense," he whispered.

"I told you not to," she said, and pulled the drawstring pants as tight as they'd go. They still hung on her hips, though, and she had to keep kicking the bottoms out from under her feet.

"I should have done it, anyway. Maybe you wouldn't

have so much fear inside you. Maybe Natalie would still be alive."

"Maybe. Or she would've killed you. Noah wasn't even a threat to her and look what happened. How it spread."

"You're right," he said, looking down as Sophie stretched her arms and burbled. "We shouldn't waste any more time. We can go as slow as we want with everything else, but . . . " With a face-spanning grin, Paul dropped to one knee. "I love you, Avery. As you were, as you are, and as you will be, I love you. I couldn't imagine a life without you when we were apart, and now that we're together, I refuse to even listen to the idea. Especially from my future wife."

She giggled. "What happened to being strangers?"

"Strangers get married."

"This is Boston, not Las Vegas."

"But it's as close as we might get." He kissed her hands, then scrunched his face. "Actually, forget that. We *will* go to Las Vegas someday. And New York City. And California. Anywhere you want, just as long as we're together." He zigzagged her face with pleading adoration. "Marry me, Avery. Be my wife."

She coaxed him to stand and pulled him into her arms. Running her fingers through his hair and down his back, she tried to picture a world in which she refused his proposal. As it was, Avery's life felt cold and dark and every declaration of love a cruel lie constructed to control or undo her. But the picture of her life without Paul was bleaker, like living in solitude on the other side of the universe with every word devoured by the vacuum of space. Yes, marrying Paul was impulsive, even dangerous, but she saw no point in battling between love and rationality.

"Yes," she whispered through a trembling smile. "Yes, of course I'll marry you."

Paul lifted Avery into the air with a joyous holler and spun her around the room. She laughed with more abandon than she had in years, and though anxiety rode close behind, it couldn't possibly complete with the bliss in knowing she and Paul had a chance. Even when Sophie started crying, Avery's unease remained suppressed by hope. And for the first time in a long time, *possibility*.

Paul scooped up his daughter and rocked her gently until her wails dampened to soft coos. "Would you like to hold her?"

Avery's body stiffened. "I've never done it before."

He hummed in amusement, then passed Sophie into Avery's arms. "I hadn't, either. You'll get used to it," he said, guiding her hands to the proper places. "You'll be her mother soon."

"Stepmother," Avery said, staring into the girl's massive blue eyes as she fumbled to cradle her.

"You have the same blood. I don't think it's unreasonable for you to raise her as your own."

"And cut Natalie out of the picture?" She swayed Sophie back and forth, and amusement flickered across the girl's rosy lips. "No. That's what Faye wants to do. I'll be a mother to her, always, but she needs to know about Natalie. And what happened to her."

Sophie yawned, and Avery gingerly laid her in the bassinet.

Paul smiled as he watched them, the color rising in his cheeks. "Whatever you want, as long as we're together. Speaking of which, how about tomorrow?"

"For what?"

"Getting married."

Her jaw dropped. "Are you serious?"

"Absolutely. We'll take my parents' ketch, sail down the coast, and find a captain to marry us at the first port."

Avery chuckled. "And here I thought I was supposed to be the crazy one."

Popping up from his knees, he pulled her into a kiss. "Never again. You're not that girl anymore. You never were to me."

"Thank you, Paul. For everything."

He kissed her forehead, then rolled off the bed. "You must be exhausted. Take the bed. I'll sleep on the sofa."

"Are you kidding? I want to sleep next to my fiancé." She climbed under the covers and patted the space next to her. As she curled up on the left side, Paul crawled in behind her and held her tight. As she relished their breath rising and falling as one, she wondered if she'd chosen the same side of the bed as Natalie. Had her sister curled up in that spot, her knees tucked to her chest, and dreamed of her future with Noah Hanson?

Tears stung Avery's eyes, and she pushed the imagery from her mind. As she emptied her lungs in weariness, she allowed her face to sink into the pillow, her body into the mattress, and her mind into the healing dark.

Paul's bed was significantly more comfortable than any Avery had in Taunton, and the sheets were heaven in comparison to the scratchy linen planks used by the hospital. When she rolled onto her side, it was strange and wonderful not seeing a blank wall or a roommate's bed, nor the lengthy shadows cast by a moon shining through barred windows. She woke often, disoriented by her surroundings and startled by hunched shadows in the crooks of the room. Sophie's dreamy warbling jostled her out of sleep more than once, but it eventually pacified her. And when Paul draped his arm over her waist, his breath flowering over her neck, she felt safe.

The next morning, when Avery rolled over to greet her fiancé, she found his side empty. She sprang up in dread, clutching the comforter.

"Paul?"

She crawled to the bassinet. Also empty. Panicked, she scrambled from the bed, her mind awash in horrible scenarios—until she saw the note from Paul pinned to the bedroom door. She plucked it free, a relieved breath fluttering the paper.

"Good morning," it said, "I hope you slept well. Sophie

and I are out running errands and should be back within the hour. Help yourself to anything in the kitchen." Just as she was reading "I love you" written grandly at the bottom, the front door opened.

Avery tossed on a robe and galloped down the hall.

"Good morning," Paul called, lugging shopping bags through the door. He clutched Sophie to his chest as he heaped them on the counter, already overloaded without Avery wrapping her arms around his waist. He laughed until she looked up at him, her lips trembling.

"Avery, you're as white as a sheet. Are you feeling all right?"

"When I woke up and you two were gone, I was so scared something horrible happened to you."

"Didn't you see my note?"

"Yes, but before that . . . and then seeing you, knowing I could've lost you . . . " She sank to the floor, and Paul followed.

Sophie gurgled and waved her chubby arms in Avery's face. She lightly grasped the girl's fingers and kissed her small, diaphanous nails. "I'm so close to getting everything I've ever wanted, and I'm afraid someone's going to take it away."

"I know exactly how you feel, believe me, but we won't have to worry about that for much longer." He plucked a large bag from the counter and dropped it in Avery's arms as she stood. "Clothes. I hope they fit."

"Thanks." She smiled as she pawed through the bag, then crinkled her brow as she removed a bottle of peroxide and Miss Clairol.

"Just so you know, I love your natural color," he said. "But if we don't want anyone to recognize you . . . "

"You're right. Changing my clothes isn't enough. I'll have to make the sacrifice. It's just hair, after all." She said it with conviction, but she didn't believe it, and neither did Paul.

He cradled her face, pouting. "You'll be beautiful no matter what color your hair is."

She sniffled and staunched her rising tears with her sleeve. Clutching the peroxide and blonde dye in panicky fingers, she turned for the bathroom.

"Wait, I have something else for you."

Paul removed a small white box from his coat pocket and flipped the lid open. The gem was small, but it caught the light with a flirtatious twinkle.

"It's not a real diamond, but it's all I could afford. It's a little nicer than the first ring I gave you, though. What ever happened to that thing, anyway?"

Avery sucked on her cheek, imagining her beloved brass ring below the floorboards of her room in the juvenile ward—if the ward still existed. She assumed she'd never see it again, but it made her heart sing knowing at least it wasn't in Faye's hands.

"It's still out there," she said. "And both rings you've given me are beautiful. Thank you." She held out her hand, and Paul guided the ring onto her finger. Grinning, she wiggled the lustrous gem in the air. "It's perfect."

He kissed her hand. "It is now."

Sophie cooed at the sparkly ring and giggled when Avery held it up to her face.

"I'd say she approves." Paul kissed his daughter's cheek, then kissed his fiancée's. "I'm going to put her down for a nap before we leave. The bathroom is all yours."

It was funny how much that simple phrase delighted her now. After nearly six years of sharing a communal bathroom with a dozen other girls and several very attentive nurses, the simple notion of privacy stirred her heart in whirling euphoria.

Unfortunately, her next task brought happiness to a halt. With shaking hands, she parted her hair and applied the peroxide. The overpowering fumes made her eyes water, and the tears increased as she watched her ebony hair change to a pale, sickly orange. Her reflection frightened her each time she looked in the mirror, so she sat on the edge of the tub while the peroxide did its work. The Miss Clairol dye was supposed to make Avery a frosty blonde, but once the process was complete and her hair blown dry, she was more of a dirty blonde—and a dead ringer for Natalie. Avery's heart pounded like it might break free of her chest. The mirror became a window into the afterlife, where Natalie looked sadder and more wretched than ever.

Paul was standing in the hallway, frozen by the resemblance.

"I won't be recognized as Avery Norton," she said, running her fingers through the strange straw-colored mane. "But people might think I'm her dead sister."

He beckoned her into a hug, then stroked her back. "No one is going to recognize you."

"I hardly recognize myself."

"You will again. We can dye it back before the wedding." He pinched Avery's chin and kissed her forehead. "I'm going to give Anna a call and let her know that Sophie won't need a nanny anymore. Then we can go."

Avery tried to avoid her reflection while Paul called Anna Mulberry and terminated her employment as kindly as possible, but it caught her by surprise, like a ghost in the glass of framed pictures and windows, even in the golden latch on Paul's suitcase as she packed up Sophie's clothes.

"Yes, I know it's your day off," Paul said into the receiver. "Oh, you are? We're headed that way ourselves. No, just a vacation. That's why I'm calling. I'm afraid we won't need a nanny anymore, at least not while we're away." He paused, his lips tightly pinched. "I know, I know. Yes, Sophie's going to miss you, too. Thank you for everything, Anna, and I'll be sure to call you if we need your help in the future. Thank you again."

He strode into the bedroom as Sophie woke from her nap. Avery scooped her up and patted the baby's back.

"How'd she take it?"

"Pretty well. She wasn't home, so I had to call the other number she gave me. It turns out it's her boyfriend's number on the island. That's where she is right now."

"It sure is a small world. Too small, if you ask me."

"Not for us. Not anymore," Paul said, wrapping his arms around Avery and Sophie.

Try as she might, Avery couldn't maintain her scowl, and her expression brightened to match Paul's. "The eternal optimist. Even after everything we've been through. I'd say it was foolish if I didn't admire it so much."

"How can I not be optimistic? I have you, I have Sophie, and together, we will have the world. As soon as we set sail, so will every shred of pessimism in that beautiful blonde head of yours."

She giggled and smacked him as he tucked her hair behind her ear. With his daughter and fiancée, Paul Dillon closed the apartment he'd shared with Natalie for the last time. They only had two suitcases, which held Sophie's belongings more than anything else.

"Are you sure you don't want to bring more?" Avery asked him.

"We're starting a new life. We don't need the trappings of the old one."

"But you're leaving so much behind."

Paul kissed her softly and said, "Not the important things."

CHAPTER TWENTY-FOUR

VINEYARD HAVEN MARINA was bustling with summer people. Paul swerved between the hordes with little effort, but Avery had gotten rusty in her years off-island. It wasn't easy walking with her head down, either. The crowds might've trampled her if not for Paul guiding her by the hand and the occasional cooing from the baby in his arms. People waved to Paul as he navigated the marina, but they were far more interested in Sophie. He carried her like a blessed relic during the Holy Ghost Festival; the masses couldn't help but part to pay homage to the child shining so bright, the mysterious companion closely following Sophie's father was of little importance. Still, she didn't release her grip on her fiancé's hand until they reached the Dillon family's fifty-seven-foot ecru ketch moored inside the breakwater.

Paul bounced Sophie in his arms. "It's your first boat trip, sweetheart!" When he tickled under her chin, she shrieked joyfully, grabbed his finger, and stuck it in her mouth.

"How are we going to steal the boat?" Avery whispered.

"Who said anything about stealing it? I have a set of keys," he said, wiping Sophie's drool on his pants.

"Do your parents know we're taking it?"

His cheeks reddened as a smirk curled up his cheek. "Okay, I guess we are stealing it, but not in a hijacking, heist-y sort of way. You remember how to sail, don't you?"

"Gosh, I hope so."

"That's okay. Sophie can take the wheel if necessary. Can't you, baby?" he sang, dancing her through the air.

"I hope you have a box she can stand on."

"No need. She can't even stand yet." He tickled Sophie's arm, and she squealed in delight as they boarded the ship. Cuddling her to his chest, Paul extended his hand to Avery.

She fanned herself demurely, then took his hand with a dramatic curtsy.

"Thank you, Captain." She boarded and leaned in to kiss Paul, but Sophie reached up and pinched Avery's chin, causing them both to burst into laughter.

She kissed the top of Sophie's head. The sea's salty aroma was strong as they stood in the playful summer breeze, but when Avery inhaled deep, she could swear she detected the clean scent of daylilies radiating like sunshine from her niece's skin.

"I dreamt of this," Avery whispered, and when Paul pressed his lips to her neck, the ocean rocked them closer to freedom.

"Paul Dillon!" A cheerful, squeaky voice rang across the marina. "Paul, is that you?"

Avery hunched and hid herself as a stout woman waddled down the pier toward the boat. Her face was beet red, and she panted as she waved up at Paul. "I thought that was you."

"And you were right. Hello, Mrs. Pilsbury."

"Why didn't you tell me you were on the island? Is your mother here?"

"No, she's substituting at the school today. We're just taking the boat out for the afternoon."

"I see. And this must be little Sophie! Oh, she looks so much like you. Such an angel." Her mouth downturned. "But her mother is an angel, too, isn't she? Poor dear."

"Yes, ma'am, she is," he whispered.

The sorrow only affected Mrs. Pilsbury's face for a minute. She quickly slapped on a fake smile and turned her attention to Avery. "And who is this?"

"The nanny. Sophie's nanny," Paul said. He was about

to launch into an explanatory speech he'd prepared for such a situation, but Mrs. Pilsbury shot him a subversive little wink and pressed her finger to her lips.

"Say no more, sweetheart."

Paul crinkled his nose in offense masked as gratitude. "We should be on our way."

"Of course. Maybe I'll drop in on your mother when school lets out. They didn't ever get that house in Menemsha, did they?"

"No, they're at the same place on Huntington Avenue."

She tapped her forehead. "How could I forget? It's the same street as the Nortons. And Natalie . . . poor dear . . . "

"Yes, ma'am."

"I honestly don't know how anyone can stay on that street after what happened in that house. I don't believe in ghosts, but if they do exist, that house must be full of them."

"I'd imagine so."

Her lips peeled back from her teeth. "It was lovely seeing you, Paul. Enjoy the day. It's supposed to be a nice one."

"You too."

Once she was gone, Avery lifted her gaze.

"Are you all right?" Paul asked.

"What Mrs. Pilsbury said," Avery whispered, a smile spreading slowly across her face. "I hope she's right. I hope there *are* ghosts in my mother's house, and I hope they haunt the shit out of her."

The resulting imagery in Avery's mind both amused and mollified her. Raising her head high, she gratefully accepted Paul's kiss and shifted her sights to the horizon.

"Grab that winch, Captain, and let's get moving," she hollered, and Paul saluted as he jumped into action.

The wind was with Avery, Paul, and Sophie as they set sail toward uncertainty. Their destination was the same open ocean as everyone else, but there was a new world within the water only they could see. It seemed an eternity since the ocean left its taste upon Avery's skin. It tossed and twisted her blonde hair, and her eyes teared—both from the pain of the wind and her gratitude in it. Sophie was surprisingly at ease with sailing and squealed in delight at each tilt and shudder. At the bow, looking out across the vast, sparkling Atlantic, Avery and Paul held each other.

"It's not a dream, is it? It's really happening," she said.

He squeezed her and kissed her rosy shoulder. "Yes, it's happening."

She looked behind her, past Paul's beautiful tan face, and squinted for the shore. "I can't see land anymore. Everything's far behind us, and what lies ahead—well, maybe it's best we don't know. There are no expectations."

"None?"

She shrugged. "Some, sure, but not about the big stuff. I just want our lives to be new. Better."

"Those are expectations, too."

"You're right. Maybe I don't know the difference anymore. When it's all seemed so impossible for so long, staring out barred windows—"

"Stop torturing yourself. You're not there. You don't have to think about it. As far as I'm concerned, none of it ever happened."

"You can say that as much as you want, but it'll never be true. As much as I try to forget, it's an everyday struggle not to think about it. It's part of me."

"But it's not part of us."

"I love you so much, Paul. And I desperately want to believe that."

"What can I do to convince you?"

She faced him. "I don't want to wait. I want our new life to start now."

His brow crinkled. "What are you saying?"

She unbuttoned his shirt and glided her fingers over his chest. Her lips parted when excitement rippled through her; it was amazing how natural it felt, how possible. She kissed him, ravenous with desire, and delighted in the sun on her bare skin. But as much as they wanted to rush below deck and lose themselves in the moment, they had a baby and a boat to tend.

"It's a little chilly down here," Avery said, laying Sophie in the bassinet. "Do you have a blanket for her?"

Paul opened the closet door and started rifling through its contents. Then with a jolt, he scrambled backward and nearly knocked Avery over.

"Paul, what is it?"

He pointed at the closet, and his voice trembled. "Anna Mulberry."

Avery peered into the closet, where the lifeless body of Sophie's nanny was twisted up against the back wall. Her face was petrified in a ghastly expression, her neck deeply bruised and lacerated, but the paisley bag sitting on Anna's lap terrified Avery most.

Breathless, she backed away. "My mom's gardening tools."

It was unzipped, and Paul cautiously peeked inside. Spinning around, he said, "Take Sophie and get to the life raft."

"What is it?"

"Just go, Avery. Now!"

Avery grabbed the bassinet and dashed above deck. She tried to calm the wailing baby as she opened the life raft storage, but Sophie only quieted when she saw her father zip past. With the gardening bag in hand, he hurried to the stern and cocked his arm back. His head raised as well, and he saw Avery staring at him with fear colonizing every inch of her body. But he smiled at her, certain everything would be all right.

Faye Norton thought she'd tied up the last few loose ends when she placed her gardening tools on the boat, but she'd failed. They were going to be fine. They were going to make it to shore and there, Avery and Paul would finally be married. They would be a family, as they were always meant to be.

Avery saw every moment of their future spread out before her like an ocean of time, with each swell and milky crest bringing a happier day than the one before. But when the waves broke, so did her reverie. Seconds after the paisley bag left Paul Dillon's hand, the world caught fire, and Avery's hope for a happy future fell to ash.

It happened too fast to process. One minute Avery was standing with Sophie in her arms, basking in her fiancé's reassuring smile, and the next, she was in the water, struggling to stay afloat. The raw burns on her hands and face drank up the sea with bolts of pain that made it difficult to tread water. Avery clung to the nearest plank of wood and kicked madly to propel herself through the wreckage littering the sea. At first, all she could hear was the explosion ringing in her ears, muffled and throbbing like her head was full of cotton, but a distant sound soon broke through the agonizing din.

Crying. A baby crying.

Sophie.

Avery pushed through the debris in the direction of Sophie's cries until she spotted the bassinet floating among the wreckage. Parts of it were melted, but as long as Sophie was crying, she was alive. When she reached the bassinet and verified Sophie had escaped with only minor burns, Avery allowed herself a moment of relief in the tumultuous sea. It was slight, however, and the sigh stuck in her throat when she saw her future floating face down between the charred debris. Her heart pounded and lungs burned as she swam towards Paul, pleading to whomever could hear her, "He needs to be all right. Please let him be all right."

But she knew. She knew before she touched his body and it bobbed like a burnt apple. She turned him over, anyway, foolishly hoping, and the cry that blasted from Avery Norton's throat was like no sound she'd ever made. Fueled by rage and grief, the sky appeared to shudder when she released her scream, and even once silent, it hung about her like the smoke wreathing the ravaged ship.

There wasn't much left of the face she adored, but Avery stroked it as if the fire hadn't robbed Paul of his beauty. She traced the paths of destruction that hardened his cheeks, and she kissed the memory of his perfectly soft lips. Allowing one more wail to erupt, Avery forced herself to swallow her immense pain. It solidified and juddered down her throat, feeling like a lump of iron in her chest that, if she let go, would sink her all the way to the bottom of the ocean. If not for Sophie, she would've let it.

Avery wrapped one arm around the bassinet and draped the other over Paul's body. Though unconsciousness claimed her, she held onto them for dear life. And that, she believed, was what made her dreams so pleasant. They stayed with her in the swaying dark. Even when the coastguard came, and the reserve boats loaded them up separately, Avery's mind never let go.

"I'm not leaving you, Avery. You'll never be alone. Never again." Paul looked as beautiful as ever as he sat beside her, holding her hand.

She whispered to him, her mind reeling with confusion. "I thought it was over. I thought this was the end."

"End?" Paul kissed her hand. "No, Avery. This is just the beginning."

RABBITS IN THE GARDEN

CHAPTER TWENTY-FIVE

AN ANTISEPTIC SMELL wafted in Avery's dreams and roused her from sleep. She knew that smell—she'd woken to it before. Though her senses sharpened, she refused to observe her surroundings for fear she was back in the electroshock room at Taunton Asylum.

"It's okay, Avery. You can open your eyes," Paul said softly.

She obeyed, expecting to see her fiancé at her bedside. Instead, an unfamiliar face greeted her.

The nurse bent down and offered Avery a half-smile. "Finally decided to come around, I see."

"Where am I?" she croaked.

"Martha's Vineyard Hospital," the nurse said. "You were very lucky. Someone must be watching over you."

"Someone always is," Avery said, then shuddered with a sudden burst of panic. "Where's Sophie?"

"The baby? She's in the ICU, but she's going to be just fine. It looks like you got the worst of it. Except for . . . " The nurse cleared her throat and jotted something on her notepad. "I'll let the doctor know you're awake."

Avery watched her leave, only then realizing a shadowy figure stood in the corner of her hospital room. She tried sitting up to get a better look, but the straps tethering her to the bed's handrails inhibited her movement.

"Don't struggle," said the shadow. "You have a lot of burns, my dear. Though I suppose a few were there before today.

Bandages covered the wounds on her wrists and forearms, but burnt flesh was the least of her worries when she noticed something important missing from her hand.

"Where is it?" she snarled.

As Faye stepped into the light wearing a satisfied grimace, Avery tugged her restraints and shook the bed.

"Where's my ring?" Avery bellowed.

Faye hushed her. "Settle down. Just because I took the first ring doesn't mean I took the second one," she said, too proud to fake indignation. "What does it matter now, anyway? You can't marry a corpse."

Avery growled as she fought her shackles and clawed at her mother, but when Faye reacted with lilting laughter from a safe distance, she flopped back and screamed in frustration.

"Don't act like such a child, or I'll have to fetch the nurses to put you out. They know and respect me here," she replied. "Besides, you know as well as I do that this place won't hold you forever. You escaped from Taunton; this is nothing." She twiddled her fingers in the air as she paced the room. "Congratulations on that, by the way. And thank you. I appreciate you implicating yourself in the other explosions by setting the hospital on fire. Like mother, like daughter, I suppose."

"I'm nothing like you."

"No? Tell that to the innocent people you burned alive in Taunton." She drew closer, her breath like that of a dragon slow cooking its prey. "Was it worth it, killing all those people just to end up here? Or—and this is just a theory—maybe you're here right now *because* you killed those people? Maybe God took Paul away from you because of what you took from so many others."

"If God worked like that, you'd be suffering worse than me."

"That's where you're wrong. My actions honor God. You killed those people for *you*, and there wasn't a scrap of honor in it."

"Where was the honor in killing Anna Mulberry? She was just a nanny."

"Nobody is *just* anything," Faye said. "From what you knew of her, I can imagine why you'd think she was an innocent, but she had her demons like anyone. And though they have been helpful demons at times, I did her a favor by releasing her." She exhaled, her eyes coasting to the window. "I'm not the monster you think I am, Avery, and you're not the victim you think you are." Her gaze returned to her daughter, and she pinched a lock of Avery's dirty blonde hair. "Look at you. I don't even recognize you anymore."

"On that we agree," she whispered.

"Can't we also agree it's time for this to stop? Don't you want it to be over?" Faye said, her voice possessed by sympathy Avery wished she could trust. "You're the only one left. You can't lose any more. Don't you think it's time to cut and run?"

"As if you'd ever let me go," she said. "I wouldn't be surprised if you've hidden your special gardening tools under this bed."

"I'm done trying to teach you lessons you refuse to learn. I gave you the chance to be with Paul like you wanted, but you had to be difficult. You had to fight against what was best for you."

"You would've never let us be together."

"Wrong!" Faye boomed. "I gave you the chance to be together in death." She swung her head sadly and tried to touch her daughter's hand, but Avery snapped her jaws at her mother's fingers.

Recoiling, Faye whispered, "Please don't do this, Avery. You can't win. Even if you go to prison, you won't escape me. I've been there. I did well there."

"You're sick."

"In the best way possible," she said. "Which is why you should disappear. Before the police come, get out of here, leave the island, go as far as you can, and maybe you can carve out a little happiness for yourself, even if it's a life on the run."

"What about Sophie?"

"Sophie stays with me. That's the deal."

"You tried to kill her!"

"That doesn't mean I don't love her, or want what's best for her. And yes, when she was with you and Paul, death would've been best. But she's with me now, where she can grow up right. I care for her deeply, just like I care for you."

Avery reared back and hocked a wad of phlegm at her mother's face. It hit her chin and began to slide, but Faye slapped Avery across the cheek before wiping the offense away. Balling up her wet handkerchief, she chucked it at the girl with a snarl.

"You brought this on yourself. You started it all those years ago when you let Paul have his way with you."

"We were just kids. We didn't do anything wrong."

"That's what they all say," Faye hissed. "They clutch their chests and feign shock at their litany of sins, but they know. They know with every smile, every kiss, every dirty little touch that they're poisoning themselves and the rest of the world. They know every time they walk out the door that they're heading through another, one that would lead them to another woman, another man, another sin upon sin upon sin."

Avery exhaled a clipped breath. "Dear God, Mom. You really have lost your mind."

She snorted in amusement. "No, Avery, you're the one who's lost something here. And if you don't believe that, you must believe this: if you ever come after us, if you ever try to get Sophie, I will make your life a living hell. I will lead the world to your doorstep. I will tell them the things you've done—things you don't even know yet. And when they capture you, they won't just lock you up. They'll lobotomize you, so you can never hurt anyone again."

Stinging tears spilled down Avery's cheeks. "Why do

you hate me so much? It can't just be about Paul. Why are you torturing me like this? Please, just tell me."

"What, and put you out of your misery?" Faye sneered and spun to the exit.

"Wait!" Avery sat up as much as she could, her arms twisted behind her. "Where's my ring?"

Faye shook her head sadly. "At a time like this, that's all you can think about? Don't press me, Avery. Don't push me. Don't throw your life away. You're young, and now that you're blonde you shouldn't have trouble picking up some pathetic man willing to suffer your baggage in exchange for—" She smirked. "Well, you know perfectly well, don't you?"

"You're so wrong about me, it's scary. You think I'm some kind of tramp, but I haven't even . . . I've never . . . " She wilted onto the bed as tears charged down her face. "You robbed me of that."

"You're better off, trust me. When they're trying to get it, you're something special, but once they've gotten it, you're just another place they've already been. Paul wouldn't have been any different. One night he would've told you he was working late, while you were home with a baby or two, but he'd be off screwing someone else. That was your future until I stepped in and rescued you, and I'll do the same for Sophie. As soon as she's recovered, I'll start teaching her. That's the key. I waited too long with you and Natalie, but I'll have Sophie tending the garden before she's walking."

"You're going to ruin her just like you ruined me."

"You did that to yourself when you rebelled. Oh Avery, you don't realize what promise you had before then." Faye hung from the door as if dancing with it, her eyes to the heavens as she warbled her woes. "You could've been an amazing asset to our family. All the good you could've done—it breaks my heart to see how far you've strayed, all the people you've hurt. Sometimes I still think you could change, maybe even remember how strong you used to be, but I'm afraid that girl is lost forever."

"I don't know what you're talking about."

"You will one day. But no matter what happens, I'm warning you to stay away from us. Sophie and I have a chance to build something meaningful in this world, and I will not allow you to ruin my plans for a second time. I don't want to see your face. I don't want to hear your voice. Am I clear?"

Avery tried to look her mother in the eye, but a lovely apparition behind Faye stole her attention.

"Say 'yes'," Paul whispered to her. "Tell her you understand."

"Yes," Avery said robotically. "Yes, I understand."

When Faye smiled in victory, so did Paul. She started out the door, but before Avery could relish the bittersweet warmth of solitude, her mother stuck her head back in the room with a blazing grin.

"By the way," she chirped, "you didn't say anything about my new necklace. I wore it especially for you." She held out the silver chain, and Avery's engagement ring swung from it like a sparkling pendulum.

Avery exploded with rage and fought her restraints, prompting Faye to call the nurses into the room. She hid her smile as she marched out, but Avery could swear she heard her chuckle, even as she disappeared down the hall.

Avery battled the nurses at first, kicking and struggling to break free, but she stopped once Paul sat beside her on the bed. He touched her leg gently, and though it made her weep, it also blanketed in her a sort of lullaby calm. As one of the nurses leaned over her, she spotted the emery board in her front pocket, but Paul told her how to swipe it. He also showed her how to position it to slice her restraints later that night. And when the straps dug into her burns as she filed them thinner and thinner, he sang to distract her from the pain. When only flimsy strings remained, she pulled free. Her head pounded like a bass drum and swam with nauseating splotches of color as she stumbled into Paul's arms.

"I thought you were dead," she sobbed, and he petted her hair as he peppered her forehead with kisses.

"Never, my love. I'll always be with you." He gulped hard. "But you have to do this next part alone, okay?"

"I don't know if I can. It hurts, Paul."

"I know, I'm sorry. Here . . . " He sat her down and ran around the room, tossing various medical supplies into a garbage bag. Twisting it up tight, he tucked it under her arm, pulled her to the window, and opened it wide.

"Where will I go?" she whimpered.

"Do you remember our camping trips? In the Oak Bluffs woods?"

"I could never forget them," she said. "Do you think I can make it all the way there?"

"You have to," he said, kissing her bandaged hands. "Go now. I'll be waiting for you, and I won't be alone."

Avery held her breath as she climbed out the window, and though she knew it was impossible, panic made her feel like she didn't breathe again until the building was miles behind her. She'd taken the longest way possible to Oak Bluffs, disobeying her internal compass despite her increasing pain. She betrayed the back paths only once when she dipped into a cluster of backyards to steal clothes off a line, water out of the hose, a canvas Boy Scout tent, and a half-can of Sterno.

With damp clothes donned and the tent rolled up, she set off toward the woods where she first realized her feelings for Paul Dillon. It saddened her to recall those days, knowing they could never rise again, but when Paul's voice entered her mind, she dried her tears and picked up her pace.

"I'll be waiting for you, and I won't be alone."

But no one was waiting when Avery reached the campground. She pitched the tent alone, watched the sunset alone, and as she settled down to go to sleep, she had to resign herself to the possibility that, no matter what her mind insisted, she would spend the rest of her days alone.

The night whispered in a hundred different voices, but none of them were the voice she longed to hear most. Paul's presence in the hospital had cast a spell over her, and now that he'd been gone for several hours, the spell had frayed. Once again, Avery questioned something for which she'd recently regained confidence: her sanity. Was she crazy to think Paul was still with her? Or was she crazy to think he wasn't?

She tried losing her worries in sleep, but the wind was a bothersome bedfellow. It nipped her feet, shook the tent, and imitated all manner of monsters, keeping Avery's eyes peeled and her heart racing. Only when a warm hand grazed her cheek did her pulse slow to a delicious throb. Soft lips touched her forehead, and her grateful smile bloomed in every inch of her body. Paul's eyes glittered of their own volition, lighting his face with a soft glow that bled over her skin when he lowered to kiss her. She enjoyed every gentle touch, but even so, a mysterious alarm rang through her mind, louder and louder until she couldn't take it anymore. She rolled away from Paul and sobbed into her hands.

"What is it?" he asked. "Avery, what's wrong?"

She sniffled and tucked herself into a ball in the corner of the tent. "Do you really have to ask? You're dead, Paul. I saw you. I felt you."

"But I'm here. I don't know how, and I don't *want* to know how if it means leaving you." He gritted his teeth as he cupped her face, his voice a desperate whisper. "Please don't start thinking I'm not supposed to be here, Avery. I'm afraid it'll send me away."

"I can't help it. Part of me wants to give in and believe that it's really you, but the other part . . . "

"The other part doesn't matter. The other part is logic, and there's nothing logical about love." Chuckling, he dotted her face with kisses, and she melted against him. "I love you, Avery. I refuse to let a little thing like death stop us from being together."

She clutched his shirt and wept. "It's not fair. We were so close to having everything."

"We can be even closer," he said. With his hand gliding to the back of her neck, Paul pressed his lips to hers, and she surrendered gratefully to the boy of her dreams.

It no longer mattered whether it was sane or not. He tasted too good to pull away. There, in the same woods where their love blossomed, Avery came full circle in a variety of ways. Paul's love was deeper than she'd envisioned on those lonely nights in Taunton, and her mind emptied with each delicious surge of passion until there was only him: the boy who always believed in her. And she believed in him. She believed in each caress and thrust and declaration of love he whispered achingly into her ear. It didn't last long, but it was everything she needed—to be with him in a way she thought Faye had stolen from her forever. When they broke apart and lay side by side, tangled up in each other's arms, Avery closed her eyes and played it over and over in her mind.

"You're beautiful," he said, rolling back on top of her and stroking her face. "Open your eyes."

Her eyelids lifted slowly to reveal the blue irises she'd always adored, but looking beyond them wrenched a terrified scream from her throat. She smacked him and kicked him and tried to wiggle out from the sloppy, disfigured corpse he'd become.

"What's wrong, Avery? Don't you love me anymore?"

The boy she knew all her life was gone. The explosion on the boat had peeled back the flesh on his face, and what remained was soggy with seawater. His teeth were blackened, his hair burnt down to sticky stubble, and when he caressed her cheek, charred bone scraped her skin.

"No . . . " Avery moaned as she covered herself with a blanket. "Please God, no . . . "

"We're together, Avery. That's all that matters. You and me."

"And me." A familiar voice purred from outside the

tent, and chapped ebony bones parted the flaps. Natalie was smiling, but the grin was only discernible on the right side of her scorched face where bits of ropey muscle remained. She cocked her head and stared down at her sister with lidless eyes. "You didn't want to be alone, right?"

Avery howled and pushed Paul and Natalie aside. She flew out of the tent, but she halted abruptly in the clearing, her brain sweating ice as her gaze whipped across the mob of charred corpses.

She recognized only a few disfigured faces out of the dozens, but they all knew her. They pointed at her and grasped at the air, but they didn't charge. They rocked from side to side, moaning and muttering, while maimed rabbits hopped around their feet.

The rabbits weren't the only animal present. A large creature chased them, but Avery couldn't figure out what species it was. In addition to its extensive burns, its characteristics didn't resemble any animal she'd ever seen. It stormed horns-first at the rabbits, its ears flapping and tail flicking wildly, but when a seared girl scuttled over, the animal skidded into reverse and pounded the forest floor with its massive hooves. The girl lifted the animal into her arms, and Avery at last recognized them as Brianne and her imaginary cohort, Tyler.

No, not imaginary; and not even invisible anymore.

She recognized them all then. From Frankie and Darian to patients who were more scenery than performers on the Taunton stage of Avery's life. Violet, for instance. She sat on the ground, half-hidden in the flock with her head slanted and eyes vacant as ever. Oddly, though, Violet was one of the few untouched by flame.

"Avery."

The young woman who spoke barely had a face left, but the way she fidgeted with her charred clothing gave her away in an instant. Avery wanted to embrace Flint, but she was too afraid.

"We're here for you, Avery, forever," Paul said. He tried to wrap his arms around Avery's waist, but she shoved him back.

She sobbed as she crumpled to the ground. "Please don't hurt me," she stammered, as Flint crouched beside her.

"We don't want to hurt you."

"It's true," Nurse Meredith hissed through a broken smile. "We're here to help you."

Avery scrambled away until her back slammed against a tree trunk. "Stay away from me, all of you!"

Natalie knelt beside her. She placed her hand on Avery's knee as delicately as possible, but the crispy skin on her leg made her sister cringe and curl herself into a trembling ball.

"Please, don't be afraid of me," Natalie said. "I know this is hard to understand, but we really have come to help you. No one here despises or blames you for anything. There's not a death here that didn't originate with Faye. You're safe, I promise."

"What do you want?"

"You have a lot of work to do. You can't let Mom get away with what she did to us."

Avery held her head in her hands and whined. "I can't stop her. Every time I try, someone I love dies. Sophie's all that's left, and I don't want Mom to hurt her."

"I'd rather have my daughter in my arms than allow Faye to corrupt her," Natalie said.

"I can't. She's too strong."

"You're stronger," Paul said. "We all believe you are. We all believe you can defeat her."

"Really?"

They nodded in unison, and Natalie added, "And we're not the only ones."

The throng parted, and a person Avery hadn't seen in over a decade stepped forward. Lacerations marked the man's face, there was a massive gash along his throat, and blood soaked his clothes, but Avery recognized him immediately. She stood, her arms outstretched, and he ran to lift her up. In the air, in his arms, she never wanted to return to the earth.

"Avery, my little girl, my little button." Jason Norton lowered his daughter and cradled her face. Several of his fingers were missing, but Avery savored the marvelous feeling of her father's hand upon her cheek.

"Daddy, is it really you?"

"Yes, sweetheart. God how I've missed you. How I've longed to see you like this. You're so grown up, so beautiful, so powerful—and you're ready to take Faye down once and for all."

"I don't think I can."

"I know you're scared, but you're the only one with the strength to stop her. None of us can rest until Faye gets her comeuppance, you included."

"But I don't know how."

"We'll help you," Paul said, his hand upon her shoulder. "We won't let you do this alone."

Cold sweat glazed her skin, and terror still swamped her stomach, but when Paul opened his arms to her, she fell into his embrace. She ignored how his chapped hands caught in her hair, and pulled his scorched arms tighter.

"I'll do it," she said.

The right side of Natalie's face spread with a grin, and she threw her arms around her sister and Paul.

"But I still don't know how I'm supposed to beat her."

"Search your mind," Flint said. "Think of everything Faye put you through. Every torture you didn't deserve, every punishment and pain. Six years in Taunton was a long time to suffer those abuses, Avery, but we have a feeling you can condense it."

"Fine," she said. "Let's do this. Let's get it over with."

"You can't act in haste," her dad replied. "If you rush, you might make a mistake, and we can't afford any mistakes."

"Take your time, my love," Paul whispered. "Maybe that's where we went wrong. We waited so long for freedom to be within our grasp, and we ran for it. We can't risk running again. We must coax it into our hands—into *your* hands."

"We believe in you, Avery," the ghosts chanted.

"What if I fail?"

"You won't," Paul said. "All you have to do is be the 'Little Avery Norton' the world thinks you are."

With a deep inhalation, she steeled her resolve. She'd spent so long warring against the idea that she could harm other people, but Paul was right; she needed to embrace what so many thought she was. There were times their notions of her made her feel sick deep in her gut, but other times it warmed her belly like chicken soup, and this was one of them.

Pride like a bonfire stroked her insides as she said, "Teach me how."

"First thing's first," Natalie said. "Repeat after me, and try to imitate my voice."

She listened several times, homing in on the inflection in her sister's every word, then repeated in Natalie's voice. Then Paul's. And her father's.

Under the starlight, speaking in spectral tongues, the corpses and Avery Norton wore the same smile.

Compared to her years in Taunton Hospital, living in the woods of Oak Bluffs for three months was a breeze. She remained on alert, though, listening for the ghostly warnings that had become part of nature's music. She avoided her mother's usual haunts, and although she had to resort to theft for food and other essentials, she justified it as easily as the arson. She had moments of doubt, of course, but she also had dozens of dead friends promising her that her bad deeds were for the greater good.

Avery slipped around the island like a phantom, stealing in and out of the shadows, hiding her face behind scarves and sunglasses. If anyone recognized the gaunt young woman with scraggly blonde hair and black roots, they didn't show it, and it delighted her. She felt especially sly donning her old patient gown to sneak back into Martha's Vineyard Hospital and help herself to what she needed. Despite her proximity to Faye's stomping grounds, she spotted her only once, coming out of Hilliard's with Sophie. She wanted to confront her right then, rip Sophie out of her arms and make a run for it, but Natalie stopped her, urged her to wait, and like a dutiful little sister, Avery obeyed.

She studied well. She listened and watched, and she believed her phantoms more each time they spoke of her victory. She soon knew their minds as well as her own and could speak in their voices without prompting. As the weeks passed, Avery reveled deeper in the bloody scenarios centered on Faye's destruction and prayed every morning it would be the day she'd finally enact her plan. But every day, the spirits told her to wait. She whispered to herself in Paul's voice, "Soon, my love," while Flint's fiery anticipation twitched in her fingers.

When the ghosts gathered one September morning and told Avery the time had come, she didn't hesitate for a second. She didn't need much in the way of clothes or creature comforts—just the bag she'd been filling over the past three months with her own variety of gardening tools—and tickets for the ferry.

At the Steamship Authority, her hands trembled with excitement as she dialed her mother's number from the payphone. When Faye answered cheerfully above the sound of Sophie crying, it took all of Avery's will to maintain her composure. But as naturally as breathing, Natalie stepped into Avery's mind and took the reins.

"Why is Sophie crying?" she asked.

"Who is this?"

"What have you been doing to her?"

"Who is this?" Faye demanded again.

"Don't you recognize my voice, Mom? Or did you think it would sound different after you burnt me to a crisp?"

Faye grunted. "Stop this immediately. This isn't funny."

"It's not supposed to be funny. Murder is never funny," Natalie said. "Not to the victim, at least. For you, I suppose it could be a different story."

Paul piped up next. "I bet you laughed your ass off when the boat exploded. I bet you thought you'd finally won. But killing someone doesn't guarantee they'll disappear, Faye. No one disappears completely. Like me. Like Natalie. Like Jason. We're still here, Mrs. Norton, and we're waiting for you."

Faye whined into the receiver. "Avery? Dear Lord, Avery, is that you?"

"We need to see you, Faye, and I think you need to see us."

"Oh my poor girl, what's happened to you?"

"Nothing that didn't begin with you," she said. "You wanted the garden tended, and it will be, but there's something we need to discuss first."

"When?"

"Now. There's a ticket for you at the Steamship Authority. Drive onto the ferry and meet me here. We'll be waiting for you."

"Waiting where?"

"Where else? Taunton Asylum," she replied. Then, in her own voice, Avery said, "I'll see you soon, Mom."

CHAPTER TWENTY-SIX

CROUCHED ON THE floor of room eight, Avery set aside her diary and removed the object hidden beneath. Shining like a piece of gold at the end of a bloody rainbow, the first ring Paul Dillon gave her waited in the ashes of a former life. Holding it to her chest, Avery remembered how much it had meant to her and her overwhelming rage at her mother's thievery. But it felt different now. Heavier, denser, as if linked to her many sorrows. She wished Paul was there as she unearthed it, but he'd refused to join her in the dilapidated hospital. They all had.

"What if I need you?" she'd asked, tearfully, on the perimeter of the property.

"This is your day, Avery. Enjoy it for all of us," her father said, as he handed her the bag of gardening tools. "We'll be with you all the way."

She felt stronger when he hugged her but still too weak to face Faye alone. Then Paul kissed her, and Natalie wrapped her arms around her neck. Flint held her hand, and even Brianne's sidekick stopped chasing rabbits as doctors, nurses, and patients of Taunton encircled her. Despite their manner of death, there was no animosity in their expressions. Instead, they radiated worship, along with the unwavering faith that she would triumph over her mother. It was a poignant, albeit surreal feeling standing in her old bedroom blackened by the fire of her freedom, looking down upon those the blaze had claimed. She felt it still as a car pulled up the drive and parked in front of the hospital. She wrung the corroded bars as Faye exited and scanned the burnt-out husk for several minutes. She wasn't certain if Faye saw her, but it didn't much matter. The only eyes she needed remained fixed on her, their savior and avenger, as Faye fetched Sophie from the backseat, loaded her into a stroller, and rolled her past the ghosts.

The wheels squealed and clicked on the sun bridge floor, drawing nearer to the charred juvenile ward. Squeezing the brass ring in her pocket, she turned from her friends and set her mind on her enemy. She had work to do, and failure wasn't an option. She owed that to every rabbit in her garden.

Avery's name rang from her mother's lips, echoing off the corridor walls like a pinball. She picked up her gardening bag, strode from room eight, and leaned against the remnants of the common room sofa as the ward doors creaked open. Faye Norton entered with her granddaughter's stroller preceding, observing her daughter's handiwork—almost proudly, Avery thought. But Faye's expression dropped to a frown when she spotted Avery smiling from the burnt sofa.

"Hi, Mom. I'm impressed you had the courage to show up."

Faye stepped out from behind the carriage and marched forward with her chin raised. But when Avery lifted her own, and their eyes met in identical defiance, Faye stuttered a step.

"I had to come." Faye tried to mask her trip-up by fiddling with her shoe, but Avery knew better, and it made her feel like the sun was shining out of her grin. Faye's face scrunched at her daughter's radiance, and she shook her head in pity. "I didn't realize you were so far-gone. I thought you were just being rebellious. But you really are sick, my dear. My love, my lamb, my last child in such anguish."

"Yes, I suppose I am. But it took this place to do it," Avery said. "And you, of course."

"Me?" she squealed in dramatic outrage. "All I've ever tried to do is raise you to be a good, decent woman."

"You raised me to be like you: puritanical, judgmental, and most of all, a murderer."

Faye roared, "Wrong!" and Sophie began to cry. Picking her up, she bounced the baby gently until she quieted. "Yes," she continued calmly. "I won't deny that I wanted my children to share my ideals. But I didn't raise you to be a murderer. I raised you to be a teacher, as I have been a teacher to you. Sometimes when students get out of line, they need a smack on the knuckles. A quick castigation to help them learn. You wouldn't take root, so I girdled you."

Avery flared her nostrils and spat. "You really are fucking crazy."

"Enough of that. I won't stand here and listen to that filth."

"You won't be standing for much longer, anyway," Avery said with a sneer. "You know this is the end, don't you?"

"Yes, I do." Faye removed a pistol from her jacket pocket and took aim.

"Where the hell did you get that?"

A smile snaked up her mother's right cheek. "I have my ways of procuring things. I always have."

"I know. And I know how you outmuscled people twice your size and half your age, too, because it was done to me repeatedly in here." Avery advanced on her mother, unafraid. "You drugged them. You injected them with a sedative. Whatever you could get your hands on. You stole drugs from Dad and from the hospital. You coerced people into giving you things out of fear and blackmail, and you've worn that superiority like a holy relic."

"Those are your perceptions, dear. Delusions. You've built me up into this menacing caricature of myself, and it's just not true." Faye crossed herself and clasped her hands in prayer, her face tilted to the heavens. "Dear God, must I constantly be tested as you tested the Immaculate Virgin? Have I not paid enough? Have I not adequately proven my devotion?"

Avery snorted. "If God exists, He must hate everything about you."

"What have I done that any loving parent wouldn't do?" Faye asked. She clutched the gun to her chest as if trying to stop her heart from slipping out a fresh wound. "I tried to teach you right from wrong. Is it my fault you chose poorly?"

"You have a fucked-up idea of right and wrong."

"Enough!" Faye screamed and pointed the gun again.

"Are you going to shoot me for cursing, Mom? Is that part of your criteria for justifiable homicide? Is this another of my delusions?"

"No. It's a lesson. Sophie's first real lesson," she said. "To see real madness up close, that's something you never forget. And from her aunt, no less. Or are you still pretending you're Natalie?"

"I wasn't pretending," Avery said. "She was with me. So was Paul and Flint and—" Her chin trembled as she spoke. "And Dad."

Faye's eyes widened, and her face blanched as she lowered the gun. "You saw your father?"

"Yes. He looked . . . well, you know. You really did a number on him, Mom. You cut him up. You slit his throat."

"Oh, Avery, you're sicker than I thought," Faye whispered.

"You made me this way! You made me see these things!"

"You can blame me if you want, but this started before our little spats. This started with *him*," she snarled. "With Jason and Lily."

"Lily? *Aunt* Lily? What does she have to do with this?"

Faye's nostrils flared with a puff of breath. "Why do you want to go back there, sweetheart? Why do you want to get into something like that when we both know it won't make a lick of difference?"

"It could help me understand your motives—"

"I don't care if you understand. I gave you all the tools, and you wasted them in the worst way. You denied me. You fought me. You learned *nothing*." Sorrow tightened her voice, and her arm wobbled so much she had to lower the gun. "I thought you would grow into the most blessed of women, but you're still that little girl: eager to please but too shortsighted. Naivety is endearing for only so long."

As Avery backed up, she said, "Take your shot if you think it'll make a difference, but to be honest, Mom, we all know it's an act. You seem big and tough, but that's because you go out of your way to make people feel small and weak. And once you've done that, yes, the grasshopper will intimidate the ant. But the grasshopper is alone. You're alone. I have an army behind me."

Faye snickered, then glanced at her granddaughter. "Not completely alone."

Avery's next breath felt more like a collective inhalation from all the ghosts who believed in her. Their confidence didn't obliterate her fear, but it made her strong enough to stand firm when Faye pulled the trigger. The pistol roared, and the scorched walls shuddered, but the bullet went astray. As ash and dust swirled between mother and daughter, Avery reached into her gardening bag. She lunged at Faye, stabbing a syringe into her chest and continuing past her, moments before her mother fired again.

The thud that followed Avery's attack incited a boisterous cheer from her friends that vibrated deliciously in her mind as she advanced on her mother.

Faye, on the floor, her head flopping heavily, scooted away from her daughter and ripped out the syringe. The vitamins were already at work, though, and once Avery emptied the contents of the second hypodermic into Faye's veins, a clarity as Avery had never seen before settled into her mother's expression.

"It hurts, doesn't it?" she said. "Realizing you've lost?

I know that feeling well. It's like the best parts of you are slipping away, you've lost all control, and you don't know where or when you'll get it back. Maybe you never will. It's a horrible thing to experience, especially on a daily basis like I did here." As Avery whispered, Faye's eyelids fluttered. "But it wasn't the worst of what they did to me. You'll feel those soon."

With a grunt, her mother fell asleep, and Avery went about her business.

Ash blanketed the bathroom, and several tubs were cracked, but it was no more unpleasant than Avery remembered. At least the fire had burned away the mildew. After dragging her mother to a tub, she peeled off Faye's coat and scowled at the object gleaming around her neck. She grasped her engagement ring but halted before tearing it free.

No. Not yet. She wanted the pleasure of seeing Faye's reaction when she took it back. When she took everything back.

Avery felt like she must've looked as animalistic as her mother when she loaded those bodies into her trunk, all muscle and grit as she poured Faye into the tub and tightened her restraints. Sophie cooed from the stroller, and Avery thumbed her niece's rosy cheek. Dipping her hands into the carriage, she lifted Sophie into her arms. The baby uttered a soft warble of concern, but as Avery rocked her back and forth, she nestled against her shoulder and fell asleep. Rubbing the baby's back, she prayed for the nap to last. If Violet was telling the truth about the hospital's basement, it was the last thing she wanted Sophie to see.

Before Avery entered the hospital that day, Violet instructed her where to go. Both exhilarated and frightened, she proceeded cautiously into the bowels of Taunton to finally see the source of the agonizing screams she'd heard every day of her incarceration. They'd become white noise over the years, but the memories howled singularly now, each a desperate, ghostly cry from a patient enduring the tortures of the asylum basement.

The fire hadn't reached the lowest level, and the electricity still worked—a small mercy thanks to the city's plans to repurpose the eastern wing in the coming months. But when Avery flipped the light in one of the rooms, a part of her wished she'd remained in darkness. Just because the fire hadn't touched the basement, didn't mean the staff hadn't left in a hurry. Hastily scattered scalpels and bloody rags littered the benches and floor, but the most carelessly discarded objects were the gaunt corpses on the operating tables.

Avery covered her mouth when she spotted a familiar face. Violet's head hung upside down over the edge, her cheeks scarred and clotted with gaping brown wounds. Unlike most of Avery's ghosts, she died because of the fire, but not on the day of the fire. When the doctors smelled smoke, they did what any sane person would do. They ran, leaving the victims of their experimental surgeries to bleed out.

Avery knew the cadavers in the hospital basement couldn't be real, but her remorse was real enough—for indirectly leading to their deaths, and for the countless times she'd tuned out their screams. For the times she'd tuned out everything, in fact.

Violet's corpse blinked, and she wheezed. "Keep moving."

Avery swallowed the lump in her throat and tenderly rubbed Sophie's back as if she were the one who needed comfort. Finding the utility room Nurse Meredith had mentioned, she flipped on the light with a grateful sigh. The ice machine was still operational, and several buckets sat nearby. With Sophie curled against her shoulder, she shoveled ice into the buckets and lugged them upstairs. It took several trips, but Faye never batted an eye. And as Sophie slumbered peacefully against her chest, Avery felt like the thud of the child's tiny heart was mending her own. After she lined up the last bucket of ice, she stood in silence, her arms enfolding her niece. Taunton Hospital had never felt more therapeutic.

CHAPTER TWENTY-SEVEN

"**T**IME TO WAKE UP."

Avery emptied two buckets of ice into the tub, and her mother awoke with a wheezing gasp, thrashing and tugging madly at her tethers. But she didn't stop. She tipped bucket after bucket until the ice bath overflowed, and Faye's screams filled the room. Then, with one hand gently rolling Sophie's carriage back and forth, she sat quietly and watched, as so many nurses had watched her. As Faye whipped herself against the tub, chunks of ice sloshed in the freezing water and spattered Avery's face, but she remained serene as she wiped the droplets away.

"Why are you doing this?" Faye screeched. "Why are you torturing me?"

"At least you still have your clothes on. I doubt it makes much difference temperature-wise, but at least you don't have the added embarrassment of being stripped naked by strangers."

Faye's lips turned bluish-gray, and her teeth chattered as she spoke. "What do you want from me? What will make you stop this madness?"

"I want a lot of things, Mom. For starters, I want to be twelve again. I want to live those six years as I should have, to be at home surrounded by my friends and family. But I know that's impossible. Even if I could change what happened that day in the garden, it wouldn't change the kind of person you are. If it hadn't happened to me at twelve, it would've happened at thirteen. Or fourteen. You never would've left me alone."

"What kind of mother would I be if I did? I knew the kind of things Natalie did when she was alone," she said, her face screwed up in disgust. "I could tell you were heading down that road, too."

"What road?"

"The one that leads to the foolish mistakes that would've ruined your life."

"You mean mistakes that would've ruined *your* life," she said. "You're too selfish to have genuinely cared about mine."

"That's not true," Faye stammered.

"How can it not be? You ran me off that road, right into an asylum, and my life *is* ruined. Because of you." Avery crouched at the tub's edge, staring into her mother's bloodshot eyes. "Natalie's life, too. And Paul's. And Dad's."

"What you call ruin, I call salvation."

"Why did Dad need salvation?" she asked, a dull ache striking the back of her head. "I want to know what happened."

"You know what happened. You were there."

"I know he didn't run off, and I didn't kill him. Just tell me the truth."

"The truth is all I've ever given you. What you really want are facts. For instance, I am your mother, Avery, and I love you. Those are facts."

"Not ones that interest me," she replied. "Tell me, Mom. If not for me, then for the off chance that God needs to hear your confession, one last time."

Faye clenched her trembling jaw and glared. "It doesn't matter what you think of me. In all my life, in everything I've done, I've worked in the best interest of my faith and my family.

"But it wasn't only your family; there were four people in it—five if you count Aunt Lily. It should've been *our family.*"

"Lily was nothing! Your father was nothing! They tried to rip our family apart!" Faye stretched her aching, frozen jaw and whined in pain. "It doesn't matter now. It won't change anything."

"I don't care. Just tell me."

Faye groaned in defeat. "Lily wasn't your aunt. She wasn't related to us at all." Her cheeks flushed as she gritted her teeth. "I allowed Jason to make her a part of this family because—well, because I was weak. Because I loved him."

"What are you saying? Who was she?"

Faye struggled to rattle out the words. "His girlfriend," she spat. "She was his patient first, actually. I don't know anything about their 'courtship', thank heaven, but I assume it didn't take much. It never did." She squinted at Avery, her face besieged by tremors. "He wasn't a good man. He provided for us, gave us material things, but he had no heart, no patience or pity. He was exactly the kind of man I taught you to avoid."

"No. I have good memories of him. He was kind. He loved us. And Aunt Lily loved us, too."

"He told her to act like she loved you just to spite me," Faye said. "He wanted to take you and Natalie away. He tried to steal you from me as if he were stealing you from my very womb."

"What the hell are you talking about?"

"He tried to get rid of me. He tried to take you away. Him and that whore he taught you girls to call 'Aunt.'"

"Lily was sweeter to us than you ever could be."

Faye snorted. "What good is being sweet? Love, structure, hope, faith: that's what children need. Sweetness can be false, but those things are always true. They're what I strove to give you, Avery, and I'm sorry you chose not to accept them."

"Hope?" Avery bellowed at her shivering mother. "You stripped away nearly every scrap of hope when you allowed me to take the blame for your crimes. And the only structure you gave was telling me to kill anyone who didn't share your same puritanical faith. And love?" She shook her head, her teeth clenched to stop their trembling. "I can't even remember your love anymore. Your cruelty and mania have twisted those memories so much I don't know what was real. Any affection you showed me feels like it was part of a lifelong nightmare now."

"I loved you, Avery. I loved you and Natalie so much I did everything I could to prevent you from ending up with your father and Lily. She tried to tart you up, make you just like her, and I was forced to sit there and abide it. I knew he loved the two of you more than he loved me; I was fine with that, and I was fine with you loving him. But when you girls started loving Lily, too, I couldn't handle it anymore. I begged him to stop seeing her, and when he refused, I told him to leave. It broke my heart to do it—I loved him from the first night we met. The night of the storm." She howled as she tugged at the ropes again, kicking her feet against the tub. "Dammit, Avery, you have to let me out."

"Keep going. What happened?"

She grunted. "I told him if he wanted to be with her, I'd grant him a divorce, but he said he wouldn't leave without you and Natalie. He wanted to take you both far away from me, from your own mother's arms where you belonged." She licked her lips and directed her eyes to the ceiling. "I'll admit the whole situation did make me a little crazy, but I doubt anyone would blame me. How can a mother allow someone to take her children when she has the strength to stop it?"

Tears streamed down Faye's ashen cheeks, and Avery's heart surprised her with a clench of nauseating pain. She pictured Sheila on the day she gave birth, grasping for her baby as the nurses tore it from her arms. What would she have done to keep her daughter if not for the vitamins pumping through her veins?

But Faye wasn't Sheila. She didn't kill Jason because she thought their children would be happiest with her. She killed him because she enjoyed it. Because if she succeeded, she'd be free to mold Natalie and Avery into whatever she wanted.

"I'm not going to feel sorry for you. You've hurt too many people to earn my sympathy," Avery said, and overturned the last bucket of ice on Faye's face and chest.

Faye screamed and convulsed madly, and blood flowered in the water.

"What do you want?" Her voice pitched so high it sounded alien. "You asked for a motive and I'm giving you one!"

"I don't actually care about your motive. No explanation would ever change what you did or the effect it's had on me. You asked me earlier what would make me stop this madness, and unfortunately for you, Mom, nothing will stop me now."

"There has to be something. We weren't always at odds. We were happy once. Mother and daughter, a love beyond description. We were both blessed and innocent then."

"I'm still innocent. I've striven to prove that since the moment I was committed to Taunton. I thought that if I kept on trying to convince people I was sane, it might eventually get through. But it made everything worse. That's when I tapped into something I learned from you." She circled her shivering blue mother as she spoke. "I realized I needed to toughen up, and to do that, I thought of you. So austere. So unflinching in your faith. I always admired that about you." She spun on her heel and pointed at Faye. "That was before I understood true madness, the kind that drives people to believe shedding innocent blood is part of some great work. The kind of madness inside you. And because of you, the kind that's inside me. I understand it all now, and you're right, it does feel wonderful to believe in something so wholeheartedly, to know that your next move might make the world a much better place. I understand, and I believe, Mom, that killing you is the greatest work I'll ever do." Faye's eyes widened in terror, and Avery sneered as she whispered, "I'll be right back."

As she strode away from the tub, her mother craned to keep her in sight, and when the distinctive rolling of wheels across the rotted floor grew louder, Faye's fear twisted into confusion. Avery positioned the machine next to the tub and patted it like a dutiful puppy.

"Honey, whatever you're planning on doing, please don't. I can fix everything," Faye whimpered. "I can tell the world the truth. I'll even take the blame for the hospital fire if you want. Just . . . please, you can't kill me. There's still so much to do."

"You're lying. You won't admit to anything."

"I will!" she screeched. "I promise!"

"Ssh . . . you're disturbing Sophie."

"Yes! Think of Sophie! Would you really kill her grandmother in front of her?"

Avery cocked her head. "Did you kill Dad in front of me and Natalie?"

"Do you remember that?"

"No, but it wouldn't surprise me," Avery said as she untangled the electrode wires. "How do you reconcile that, Mom? How can you believe God loves you after all you've done?"

"Because God commanded it," Faye said, smiling as much as the cold would allow. "With all those voices in your head, are you really telling me there isn't one that feels divine?"

"With all these voices, I'm still too sensible for that, Mom." She chuckled as she liberated the last electrode, but the dull pain now cracking hard through Avery's brain robbed the laugh of authenticity.

"You poor girl," Faye hissed. "You're damned, and divinity is the only thing that can save you. You must be penitent. You must be castigated. You can kill me and hundreds more, but it will never satisfy the fire inside. Your soul is drenched in blood. You will never be happy, Avery. You will always be a killer."

"Fuck you!" Avery gripped her pounding head and

moaned. "How's anyone supposed to keep from going insane with your constant lying like a screwdriver to the brain?"

"Why should that matter to you? You've never been sane," Faye said matter-of-factly. "I've never lied about your bloodlust or your blackouts. I'm afraid you'll discover that soon enough."

Drawing her face close, she snarled. "That's not what you should be afraid of, Mom."

She dipped the electrodes in the bathwater. With one hand cradling the left side of her mother's head, she forcibly stuck the electrode to her right temple, then repeated the process on the other side. Crouching beside the tub, she looked her mother square in the eyes. Her anger had never been so focused—or so wild. The voices of her dead companions allowed her to speak with violent eloquence, but her mind was a manic whirlwind of rage.

"You are a liar, a murderer, and an abysmal excuse for a mother," she said. When Faye moaned, she hushed her and tenderly stroked her hair. "Quiet now . . . there's nothing you can do. You led us here, and you deserve to die for it. And just like your victims, no amount of begging will save you."

"They weren't victims," she said, brutally spitting the words at her daughter. "Maybe I do deserve to die, but so did they, and so do you. The difference between you and me, Avery, is that a higher power has already absolved me. If I die today, I will die a martyr. I will die strong and proud like St. Agnes."

"You're not even making sense. I just hope Sophie doesn't remember you. I don't want to imagine what your parenting would've done to her."

"Lucky for you, you don't have to," Faye said. "You've come full circle. From child to adolescent to adult, with everything you've done to distance your life from mine, you've succeeded in becoming exactly like me."

"That's not true."

"Listen to you, acting as shortsighted as those who refused to hear your protests of innocence. I say I'm sane, and you say I'm not. We're two peas in a pod, little lamb. You thought the austerity in my faith was admirable when you were young, right? But you were like that, too. Your memories of being a joyful, innocent youth are false, Avery. You have always craved the dark."

"I don't believe you."

"Of course you don't. Your psychosis won't allow you to be wrong." Faye chortled and coughed haggardly. "But while you were creating those ghosts in your head, you took what you needed from us. You became strong like me, romantic like Natalie, convinced of your virtue like Paul but tortured by compulsion like your friend Flint. What you become during your blackouts—it's a monster that's stolen pieces from us all."

"Stop it! You're lying. You're trying to save yourself."

"What would be the point? You've made it perfectly clear I'm not getting out of here alive. So go ahead and flip your switches, and while you do, protest your innocence one more time. Maybe someone will finally hear it echoed in your mother's dying screams."

Avery turned away to blink back tears. Shaking her head, she whispered, "Innocence doesn't matter to me anymore. But I'll take the screams." Facing her mother again, she fondled the electroshock switch. "Before I strike the match, there's just one more thing I need from you."

Faye snarled and kicked the icy water. "What?!"

Avery leaned over her, wrapped her fingers around the engagement ring, and ripped it free so violently the chain sliced her mother's flesh.

Wincing, Faye shot her daughter a hostile glare. "Do you have everything you want now, Avery?"

"Almost," she said, tucking it away. "What about you, Mom? Is this what you hoped all your lessons would teach me?"

Faye's lips curled upwards when she opened her

mouth, but she didn't answer. Instead, she tilted her head back on the tub and opened her hands in acceptance. Avery's brain rumbled with anger, and she looked down on her in the hard, haughty way she'd learned from her mother.

But it didn't work. Waterlogged in the ice bath, with tears running down her cheeks, Faye Norton was still in control. Her fingers gripped the sides of the tub in disturbing and righteous anticipation, and she grinned as Avery pinched the switch.

It was a grin they shared once the switch flipped.

The current hit Faye's brain with sparks that crackled loudly as they traveled through water and flesh. Her body slammed against the tub in violent convulsions that broke her bones, and she clenched her jaw so tightly her teeth shattered from the pressure.

Avery's heart ballooned with joy, but the smoke and searing stench soon became too much. She turned away from her mother and hurried to Sophie. The current continued surging after its human conductor was nothing more than a slack lump of sizzling meat, but even though Avery didn't wish to stew her mother's body, her vengeance prevented her from stopping it. It was all too lovely.

She slipped on Faye's coat and withdrew her car keys. As she rolled Sophie's carriage out of the room, she fixed her focus on what lay ahead, but her ears strained to catch every delightful hiss and pop.

CHAPTER TWENTY-EIGHT

AVERY EMERGED FROM Taunton Asylum, and resounding applause rose from her ghosts. She smiled and placed a finger to her lips, hushing them as she wheeled the baby past. Rabbits ran around the stroller, crisscrossing and clearing a path to where Natalie stood with her scorched arms open. Avery lifted the slumbering baby and passed her to her sister, who rocked and kissed and wept over her.

"I'm sorry, Natalie."

"Don't. Just promise me you'll take good care of her. Raise her as your own. Don't let her know what happened here. I'm afraid the story alone will poison her."

"We don't have to worry about that anymore," Avery said as Natalie laid her daughter in the stroller. "We're together now. We're free."

Paul held her hands and kissed them tenderly, but he avoided her gaze.

Fear sprang into Avery's throat, bitter and cold. "What is it? What aren't you telling me?"

Paul and Natalie glanced at one another, and she hung her head in sorrow. Even with the missing panels of flesh and muscle, lament noticeably registered on Paul's charred face.

"Avery, we can't come with you," he whispered. "Our work is done, and yours is just beginning."

"You're not serious," she said, looking from her true love to her big sister. "I need you. I need all of you. You were the only thing that made me think clearly. I couldn't have done this without you. How are we supposed to survive the rest of our lives if you're not there?"

"We'll still be there," Flint said, resting her scorched hand on Avery's shoulder. "You won't always see us, but we'll be there."

"And you were right, sweetheart," her father said. "We're free now, and we owe it all to you."

Avery shook her head and stared pleadingly into Paul's piercing eyes. "You can't abandon me like this. What about everything we promised each other? What about your daughter?"

"She'll have a good life with you. I know you'll love her just as much as we did." He cupped her face and skated his thumb over her cheek. "There's a whole world out there, and it's yours now. I know you wish it could be ours—I wish that too—but we have to be realistic. This is your time to live, to become the woman you were born to be. You must make our sacrifices worthwhile. You must share what you've learned." He raised his eyebrows and smiled. "Faye was crazy, but she was right about one thing: the world is a garden, and it must be tended."

"I can't. I need you. I need your love."

"And you'll have it," he said. "We'll all be loving you from afar, guiding you from our heavens. But the battle is over. There's no more need for sadness or regret."

"But I do have regrets. I regret we'll never get our chance to be happy. I regret that every ring you gave me means nothing now. I regret everything that led to this, to one harsh fact, the only thing I know for certain." She exhaled in shuddering lament. "I will always be alone, Paul. If I tell anybody what happened or who I am, they'll lock me up forever. I can't be *me* anymore." She stared down at Sophie, who cooed in her sleep. "Even with her, I'll be alone."

"Look at me," Paul said, and she tearfully obeyed. "Those rings aren't meaningless. We may have never exchanged vows, but you are my wife, Avery. I don't need a priest to confirm it, and neither should you. As long as you remember that, it doesn't matter who you become. You are the love of my life *and* whatever comes after. You'll never be alone." He thumbed away her tears, streaking her cheeks with ash. "But the brass ring is a different story. It should be passed along."

Sophie opened her twinkling blue eyes and smiled. Avery's heart quickened as she removed the brass ring from her pocket, slipped it onto the chain, and dangled both rings over her carriage. The baby giggled and reached for the rings, which Avery slowly lowered into her daughter's chubby fingers. Sophie latched onto the brass ring and shoved it in her mouth, causing the crowd to chuckle in adoration.

"It is as it should be," Paul whispered.

Looking back, Avery said, "Nothing is as it should be."

Sophie hummed happily as she sucked on the ring, her eyelashes fluttering as she stared at her mother, and Avery added softly, "But I'll take it."

She didn't want to say goodbye, so she tried to leave without another word. But before she could load Sophie into Faye's car, Paul latched onto her arm. He spun her around and pressed his lips to hers. It was a good kiss, one of the best he'd ever given her. Only his waning solidity prevented it from topping the charts.

He was fading fast. They all were.

Avery rushed to embrace as many as she could before they disappeared. She even hugged the nurses she hadn't liked; while they'd stifled and harmed her in life, their encouragement had been invaluable to her in death. From her father to Flint to the vacant girl in the purple chair, she felt she absorbed them with each embrace. By the end, she believed it was true: she would never be alone again. By the time the last dead rabbit vanished, Avery's mind was at peace.

"My dear Sophie," she said, curling a finger against the child's milky cheek. "This garden has been slashed, burned, and salted, and God willing, nothing will ever grow here again."

Yes, she thought. The world was a garden, glorious and free, with no fences to lock it in or stones to obstruct its growth, and it was a truth that filled Avery's mind as she pulled away from Taunton Hospital. She wanted to say something to the baby that would adequately portray her feelings, but "I love you" wasn't enough. Instead, she spoke the four words that made her feel loved while she was locked away.

"I believe in you."

As Taunton Asylum shrank in the rearview mirror, dozens of weights lifted from Avery's mind. But with them, secrets they'd long entombed squirmed to the surface. She tuned the radio to a station far from her mother's favorites, and patted Sophie's belly as Elvis Presley crooned, "Love Me Tender." With a joyful squeal, Sophie removed the brass ring from her mouth and slid it onto her new mother's finger.

Paul was right. It was time for Avery to live. It was time for her to become the woman she was born to be.

With that glorious thought, every sin felt absolved, and every mile between Avery and her old life was a step toward a greater propagation.

JESSICA McCANN

EPILOGUE

THE HOTEL HAD a color television, but the novelty was wasted on someone with a baby to bathe. She might as well have been listening to a radio as she wrung a soapy sponge over Sophie's head. The baby squealed in delight, and Avery tickled her under the chin. TV, radio, it didn't matter; she was thankful for any opportunity to choose.

Choice wasn't something she experienced much in Oak Bluffs or Taunton Asylum. She'd been controlled there. She'd been denied.

But Sophie wouldn't live that way. There was nothing she would deny her daughter. Avery would be the kind of teacher Faye should have been, the kind who listened as often as she decreed. She would pause between lectures and allow her student to contribute. She would help her daughter evolve and allow Sophie to help her in turn.

Oh, she had such lessons to teach the girl! Love, structure, faith, hope . . .

She still had doubts, though, and she understood they might always be there. But they hadn't knotted up her insides as much as they did that night in the hotel, when she laid Sophie down to sleep. Massaging her aching temples, Avery gazed at her daughter and wondered if she could hide everything from Sophie like Natalie wished. She wanted to be honest with the girl about where she came from, but how could she explain the life-changing events that pushed them farther and farther from home? How could she tell her what her grandmother had done? How could she admit what *she'd* done? And most terrifying of all, what would she say if Sophie turned out just like her?

The television drew Avery's attention when the nightly news launched a breaking report about a missing woman found just outside of Boston. She sat on the edge of the bed, waiting for the details, but she didn't need them. She knew how the story would end, and a strange sort of pride untied her internal knots in an undeniably delicious way.

"Today, police identified the body of twenty-two-year-old Olive Reardon who was discovered along route 128 to Boston, more than three months after her car was found abandoned. Although originally labeled an accident, it has now been declared a homicide."

"Do you have any suspects, Officer O'Malley?" the correspondent asked.

"Not officially, but we believe the murder occurred around the time of the Taunton Hospital fire. Several patients escaped during the blaze, including convicted murderer Avery Norton, who is still at large."

Avery switched off the television and her focus drifted to Sophie on the bed. Curling up beside her, she tensed every muscle in her body as the mounting pain of a hundred lost memories careening home. But there was beauty in the agony, in being remade by the brutality of truth.

Sliding her finger over the velvet cheek of the daughter to whom she would deny nothing, she decided, perhaps, some things were better off being denied.

ABOUT THE AUTHOR

Jessica McHugh is a novelist, a 2x Bram Stoker Award®-nominated poet, & an internationally-produced playwright running amok in the fields of horror, sci-fi, young adult, and wherever else her peculiar mind leads. She's had twenty-nine books published in fourteen years, including her bizarro romp, *The Green Kangaroos,* her YA series, *The Darla Decker Diaries*, and her Elgin Award nominated blackout poetry collections, *A Complex Accident of Life* and *Strange Nests*. For more info about publications and blackout poetry commissions, please visit McHughniverse.com.

SPOOKY TALES FROM GHOULISH BOOKS

☐**BELOW | Laurel Hightower**
ISBN: 978-1-943720-69-9 $12.95
A creature feature about a recently divorced woman trying to survive a road trip through the mountains of West Virginia.

☐**MAGGOTS SCREAMING! | Max Booth III**
ISBN: 978-1-943720-68-2 $18.95
On a hot summer weekend in San Antonio, Texas, a father and son bond after discovering three impossible corpses buried in their back yard.

☐**LEECH | John C. Foster**
ISBN: 978-1-943720-70-5 $14.95
Horror / noir mashup about a top secret government agency's most dangerous employee. Doppelgangers, demigods, and revenants, oh my!

☐**RABBITS IN THE GARDEN | Jessica McHugh**
ISBN: 978-1-943720-73-6 $16.95
13-year-old Avery Norton is a crazed killer—according to the staff at Taunton Asylum, anyway. But as she struggles to prove her innocence in the aftermath of gruesome murders spanning the 1950s, Avery discovers there's a darker force keeping her locked away . . . which she calls "Mom."

☐**PERFECT UNION | Cody Goodfellow**
ISBN: 978-1-943720-74-3 $18.95
Three brothers searching the wilderness for their mother instead find a utopian cult that seeks to reinvent society, family . . . humanity

☐**SOFT PLACES | Betty Rocksteady**
ISBN: 978-1-943720-75-0 $14.95
A novella/graphic novel hybrid about a seemingly psychotic woman who suffers a mysterious head injury.

☐**HARES IN THE HEDGEROW | Jessica McHugh**
ISBN: 978-1-943720-76-7 $21.95
15 years after the events in *Rabbits in the Garden*, Avery
Norton is a ghost. 16-year-old Sophie Dillon doesn't know
anything about the alleged murderer, yet she's haunted
nightly by the same dark urges, which send her on a journey
to uncover her past with the Norton family and to embrace
the future with her spiritual family, the Choir of the Lamb.
But Sophie's devotions can't protect her from the ghosts
waiting in the wings. After all, she's the one they've been
waiting for.

Not all titles available for immediate shipping. All credit card
purchases must be made online at GhoulishBooks.com.
Shipping is 5.80 for one book and an additional dollar for each
additional book. Contact us for international shipping prices.
All checks and money orders should be made payable to
Perpetual Motion Machine Publishing.

Ghoulish Books
PO Box 1104
Cibolo, TX 78108

Ship to:

Name _____

Address_____

City_____State_____Zip_____

Phone Number _____

Book Total: $_____

Shipping Total: $_____

Grand Total: $_____

Patreon:
www.patreon.com/pmmpublishing

Website:
www.PerpetualPublishing.com

Facebook:
www.facebook.com/PerpetualPublishing

Twitter:
@PMMPublishing

Newsletter:
www.PMMPNews.com

Email Us:
Contact@PerpetualPublishing.com

Patreon:
www.patreon.com/pmmpublishing

Website:
www.PerpetualPublishing.com

Facebook:
www.facebook.com/PerpetualPublishing

Twitter:
@PMMPublishing

Newsletter:
www.PMMNews.com

Email Us:
Contact@PerpetualPublishing.com

CPSIA information can be obtained
at www.ICGtesting.com
Printed in the USA
LVHW091248030922
727497LV00017B/751

9 781943 720736